THE MAN FROM TOMORROW

By
STANTON A. COBLENTZ

I0616829

ARMCHAIR FICTION
PO Box 4369, Medford, Oregon   97501-0168

*For more information about Armchair Books and products, visit our
website at…*

www.armchairfiction.com

Or email us at…

armchairfiction@yahoo.com

THRUST THREE HUNDRED YEARS INTO THE PAST

When James Cloud entered the offices of Professor Elliot Howard, he spun a wild scientific tale about being able to view the distant past or future with his revolutionary new device…The Fourth Dimension Machine. But it was with great skepticism that Howard and his assistant, Dr. Horn, visited Cloud's lodgings—a man they were certain was a scientific crackpot. However, within minutes, not only had Cloud proved the authenticity of his device, but he had also deposited a man from 300 years in the future into a wire contrivance on the machine itself. And when this man from tomorrow awoke, the world would never be the same again. His physical attributes, his knowledge, his clothing, and especially his arrogance, were like nothing 20th Century mankind had ever experienced before.

CAST OF CHARACTERS

JOHN WORMWOOD
Born 300 years in the future, he knew more about science than any 20th Century man—a fact he was amazingly arrogant about.

PROFESSOR ELLERY HOWARD
This esteemed Professor was well-versed in science. Little did he realize the science-shattering discovery that awaited him.

JAMES RICHARD CLOUD
An unheralded genius or a complete kook? His "Fourth Dimension Machine" turned out to be no laughing matter.

DOCTOR HORN
His urging of Professor Howard to visit a crackpot's lodgings for a demonstration proved to be a pivotal moment in science.

MISS ALICE WHITCOMB
She was young, beautiful, and very proper—and the one person from the past that the man from tomorrow had an attraction to.

PROFESSOR CHARLES WARRINGTON
Chairman of the Science Department at Gotham University, he gave the man from tomorrow free reign of the college campus

MRS. HOWARD
She was amazed to have a guest who came from the future, but even more surprised when he asked to sleep on the roof!

CHAPTER ONE
Madman or Genius?

As I glance back upon that strange and bewildering episode which not long ago was the riddle of scientist and common man alike, I have difficulty in pointing to the moment when it all began. But I believe that, had it not been for one seemingly innocent remark, which I made before the International Congress of Engineers, I would have been spared the most disturbing but most fascinating experience of my career, and my fellow men would have gone a little more calmly, if not quite so wisely, along their way.

For nearly forty years, as the reader may recall, I have held the Chair of Physics in the University of Gotham; and it was presumably in testimony to the length of my service to science, rather than in recognition of any particular attainments, that I was called upon to preside at the eminent gathering which included some of the world's foremost mechanical geniuses. At all events, I was conscious of no especial qualifications enabling me to shine before that august body; and no one, consequently, was more surprised than I, when my opening address was tumultuously received, and when certain of my remarks, catching the notice of the daily press, were printed and reprinted and criticized and commented upon with an earnestness and gusto that their banal character certainly did not merit.

"SAVANT FORETELLS SUPER-WORLD" I remember seeing in headlines in one of our metropolitan papers; and, though I winced at the blatant indelicacy of the tone, I lost no time in reading the article to the end:

"Professor Ellery Howard, speaking before the International Congress of Engineers, threw his audience into an uproar last evening by his forecasts of the future of science. 'Modern discoveries and inventions,' he declared, 'have brought us to such a stage that the world is tiptoeing at the brink of a precipice. At any moment some fresh work of genius, going only a few inches beyond what we have achieved already, may upset the balance of civilization and revolutionize human life, deluging us with blood and terror, or inaugurating the Millennium... Let us therefore regard every new invention with cautious but tolerant eyes, for who knows what harmless-seeming instrument devised by some unhonored Stephenson or Marconi may hold the key to human destiny...?' "

On and on, in much the same vein, the report continued to the length of a column. Personally, I still have no idea why remarks so utterly commonplace should have created such storms of attention; but it is certain that they were quoted and requoted with an enthusiasm worthy of a better cause, until in the end, there was no housewife or schoolchild to whom they were not as familiar as any time-honored platitude. It will be better to say nothing of the swarms of letters which came to make a torment of my life, nor of the multitude of dinner and after-dinner invitations from which I had to shield myself behind the stout tongue of my Secretary; it will be well to pass on at once to the one important aftermath—an aftermath as curious as it was unpredictable, and as brilliant in its outlines as it was alarming in its possibilities.

In a word, I should never have met James Richard Cloud, had it not been for that address before the Engineering Congress; and his weird masterpiece would not have been rescued from that oblivion wherein, perhaps, it would have been best for it to remain. It was only by an accident that Cloud succeeded in reaching me at all, for the deluge of callers following my engineering address had compelled me to refuse admittance to all whose business was not urgent. I still do not know how he managed to make his way past the formidable defenses of my secretary; my only explanation is that she had momentarily left the room, and that he had simply walked into the unguarded citadel. However that may have been, I do know that, while I sat late one afternoon in my office in the Natural Science Department of Gotham University, poring over some reports I was about to submit to the President, I was startled by the entrance of an uninvited visitor.

Or, rather, I was startled by his presence, for I really did not see him enter. Looking up from my papers, I observed him standing in front of my desk, peering inquiringly down upon me, with the meekest and mildest expression possible, as though to say, "Go right on with your work, Professor. Don't let me disturb you."

Had he arrived phantom-like through the solid walls, he could not have astonished me more. The first glance told me that he did not belong here; not often had such a character been seen within the respectable walls of Gotham University. A gray-headed man of fifty-eight or sixty, with a gray untended beard, he was clad in the scraps and tatters of a vagabond. His grimy felt hat, which he held in his hand, had been bruised and battered into the shapelessness of dough; his soiled brown shirt was ripped beneath the collar, and his scrawny neck was dark with the accumulated dust of many days. Altogether, with his tall, ungainly, underfed figure and his pallid bony face, he made a most unattractive appearance; and yet, even in that first surprised glimpse, I could not help seeing that there was something unusual about him—not only in the hard, stubborn lines of the jaw and lips, but in the black eyes, smoldering as though their obscure depths held all the unfathomable sorrow of the world.

"Well?" I jerked out, as my astonished glance met that of the intruder. "Who are you? Where do you come from? What do you want here?"

He met my gaze with an unperturbed steadiness, and only the inconsequential manner, in which he swung his hat back and forth, gave evidence of his nervousness.

"Professor Ellery Howard?" he inquired, as the bloodless lips parted to reveal a badly decayed set of teeth.

"Yes!" I acknowledged, with a growl. "What do you want?"

Instantly a thin, fleshless hand shot toward me across the desk. "Pleased to meet you, Professor Howard! Hope you don't mind the intrusion! I've been reading your books for years! Always looked on you as a master in your field! But never thought of coming here till today, when I read in the paper about your remarks. This certainly is a real pleasure!"

Perfunctorily I had taken his hand, which gripped mine with a clinging intensity. "I didn't get the name," I said.

"Oh, that doesn't matter!" he laughed. "You've never heard it before, anyhow. Cloud! James Richard Cloud! But maybe you'd better remember it. It might, for all you know, be a name to remember!"

I eyed my visitor quizzically, wondering vaguely whether he could be mad. It occurred to me to press the bell, and instruct one of the guards to escort him quietly out; and I do not know what restrained me, unless it were a certain burning eagerness in his eyes, coupled with the strange, indefinable sense, which seemed to tell me that somehow I was on the brink of an adventure.

"Now as you might have guessed," Cloud rattled on, apparently never pausing to ask himself whether I had the time to listen to his chatter, "I've come here for a reason. A very special reason. That speech of yours shows that you're the sort of man I can take into my confidence. You're a friend of inventors. You realize the possibilities of great discoveries. Why, your words might have been made to order to fit my case!"

"To fit your case?" I gasped, a little taken aback by the audacity of the man.

"Yes, exactly!"

My visitor was warming to his theme, and the glitter in his eyes was concentrated in two intense, fiery points that fascinated and yet troubled me.

"Your words exactly fit my case, Professor! Of course, you couldn't have known that. But they do you credit just the same; Talk about revolutionizing human life! Talk about holding the key to human destiny! Why, sir, that's just what I'm doing! Yes, sir, and no one but me knows about it—yet!"

Once more the thought occurred to me that the man was out of his head. "You're modest, aren't you?" I managed to mumble.

"Modest? No! Why should I be? When one's reached the point that I have, the time for modesty is past! For thirty-five years I had to be modest, while I was working for results! But now that I've succeeded, why not let the world know about it?"

In spite of the flaming earnestness with which Cloud spoke, I could not help smiling. Certainly, his raveled garments, with their ill-assorted patches, did not indicate a superb success. No doubt, I reflected, the man was harmless; but it would not have surprised me to have had him inform me that he was Newton, Darwin, or Edison.

Thinking to humor him, I murmured, mildly, "Well, then, Mr. Cloud, why don't you let the world know about your success?"

The vehemence with which he met these words astounded me. A light that was actually savage blazed in his eyes; the thin lips upcurled as if in anger or defiance; his great fist clenched and came down in a heedless frenzy among the papers on my desk, scattering ink and havoc among them. And while I opened my mouth in a vain effort at protest, my visitor fairly roared into my ear:

"Why don't I let the world know? God in Heaven! Do you think I haven't tried? Do you think I haven't walked my legs half off and shouted my lungs out trying to make people believe? Do you think I haven't thrown my last penny away struggling to get someone to take an interest? Look at these rags! Do you suppose I always went about this way? Not in the least. Once I had money! I've spent it all on my invention! But now no one will believe me. They won't even look at it, won't even see how it works! They only laugh. Can you imagine it? They think I'm crazy!"

I could easily imagine it, but forebore to say so. Once more some strange magnetism behind the man's words held me fascinated; and, at the same time, I was not unmoved at the sight of a stray tear or two that had gathered to his eyes and trickled unchecked down his cheeks.

And so, when I spoke, it was in kindlier tones than before. "Sit down," I invited. "Tell me all about it."

He slouched gratefully into a seat, sighed with relief, and then, while I waited politely, went on to explain, "I can't mention much about it, Professor, till you actually see it. It's seeing that counts, not hearing. Chances are, if I simply speak about it, you simply won't believe any more than the rest of them. Why, you'd probably laugh in my face at the mere mention of my Dimension Machine—"

"Dimension Machine?" I echoed.

He stared at me with a sheepish grin, in the manner of one conscious of a blunder. "There I've gone and let the cat out of the bag," he muttered. "Well then, I might as well go on and tell you. I always think of it as the Dimension Machine, although it is really a Fourth Dimension Machine. That is to say, an engine to put us into touch with the Fourth Dimension."

I peered at him with an incredulous smile, exactly as if he had told me that he had solved the problem of perpetual motion or of squaring the circle.

"You don't believe me, do you?" he flung out at me, in a disappointed, almost resentful, manner. "No, of course you don't! But surely, Professor Howard, you're not going to be like all the rest! You're certainly going to listen to me, aren't you?"

"Go on," I mumbled, none too encouragingly.

"Then consider this," he proceeded, his thin face drawn up into a thoughtful expression. "You know some of the modern theories about the fourth dimension. How Einstein and others suppose that the fourth dimension of space is time. Well, I don't want to claim anyone else's laurels, but that was my view even before the name of Einstein was heard of. I've been working at it for thirty-five years. It's my belief too that the fourth side of space is time, and that, in a sense, all time exists simultaneously and eternally—although on some other plane than ours—just as all space exists simultaneously and eternally. Now somewhere there must be a point of contact between the third-dimension and the fourth, just as there is between the third and the second—between a flat surface, let us say, and the cube of which it is a part. If we could find that point—as I have, in fact, found it—we could literally walk out on the fourth dimension, and see anywhere in time, or else we could reach out with a sort of fishing-line and seize anything anywhere in the past or future and bring it into the third dimension for our closer inspection."

"That all sounds very good, Mr. Cloud," I acknowledged, still unconvinced. "Then you mean to say you could watch the armies of Julius Caesar. Or gaze upon our descendants in the year 4000?"

"Why not? Why not?" returned the inventor, his lips twisting with disdain, as though to say; "Give me something hard, why don't you!"

"I've not only looked upon Julius Caesar, but upon Moses, Rameses and the Cave Man!" he insisted. "Also, I've glanced ahead as far as the year 10,000, beyond which my machine still won't work very well."

"That doesn't surprise me," I said, reverting to my original theory that Cloud was a madman.

He reached into his pocket, and drew forth a soiled paper crowded with mathematical notations. "Here are the computations that enabled me to reach my results," he explained. "It's taken years of calculation. I might almost say I've invented a new mathematics. Of course, you haven't time to go into all that just now. First you'd better take a look into my machine. After you've seen Charlemagne or Christopher Columbus, maybe you'll be convinced."

"Really, Mr. Cloud," I suggested, thinking it would be easier to be convinced that he had escaped from some institution. "I believe you'd better come around some other day. Can't you see how busy I am? My secretary will show you the way out."

And this time I reached in deadly earnestness toward the bell.

In spite of the abject, woebegone expression with which he sat regarding me, this probably would have been the end of my acquaintance with John Richard Cloud—had it not been for the untimely entrance of my assistant, Dr. Roscoe Horn, a man who had earned no small distinction by his Doctor's thesis on the non-Euclidean geometry.

Obviously taken aback at the sight of my strange visitor, Dr. Horn stood framed for an instant in the doorway and then was about to retreat, when I motioned him to me.

"Dr. Horn," I said, on an impulse that I have never been able to explain, "meet Mr. Cloud. Mr. Cloud has been conducting some experiments with the Fourth Dimension. He claims to have solved its mystery."

"Yes, and here are the figures," testified Cloud, pointing to the paper with the mathematical notations. "I have found a way of glancing out along Super-dimensional space."

To my surprise, Dr. Horn reached for the paper and began examining it attentively. At first his features were puckered in a puzzled frown, but after a moment his expression became graver and more absorbed and his eyes were glued to the page with a devouring relish... Several minutes passed. Dr. Horn uttered no word except a mumbled exclamation of surprise; Cloud stood staring at the newcomer with the eagerness of a drowning man; while I sat peering at both of them in impatience and surprise, wondering: what interest Dr. Horn could find in the scribblings of a lunatic...

"By heaven, Mr. Cloud, this is splendid! It certainly does look as if you're on the track of something!" enthused my assistant, turning to the inventor with a congratulatory nod. "It would take hours, of course, to follow all this out in detail, but I can see in what direction you're working. Theoretically, you're starting from a sound enough basis—"

"And practically I've been working from a sound enough basis!" proclaimed the inventor. "Dr. Horn won't you come with me and see my machine for penetrating the Fourth Dimension? Professor Howard, won't you come too? I won't take much of your time! But I promise to convince you!"

"What machine are you talking about?" inquired Dr. Horn.

Requiring no second bidding, Cloud launched into a detailed explanation, which I hardly attempted to follow. What startled me were not so much my visitor's extravagant contentions as the fact that Dr. Horn, while evidently surprised, was by no means so incredulous as I might have expected. "Sounds pretty far-fetched," he grunted, when Cloud had finished. "Still, I wouldn't attempt to pass snap judgment... What do you say, Professor? Suppose we go and see this man's machine? What harm can come of it? At worst, we may waste half an hour."

Gruffly I muttered something about the amount of work that lay untouched. But the jovial laughter of Dr. Horn dissipated my objections like mist. Besides, in spite of all Cloud's queerness, my curiosity had been awakened by the strange fire and earnestness of his demeanor.

And so, half reluctantly, I nodded assent; and a few minutes later, accompanied by my assistant and the inventor, I was on the way to Cloud's lodgings, where the most startling adventure of our lives awaited us.

CHAPTER TWO
A Journey in Reverse

AS THE three of us made our way together through alleys and side streets toward the poorer section of town, Cloud engaged in an almost continuous monologue:

"I don't want you to think I've been attempting anything so exceedingly strange and unheard of. In fact, the general idea that time and space can be interchanged is far from new to mathematicians. For a long while they have been accustomed to treating time as one of the dimensions of space. And that which can be represented in mathematics, must have some reality in the outside world. To take an old illustration: suppose that a two-dimensional creature was living on the flat surface of a table, but was unable to see anything above or below. And suppose that, being skilled in mathematics, it was informed by its computations that there actually was something above and below, even though something that its limited senses could not perceive. Would it not be the intelligent thing to try to invent some instrument to lift it over or beneath the plane surface and give it a different perspective? And would it not, from its new angle of vision, be able to look down upon its fellows, grasping them in their entirety, and discovering in one second what it might otherwise take years to learn? All this, you will admit, is theoretically possible. And this, on a larger scale, is what has actually happened with my Dimension Machine."

To my surprise, Dr. Horn nodded approval. "The idea is an excellent one," he affirmed. "To tell you the truth, Mr. Cloud, something very much like it has often occurred to me. It seems a strange coincidence, but for years it has been my pet dream to master the Fourth Dimension. I have seriously thought of attacking the problem with properly constructed instruments—but, somehow, I have never quite gotten down to the actual task."

In Dr. Horn's eyes, as he spoke, there was a sparkle of enthusiasm that startled me, since he was revealing a side of his nature I had never suspected before.

By this time we were walking through a street of miserable, grimy red brick sidewalks, where street venders hawked their wares and droves of noisy children screamed and played. Before one of the dingiest and most ramshackle buildings on one of the most poverty-ridden blocks, Cloud paused and mumbled, "Here we are." Then, without further ado, led us up the grim, narrow stairway to the fourth floor. Panting and puffing from the unaccustomed exertion, I was escorted into a room which, having no outlook except on a pitchy court, was even more dark and depressing than I had expected; and while our host turned on an old-style electric light, I sank into a bare-backed wooden chair to recover my breath.

"I have just two rooms," Cloud was telling us. "This one, of course, is the living room; the other one I call the laboratory. Shall I show you?"

"Just one moment!" I protested, raising my hand in a restraining gesture, while my eyes, I fear, fairly popped out of my head. Never had I seen such a living room as this! Once more the suspicion flashed over me that Cloud was insane—and this time, I thought, I had the best of reasons for that suspicion. Was I actually in the home of a fellow creature? Or was I in a museum? But no, even in a museum no room would have included so strange and varied a collection of oddities. My imagination fails me when I attempt to describe the appearance of that place: on the wall opposite me hung a broken copper sword curved in some antique fashion; beneath it stood an enormous cracked jug decorated in brilliant colors reminding me of old Grecian vases; to one side of it, I recognized the bas-relief of victorious, ancient warriors, presumably Assyrians or Babylonians; on the floor to my right was the fragment of an old Egyptian mummy case, the hieroglyphics being clearly distinguishable among the intricate swathings and wrappings. More surprising yet was an enormous rough-hewn axe, with stone head and handle, which made hideous one of the corners of the room; while what amazed me most of all was the marble bust of a woman, broken off at the chin, but showing that exquisite grace and refinement of outline which we have learned to associate with the masters of old Athens.

"Lord in heaven!" I muttered, trembling like one not quite in control of his senses. "Where did you get all these—these—"

"Oh, those? Why, they're nothing at all!" returned Cloud, with a disdainful shrug. "More pickings and findings! Debris of the ages, you might say, which happened to get entangled in my Dimension Machine, and got thrust into our dimension. They've not much value, as you can see. I'm keeping them as curiosities."

"But, by the Almighty, if such things are possible—" I began, as I rose excitedly in order to examine a scrap of tapestry depicting two helmeted knights in combat. "If such things are possible—"

"Much more than that is possible!" interrupted Cloud. "Sometimes something of value turns up. I've been living for months from the proceeds of a gold necklace from the time of Louis XIV. But, of course, that was only a lucky accident. Happening to be at the point where the Fourth Dimension verges on the Third, things sometimes get shoved into our world by chance. But don't let that surprise you. Wait till you see what my machine can really do!"

"Go ahead, Mr. Cloud! Show us!" I encouraged.

For, while by this time more firmly convinced than ever that Cloud was mad, I was willing to concede that he was a madman of an unusual type.

"To tell you the truth, Professor, he's got me guessing," Dr. Horn whispered into my ear, as he passed into the adjoining room. "I've been examining that little strip of parchment over near the door. If it isn't a genuine Roman document from the third century, it's the cleverest imitation I've ever seen!"

Unluckily, I had no time to reply. Our host had switched on the lights in his "laboratory," revealing a fair-sized room littered with coils and wires, and malodorous with chemicals and strong acids. In the center stood a tall canvas-covered object of about the size of a piano—indeed, it might have been a piano, for all that we could tell; and to this article Cloud pointed with enthusiastic gestures. "The Dimension Machine!" he announced. "The Dimension Machine!"

Being in the position of spectators at a play before the first curtain has lifted, we could only peer interestedly at the object, and nod.

Slowly, and with the significant smile of a showman about to unveil some remarkable exhibition, Cloud withdrew the covering from about his machine. "There!" he exclaimed, with every evidence of satisfaction. "There! Now you can see for yourselves!"

A momentary silence followed. It was the silence not of amazement, but merely of a blank, unimpressive wonder. My first sensation was that of a vague disappointment—what was this curious instrument that Cloud had shown us? Certainly, it did not look nearly so strange or intricate as many mechanisms designed for much simpler ends. Directly facing me at the end of the machine, I saw a large but quite ordinary-looking mirror; while other mirrors, to the number of thirty or forty, were connected with thin wires and rods, and arranged back to back and less than an inch apart. At the further end of the machine I observed a complicated mass of steel rods and levers connecting with a basket-like device of wire of the size of a small barrel—but, except for these appliances and a few electric bulbs and connections, there seemed to be nothing at all to the whole contrivance.

"You will observe the extra-dimensional mirrors," pointed out Cloud, speaking rapidly and excitedly while his dark eyes burnt with a zealot's fire. "Watch them carefully. They may do strange antics."

With these words, he pressed a small button at one side of the machine; and the whole apparatus instantly expanded like a camera, until the mirrors were several inches apart and reached almost from end to end of the room.

"Now for the current," he continued, plugging a wire into an electric light socket, following which a low buzzing filled the room, and sparks began to flash and sizzle from somewhere amid the steel rods and levers.

"I need the electricity only incidentally. Any other source of power would do as well. It has nothing to do with the real purpose of the machine," the inventor explained. "Now you'll see me get the mirrors into action. Don't take your eyes off them. Want to take a peep at past time?—or at future?"

"Past," decided Dr. Horn.

"Very well," acquiesced our host, turning to an object somewhat like a radio dial, and numbered, like such a dial, from one to a hundred. Just beneath it was a little lever, on one side of which we read the word "Forward," and on the other "Reverse." "The past is reverse, of course," we were told, while Cloud shifted the lever to the right. "Now how many years back would you like to go? I haven't got the gauge accurate as yet, but each number on the indicator represents, roughly speaking, one century."

"Oh, a thousand years would be enough," suggested Dr. Horn, in a casual manner.

"As you say!" nodded Cloud.

"Of course," he added, apologetically, "you mustn't hold it against the machine if I turn the dial a little too far, and go back eleven hundred or even twelve hundred years."

I remarked that this was a sin we would forgive.

Then, while I watched with a smile that I fear was still just a little incredulous, Cloud began manipulating various bars and levers with such rapidity that we could not follow his movements. As he had promised, the mirrors did indeed perform strange antics! Propelled on small rods and wires, they moved in all directions; some swung upward, some sidewards, some downward, some tilted at curious angles, until each reflected its neighbors in odd and unexpected ways. For several minutes their movements continued, now slow, now rapid, while the buzzing and clattering of the machine filled the room, and at the same time Cloud was trying to make himself heard above the uproar.

"It isn't always easy to get things in the right position," he assured us. "Yet everything has been calculated mathematically, so that if the mirrors are in precisely the required relation to one another, and each properly reflects the lines and angles of its neighbors, they will also reflect the Fourth Dimension, and show what is going on there... Ah...now I think we're getting near it! We may be a century or two off in our bearings, but that can hardly be helped."

So saying, he removed his hands from the machine, and all the movements and clattering instantly ceased.

"Now look carefully!" he directed. "You'll behold a scene in the tenth century or thereabouts!"

I looked as carefully as I knew how, but my smile of incredulity only broadened. All that I saw was the reflected lights of the room.

"You will have; to concentrate, Professor," advised Cloud, turning to me reprovingly. "Sometimes the impressions are blurred at first, and the vision is obscured by one's third dimensional bias. But see! Why, you're looking at the wrong mirror! Can't you be more careful? Everything is as plain as daylight to me!"

I shifted my gaze to another mirror, and lo and behold! I did indeed see something unexpected. I was not sure at first that it was the Fourth Dimension; all that I knew was that it left me dizzy and bewildered; I was confronted by a confusion of crazy, meaningless lines, as if I had peered into one of those convex or concave mirrors which are sometimes displayed for comic purposes, and which distort the observer into a ten-foot living rail or into a walking circle. What crude sort of joke was Cloud trying to perpetrate?

But even as I asked myself this question, the scenes before me commenced to grow a little less puzzling and bizarre. I began to see order amid the chaos; I made out the contours of a green field, looking a little remote and queer, and yet unmistakably a green field! And in the distance I distinguished the shimmer of water and the cloudy shapes of trees!

"See!" cried our host, leaping up and down with the agitation of a four-year-old, and literally shaking his own hands in his excitement. "See! I told you, didn't I? The tenth century!"

Although willing to concede that Cloud had used some very clever trickery, I was still able to snort in unbelief. "Hmm!" I grunted. "That's a country scene, all right! But what's to show me it isn't the twentieth century?"

Cloud stood gazing reflectingly into the mirror, and then reluctantly conceded, "Why, I guess there's nothing to show you. Unluckily, landscape scenery hasn't changed much in a thousand years. We'll have to shift the scene a bit—though, of course, there's always the danger of accidents. Some dinosaur bones, for example or else a stone or stump or some antique bit of furniture may get caught in the machine."

Once more Cloud turned to the levers, and there was another brief clattering, while the mirrors again changed places.

"Now maybe we'll get better results!" he declared. "We've gone back another generation or two!"

This time also I was aware of a confusion of lines—parallels that seemed to meet in contradiction of Euclid, curving triangles, squares that verged toward the circular, and circles that verged toward the square. Then by degrees my bewilderment subsided, and the mirror seemed to contain the reflection of a recognizable scene.

"By the eternal!" muttered Dr. Horn, beneath his breath. "It's like a picture out of a story book!" And I too muttered beneath my breath, unable to imagine by what diabolical ingenuity the inventor had produced his results.

It seemed to me that I was gazing across a black pond at a gray stone building—a building whose ramparts and turrets and watchtowers and thin spidery slits of windows reminded me of the castles I had seen on a European tour years before. At the base of the edifice a huge door suddenly opened; several coarsely garbed men appeared; a drawbridge was slowly let down across the waters; then a score of horses strode forth, each bearing a rider appareled from head to foot in steel and brandishing an eighteen-foot lance...

My observation of this astonishing scene was interrupted by the groan of our host.

"What a mistake!" he lamented. "What a mistake! I meant to make it a thousand years, and we've only gone back six or seven centuries! I'll have to try again!"

"One moment, please!" I snapped, still not quite unconvinced that he was attempting some roguery. And I began to look about the room for some concealed apparatus that might have produced the results. Could there be a hidden motion picture machine? This idea, I must admit, seemed absurd; yet it seemed less absurd than that Cloud was actually in touch with the Fourth Dimension. Accordingly, I conducted my investigation as diligently as a detective on the trail of a murder mystery. But I found no trapdoor, no disguised machinery, no sign of an abettor or confederate. All that I discovered to reward my pains were the bare walls and one small drawer containing—absolutely nothing.

Now all at once, despite all my years of sober scientific training, I was obsessed by a feeling such as I had not known since childhood. A strange shuddery sensation began to overwhelm me, as though I were in touch with something weird, something uncanny, something unhuman and appalling, a universe of black and bottomless mystery. Had I been a superstitious person, I would have crossed myself or mumbled secret prayers; as it was, I merely frowned and gritted my teeth. Irritated at my own weakness, I tried in vain to forget the chills that were creeping along my spine and was perhaps needlessly gruff in requesting the inventor to make further demonstrations.

This he readily consented to do, while Dr. Horn stood by grave and speechless, his stern features twisted into an expression of wonder, his eyes fixed upon the Dimension Machine with a telltale fascination.

It would entail endless repetition to describe all the wonders unfolded before us during the next half-hour. Skeptical as I was in the beginning, I should have had to be immensely incredulous not to be convinced by the time I had peered at half a dozen new marvels: at a Crusading army, with its pilgrim's garb and its crosses; at a Roman amphitheater during a gladiatorial exhibition; at Carthaginian warriors setting out with their trappings and their elephants; at a three-banked slave galley awkwardly cleaving the waters of the Mediterranean; at a royal Egyptian funeral procession held several thousand years before the birth of Christ. These and other sights equally unbelievable were flashed in rapid succession before our eyes, until both Dr. Horn and I were ready to grasp the inventor's hand with an almost tearful enthusiasm, and to proclaim that he was a veritable genius.

Only one final demonstration required to be made. "Your machine seems pretty efficient in scouring the past," acknowledged Dr. Horn, after we had gazed at China of the time of Confucius. "But how about the future? Can it do, as well for coming events?"

"Of course!" the inventor asserted. "I merely have to reverse its direction."

And he pulled the lever labeled "Forward," thereby opening the way for stranger results than any of us could have anticipated.

"I've really experimented much less with the future than with the past," he confided, as the mirrors paraded back and forth and up and down and around in an opposite direction from before. "But I've done enough to know I can succeed. Any part of time, of course, is accessible to one who can reach the Fourth Dimension. The difference between tomorrow and yesterday is no greater than the difference between east and west."

"Then, having seen a few men from yesterday, I'd like to see a man from tomorrow," I suggested, glibly.

Little did I suspect how literally my desire was to be fulfilled!

CHAPTER THREE
A Visitor from the Void

GLANCING into the mirrors of the Dimension Machine as they flashed with supposed reflections from the future, I was aware at first of the same insane confusion as when peering into the past. There were lines that twisted and wavered until I hardly knew whether they were jagged, circular or straight; there were triangles and quadrilaterals that appeared to meet and part and divide in defiance of all known laws of geometry; there were cubes and spheres that seemed somehow not cubes or spheres, since they were evidently able to pass through one another without touching; while their left-hand hemispheres had a habit of changing places with their right, as if by a process of instantaneous magic. Merely to glance at them, was enough to make my senses reel; and I was therefore relieved when at length the spectacle became a little less bewildering, and I was able to make out some sensible and recognizable scenes.

The first of those scenes, to be sure, were in no way remarkable. I saw a snow-capped mountain, and it did not seem to me to matter what the century might be; I saw a valley where pines were growing and cattle browsed in green meadows, and again the century was of no importance; I saw a rock-strewn desert where a hot sun blazed down on a parched infinity, and once more I did not care if the date were a thousand B. C. or five thousand A. D.

"Are we going to see nothing by way of evidence!" I muttered, impatiently—when, suddenly, I had all the evidence I wanted.

Staring at me out of the mirror, were the stone walls and towers of a city, such as I had never imagined in my weirdest dream. I cannot describe it in detail, for my view of it was only momentary; I can only say that it jutted to the height of mountains, and that a multitude of thin spires, straight and black like the standing tree-trunks of a burnt forest, pointed skyward to the height of perhaps a mile; while each was joined to its neighbors by means of heavy steel meshes and cables like the connecting masts of a ship.

"A city of the year 2900!" exclaimed Cloud, enthusiastically. "Those tall towers, I assume, are the dwelling places of the well-to-do. Probably those that live below are old at forty because of the monoxide-infested air."

"Can't you give us something a little nearer our own times?" requested Dr. Horn, impressed and at the same time repelled by the exhibition.

"Certainly," conceded the inventor, as he again manipulated the levers of his machine. "Let's try to have a look at the twenty-second or the twenty-first century."

We now caught a glimpse of an enormous airplane, with a central compartment of the size of a Pullman car, in which dozens of passengers sat at their ease. Then, by an instantaneous shifting of the scenes, we had a view of something hideous and unspeakable, where clouds of yellow vapor rolled across a blackened land, and scores of thousands of men gasped and fell dead...

"A future battlefield!" cried the inventor, in a voice of horror; and in his excitement, it seemed to me, he became exceedingly careless and lost control of his movements. For a moment he moved the levers without seeming to notice which one he was touching, and the mirrors reflected the craziest array of shifting lines and figures I had yet seen.

Now all at once, with disconcerting abruptness, there came a strange whirring and rattling from the instrument. The inventor uttered a sudden "Damn it!" and his eyes bulged with alarm; while his fingers began to work with lightning rapidity.

Whatever the trouble may have been, he was too late to repair it. While Dr. Horn and I looked on in dread and amazement, a vastly more frightening manifestation overwhelmed us. There came a flash of lightning; then another flash, and a deafening detonation; then a third flash, and, to our terror, the lights all at once went out, and, in the darkness, there sounded another thunderous demonstration, accompanied by a shattering noise and a thud as of some heavy body striking the ground...

As the echoes ominously died away and comparative silence fell upon us, we heard the irritated voice of the inventor. "Anybody got a match? Damn it! Got a match, anybody? I don't know where I've put mine!"

Energetically I searched my pockets, but not one of the desired articles was to be found.

"Here's one!" mumbled Dr. Horn; and he struck a light that flared only long enough to reveal how his hand was trembling.

"As luck wouldn't have it, that's my last!" he growled as the flickering flame went out.

"I'll have to feel my way!" groaned Cloud, beginning a groping movement somewhere amid the obscurity. "Hope you don't mind, everybody. I'll find the electric connections in a minute. They couldn't have been damaged much."

Then, while he banged against some unseen object in the dark, he called out, by way of afterthought, "Neither of you hurt, are you?"

Although I had rarely received a sharper nervous shock, I had to join Dr. Horn in disclaiming all injury.

"Sorry it had to happen while you were here. That's about the worst short circuit yet," apologized our host, as he collided with another obstacle in the gloom.

"Short-circuit?" echoed Dr. Horn.

"Short-circuit is what I call it. Naturally, it isn't really that."

For a moment, we were conscious that Cloud had halted in his stumbling movements about the room. "When some object from the Fourth Dimension gets too near my machine, it isn't simply reflected in the mirrors; it becomes entangled in the instrument, sending an electrical shock through the whole mechanism. That's what produced the lightning and thunder. But, believe me, gentlemen, I never saw things go quite so badly before. To tell you the truth, it had me scared for a minute."

"You mean to say—something from the Fourth Dimension may be in the machine now?" demanded Dr. Horn.

Even as my assistant uttered these words, Cloud gave a jubilant exclamation. "Ah! Here it is!" And, to our intense relief, he switched on the light.

"The bulb was merely jarred out of place," he explained. "No real damage done."

But we gave little thought to his words. Our attention was riveted upon the Dimension Machine. Certainly, Cloud's remark, "No real damage done," did not apply to his invention. It looked as if a storm had struck it; half of the mirrors lay cracked and broken; more than half of the rods were twisted and curved as though by an earthquake. "God have mercy!" moaned our host. "I am ruined!" And his face went suddenly white; the tears started to his eyes; he flung himself toward the shattered machine and began to examine it with the passion of a mother encountering a wounded child.

Perhaps it was because of his very fury that he failed to see the object that arrested the attention of Dr. Horn and myself. In the basket-like wire contrivance at one end of the machine, there was a large dark mass that had not been here before. Never have I had a more uncanny sensation than when I first set eyes upon it: it was almost as if something had been created out of nothingness, as if a solid reality had been shot at us from some other world! "What can it be?" I muttered into Dr. Horn's ears; while, without answering, he joined me in examining it.

Coming face to face with the object, both of us merely gasped and stared. So great was our bewilderment that we were unable to speak—was this only an hallucination? A phantom? Was it a ghost bred of our own shocked imaginations? For we seemed to be gazing at a fellow man! Although the eyes were closed; although the position was cramped and unnatural; although the knees were drawn up against the chin, in a manner reminding us of a babe in its mother's womb; although the creature was fantastically clothed and unusually small for an adult, still it was unmistakably man!

How had it found its way inside that wire basket? Found its way in without removing or breaking any of the closely placed wires?

"Cloud! Mr. Cloud!" called Dr. Horn and I, as we both regained our voices at the same instant. "Come, Mr. Cloud! Look! Look!"

The inventor, who had been examining the cracked mirrors with such mournful absorption that he had not even noticed the contents of the basket, slouched disconsolately over to us.

"Good heavens!" he wailed, as he caught a glimpse of the occupant of the wire cage; and he wrung his hands like one burdened with woes unbearable. "What have I done to deserve this? Isn't it enough to be showered with relics from the past? Now I've kidnapped a man from the future!"

The somberness with which Cloud uttered these words was such that, despite our own grave mood, Dr. Horn and I had difficulty not to laugh.

But we became serious enough the next moment, as the inventor pointed out the dangers of our predicament.

"Looks like a dead man, too," he moaned. "The shock of coming to this century has killed him! Why, I'm nothing but a common murderer. Of course, maybe he would have died anyhow. But that doesn't help us out much. What shall we do with the body? Dispose of it like a gang of conspirators? And then maybe be detected and brought to justice? Or quietly give the remains up to the police? Confess that they come from the Fourth Dimension? You know what will happen then. We'll all be able to escape the Electric Chair—on the ground of lunacy."

A long, long silence followed. The atmosphere about us seemed suddenly heavy, oppressive, gloomy, as though charged with some intense, invisible evil. Only too clearly we realized the truth of the inventor's remarks; only too distinctly I saw how we had involved ourselves in an adventure that threatened to end disastrously.

"Of course, if it comes to an investigation, I myself will take all the blame," our host assured us. "You two gentlemen are innocent—I will vouch for that."

"Come! Aren't you losing your head?" suddenly demanded Dr. Horn, in the manner of one grasping at a desperate hope. "How do you know our visitor is dead? Perhaps the shock of coming here hasn't killed him after all. Why not examine more closely? We may yet bring him back to life. First let's get him out of that cage. But hurry, hurry! His life may depend on our haste!"

"Good!" I acknowledged, inspired with fresh courage. "Very good. Got any tools handy, Mr. Cloud?"

With sudden frantic haste, Cloud fished about in an old chest, from which he produced a pair of pliers and a hammer. A moment later, we were busy freeing the stranger from his wire prison.

CHAPTER FOUR
The Awakening

AFTER we had released the captive and borne him to the couch in Cloud's living room, we began to take careful note of his appearance. He was, as I have already said, a small man, being not more than five feet in height; he was beardless and nearly bald, and yet his smooth, chalky pallid skin proclaimed him not past early middle age; his features were small and strong, and at the same time were peculiarly ugly in their irregularity, for the sharp chin projected at a twisted angle, the thin nose was bent slightly awry, and the bulbous forehead bulged more prominently on the right side than on the left. But the thing that struck us most strangely was not so much his physiognomy as his clothes. He was, it seemed to us, almost in a state of undress: he was clad only in a single-piece costume, of some curious substance which, while dark at a distance, shimmered beautifully upon close approach; and not only were his arms bare, but his legs below the knees were exposed except for the sandals that covered his feet, while the upper part of his chest boasted no raiment, and down his back there was a big V-shaped slit reminding me of a woman's party gown.

From the moment when we set to work over this singular individual, we began to feel a pulse of reviving hope. His skin, as we discovered to our immense relief, was of almost normal warmth; apparently he could not have been dead long, if indeed he were dead at all. True, no trace of respiration was visible, nor could we at first detect any heartbeat; but after we had deposited him on the couch and began to fan his face and rub his limbs to restore the circulation, I thought that I saw him move slightly—ever so slightly, but more than one would have expected of a corpse!

"Take courage, Mr. Cloud," I advised. "We may still escape indictment as murderers."

As I uttered these words, it seemed to us all that a sigh—woefully faint and thin—escaped from the lips of the sufferer.

With significant glances, we stood regarding the stranger. Then Dr. Horn, reaching for a glass from the table, held it above the lips of the stricken man. Immediately a faint but perceptible film appeared.

"There!" cried my assistant, stroking his moustache in emphatic self-congratulation. "See! He lives! He lives!"

But like a dash of cold water came the words of the inventor. "What help will that be if he's about to die? Can't you see, he hasn't any vitality at all! Why doesn't he show any pulse? If he isn't dead, then at least he's dying!"

"Wouldn't it be best to send for a doctor?" I urged.

But no one paid any heed to me, and I contented myself with reaching for the wrist of the unknown, and trying for the tenth or twelfth time to detect some evidence of a heartbeat. At first the effort appeared as fruitless as before; but after a moment I did seem to notice a faint rhythmic movement. How pitiably slow and weak it was. Yet it was strong enough to lend me new hope!

"Take courage!" I exclaimed once more. "Our friend may still recover."

Cloud sniffed incredulously; and I, disregarding him, pressed my ear against the afflicted man's breast, in the hope of still more encouraging evidence. Listening on his left side, in the supposed position of the heart, I was dismayed to hear nothing at all; whereupon, moved by some impulse that I still do not understand, I shifted my attention to the right side. And immediately my efforts were rewarded! A subdued but regular throbbing greeted my ears.

"Heavens, but this is strange!" I muttered. "His heart seems to be on the right side!"

"The most likely thing in the world," remarked Cloud, shrugging indifferently. "In making the change of dimensions, his sides happened to get reversed. It's no more peculiar than if an object falling through the air landed upside down."

Since my studies of the Fourth Dimension were much more limited than Cloud's, I did not venture to argue. Instead, I felt once more for the stricken person's pulse, which, to my surprise, appeared to offer some feeble resistance. And, to my further surprise, the pulse was noticeably firmer than before!

"Prepare yourselves, friends!" I exclaimed. "Our patient is not going to die—not, at least, today!"

As if to confirm these words, the lips of the stranger opened, in another sigh—apparently unconscious, yet louder and more distinct than before. We could now see that the chest was heaving slightly and slowly, as if with the first labored efforts at reviving animation.

Never did nurse or physician attend his charge with more trembling devotion than did we bestow upon our mysterious visitor, now that he seemed to be struggling out of his coma... Half an hour went by; an occasional sigh or moan continued to escape from his lips; once or twice he shifted slightly in position; and the time the heaving of his chest was growing more pronounced and more regular and the pulse was becoming stronger and nearer to normal; while we, hovering over him, were energetic in warming his stiffened muscles, in applying water to his parched lips, and in fanning him with many a reviving breath.

It was with unexpected suddenness that he at last opened his eyes. An anxious second passed while the dilated pupils stared at us with a dazed expression, from amid the pallid blue of the iris and the thin face were expressive of bewilderment and wonder. Then the man lifted himself slightly on his elbows, and an exclamation, half of amazement, half of terror, tore itself from his throat.

"Where am I? Who are you?" we afterwards judged to be the import of the words—though the syllables were all slurred together, and what he said might be more properly represented as, "Where'm I? Who'r 'ou?"

"Where am I? Who are you?" he repeated, as his gaze traveled in startled inquiry about the room.

And then, as his bloodless hand anxiously stroked his forehead, he seemed to us like a victim of shellshock, trying to collect his scattered thoughts. With an effort, while his breath came short and fast, he gradually drew himself up to a sitting posture; and once more his words came forth, being addressed, it seemed, not so much to us as to himself.

But this time he spoke more slowly; and though his accentuation struck us as coarse and peculiar and he still showed the same deplorable tendency to slur his consonants and forget his vowels, we were able to make out most of his words.

"What has happened to me? Have I died? Or can this be the Fifth Dimension? No! Not that, either! Where then is Maranna? And the observatory—where is the observatory? I do not see them! They are all gone! It is so strange! Who...who are these uncouth persons here?"

With a sigh, he sank back once more upon the couch. Dr. Horn and I exchanged significant glances; but no one cared to speak.

Now it was that an alarming thought flashed over me. What if we had captured a lunatic from some other age?

But in a moment this fear began to be dissipated. With an obvious effort, the man arose once more to a sitting position; for a full minute he stared at us without uttering a word; then, as he gazed, his pupils began to contract, and a keener, more intelligent expression filled his eyes. The look of astonishment and wonder had not yet left him, but it was apparent that he had been delirious before, and had scarcely been conscious of what he was saying.

"Where am I?" he inquired once more, but in a slower, more deliberate manner. "I do not know you. What place is this? What has overtaken me?" And there followed a mumbled sentence, which none of us could make out at all.

"Be of good cheer!" I encouraged. "You are with friends."

"Be of good cheer!" he repeated, as though I had said something unusual. "What a curious-sounding phrase. I wonder where you learned such an antique expression!"

There followed an embarrassed pause; after which the stranger inquired, in a hasty, rattling voice, "Would you mind telling me, am I in a museum? Why all the ancient trappings about this place?

How comes it that you use that obsolete style of lamp over there? I believe I once saw something like it, though not quite so primitive looking, in an exhibition of old heirlooms. An electric light…that's what it's called! But why not use the modern inter-atomic bulbs?"

"Inter-atomic bulbs?" we all echoed, wondering if the man was still delirious.

"Then look at those costumes of yours," proceeded our visitor, breaking into a smile that was dangerously close to laughter. "Where did you ever procure them? Are you dressing for a masquerade? Why, they remind me of survivals from the Neurotic Age! You, sir in particular…" Here the speaker pointed to me with an amused grimace. "…are to be congratulated upon your post-Medieval style. It is ugly and unsanitary enough to have pleased our ancestors. Why not take it to a specialist in curios? It should bring in at least a hundred tantrums!"

"Tantrums?" I demanded, puzzled and offended, for I had always prided myself upon the neatness of my apparel, and nothing could have been more unexceptional than the well tailored brown business-like suit I was wearing. "What are tantrums?"

"What are tantrums?" repeated the stranger, apparently no less surprised than I. "You speak, my dear Sir, as if you had never heard of the medium of exchange!"

"And you, my dear sir," I retorted, still wincing beneath the wound he had dealt me, "speak as if you had never seen a decently clad citizen. Tell us, do you expect everyone to go around like you in a bathing suit?"

Our visitor looked more puzzled than ever. "Bathing suits?" he challenged. "As if anybody needs a suit for bathing! Really, sir, you have the most ridiculous ideas! And what, may I ask, do you find wrong with me? Am I not dressed in the most modest, conservative garment permitted by the Censor?"

This was too much for me. I opened my mouth to reply; but I could only gape at the speaker and remain silent, unable to find words to express my conflicting feelings.

"Once more I ask you, where am I? Who are you all?" demanded the unknown. "Have I been kidnapped? Or have my experiments thrown me among you by chance? You all seem so strange! Your house is so strange, your clothes are so strange, and your speech is the strangest of all! You have such a coarse, un-natural accentuation, and use so many curious words! It is really difficult to follow you. I swear to you, I have not been employing a time-eliminator; otherwise, I could not believe I was still in the twenty-third century!"

"Twenty-third century?" we gasped, looking at one another questioningly.

Something in the manner in which we uttered these words must have struck our visitor peculiarly. "Why, you seem surprised," he remarked, eyeing us keenly. "What century is this, then, if not the twenty-third?"

It was Dr. Horn who broke the distressing news. "I am sorry to have to inform you, my friend," he declared in slow, hesitant tones, "I am sorry to have to inform you that you are a little misplaced in time. This is not the twenty-third century. Not by three hundred years. It is now the year 1930."

"1930!" bawled our guest, in a voice vibrant with horror. "Heaven have mercy!"

Suddenly he sprang to his feet. His fists were clenched; his knees trembled; his eyes glittered with agony and rage. "1930!" he shrilled. "What a doom! What a doom! To be back in the Neurotic age! What have I done to deserve this? What have I done? Why couldn't I have gone to some other age, any other age at all?"

Speechlessly we looked on at the poor man's sufferings, unable to help him, unable to speak a word in consolation; while his features worked with an anguish that if was pain to see, and he paced the room with the distraction of a trapped animal.

After a moment, having spent his feeble strength, he sank down upon the couch with a moan, and buried his face in his hands. Then, after rocking back and forth in frantic emotion, he arose on an impulse, and, addressing himself to me, burst out imperiously, "Sir, I demand—I demand that you transport me back to my own century!"

"Why, I—I'm sure I'd be glad to—if I could," I blurted out, a little shaken by the fury of the attack. "But you're asking the wrong man."

"We can't—really we can't," added Cloud, mournfully, as he swung open the door to the adjoining room and revealed the ruins of the Dimension Machine. "The invention that got you here is destroyed. There isn't another like it in the whole world. I'm afraid it couldn't have gotten you back, anyhow."

Even amid the frenzy of his grief, our visitor had time to peer at the Dimension Machine with lower lip curled into a sneer. "So that's the invention that got me here? You mean to say you actually used that? Oh, yes, it does vaguely remind me of our own hyperspace engines. But how rudimentary-looking. Where is its time-amplifier? Where is its plane-differentiator? Where is its distance-generator? God in heaven, it doesn't seem to have any safety equipment at all. No wonder I got caught in it! No wonder!"

Sinking back again to his seat on the couch, our visitor continued, in less passionate tones, "Of course, it's not your fault altogether. I have myself to blame too. Yes, I really have myself to blame. If I hadn't been trying to explore the Fifth Dimension, I would never have been caught in the Fourth. To be sure, I didn't mean to leave my own age. But that was one of the risks I had to take. And so here I am, among my ancestors of the Era of Decadence, nearly three hundred years before I am born! Was ever any man so punished before?"

"Really, sir, it isn't so bad as all that," suggested Dr. Horn, in the diffident manner of a schoolboy addressing his master. "The Twentieth century, as you will find, is actually a very advanced period—"

"A very advanced period!" Long and scornful was the laughter of our visitor. "A very advanced period, you say? You have an excellent sense of humor, sir! Personally, I haven't read a great deal about your age, being always concerned with cultural subjects; but our historians wouldn't agree with you. Why, don't you recall that science was only in its infancy then? They hadn't even invented such everyday commodities as ultra-violet vision, inter-atomic heating, radio intelligence-testers, automatic thought-regulators, X-ray character dissectors, and a thousand and one other necessities of civilized life. Indeed, they had created almost nothing except machines for producing neuroses, which would have led to racial suicide or insanity if a more enlightened era hadn't followed. No, sir, you can't convince me that the Neurotic Age was progressive!"

And once more the man from tomorrow broke into a blasting burst of laughter.

"But if this be the Neurotic Age," I inquired, galled by his manner, "what, pray is your own era called?"

He hugged his dwarfish knees and rocked back and forth in renewed laughter. "The day of the Superman!" he said. It was a strange sight to see this little creature diminutive as compared with us, yet so positive in his views, standing before us arms akimbo, and upholding in the most matter-of-fact way, the ways and methods of his century. He was like a child instructing his elders, for as a matter of course, he was absolutely positive, we might almost say obstinate, in his own quiet way of dilating on the great advantages of his era.

Somehow or other, the condition of things with us and our point of view, seemed to impress him as very comical, for his ideas had so much of advance in them that their oddities were really masked by it, and we could not feel that they were at all comical.

CHAPTER FIVE
The Man from Tomorrow Takes Command

AFTER our visitor's mirth had subsided, his face was crossed once more by an expression of intense pain. He began to bite his lips and to mutter to himself; and, wringing his hands, he arose and paced the room again. "Maranna!" he moaned, in barely audible tones. "Maranna! Oh, when will we ever meet now?"

A racked moment passed in silence, while he struggled visibly with his emotion, and at length, with an evident effort, managed to twist his lips into stern lines of resignation.

Then, seeing how curiously we were eyeing him, he attempted to answer our unspoken questions. "Maranna," he confided, in a trembling voice, "was my laboratory assistant. She was to have been my mate. It has just occurred to me—she is buried three hundred years in the future. Perhaps I shall never see her again!"

Despite all his efforts at a stoic repression, the tears were gathering to the blue eyes of the man from tomorrow.

But, with a desperate resolve, he finally wiped the tears away, and managed soberly to explain:

"Maranna and I, you see, conducted all our experiments together. My name is Wormwood—John Wormwood. I had charge of the International Hyperspace Observatory at Mount Holrood. We used to decide such questions as the appearance of the secondary craters on the other side of the moon, or the state of the magma two thousand miles beneath the earth; or else maybe we would foresee what was going to occur on the seventh dark satellite of the star, Vega, in the year 1,000,001. We would also explore—"

"Did you discover much about the Fourth Dimension?" interrupted Cloud, his dark eyes glowing with eagerness.

"Fourth Dimension?" Wormwood stared at his interrogator in wonder mixed with a peculiar disdain. "No, we didn't give much attention to elementary work. Our peculiar concern was the Fifth Dimension. We'd pretty nearly mastered that too, and were contemplating going on into the Sixth. It was my effort to complete my discoveries that landed me here. I had invented a machine to project myself into the Fifth Dimension, and I made my first experiment with it only last night. That is to say…" Here the man from tomorrow paused in evident embarrassment. "…That is to say, one night three hundred years from now. But I must have lost my balance, and in a moment of absentmindedness descended into the Fourth Dimension, where your machine accidentally picked me up. Though it won't happen for three centuries yet, it really seems only an hour ago when I stepped into the little aluminum compartment, saw Maranna smiling down upon me, heard her switch on the inter-atomic power, and felt myself whirled away into nothingness."

An impressive silence followed. I was on the point of saying something terse and strong, for it did not seem to me that to make a journey to the twentieth century was exactly to be "whirled away into nothingness." But I was deterred out of respect for the grief that still convulsed our visitor's rugged features.

It was Dr. Horn that put the next question. "If you know so much, sir, about super-space, surely you should be able to help us to construct a machine to send you back to your own age. Why not show us the way?"

But Wormwood, to our surprise, did not take kindly to this suggestion. He merely stared at us hopelessly, as if to say, "Oh, what's the use? What's the use?" And it was a minute before he answered, in a dull, despondent manner:

"It would be the easiest thing in the world to contrive such a machine if you had the equipment. But I'm sure you haven't. Where are your molecular compressors? Your radio-propeller gauges? Your etheric estimators? Not to speak of your inter-atomic power plants? No, I'm sure you haven't any facilities at all, and won't have any for a hundred years yet. It's all very well to ask me to make a Fourth Dimensional machine, but could one of your own mechanics construct an airplane or a locomotive with no apparatus other than the stone axes and flint cleavers of the Cave Man?"

Having uttered these words, the man from tomorrow shook his head despairingly, and fell into a brown study.

Once more I was tempted to protest, for the reference to the Cave Man seemed to me entirely beside the point. However, I restrained myself, since I realized that, after all, Mr. Wormwood was in a peculiar predicament, and one that would entitle any man to the use of strong language.

After a delay of a few seconds, Cloud took our thoughts rudely from the Fifth Dimension by offering an unexpected suggestion. "Mr.—Mr. Wormwood," he ventured, diffidently, "you have made a long journey. You must be hungry. Wouldn't you like some refreshments?"

"Refreshments?" demanded Wormwood, looking puzzled. "What are refreshments?"

"You mean to say you don't know? Things to eat. Food," explained Cloud, in a chastened voice.

"Then why didn't you say so? What a queer-sounding word, refreshments! I suppose, though, it was commonly used in the Neurotic Age, when they needed plenty of things to freshen them up. Yes, thank you. I'll have some, if you don't mind. I haven't eaten since the twenty-third century."

"There's never much in this place, but I'll get what I can," promised Cloud, as he began to ransack the cupboard at one end of the room that served him for kitchen and pantry.

A few moments later, he had managed to produce two good solid-looking ham sandwiches, which he set with an apologetic air before our guest.

For a hungry man, Wormwood showed a surprising reluctance about setting to work on these morsels. A questioning glitter came into his eyes; his slender nostrils were wrinkled as if in distaste; his thin lips curled with an expression dangerously close to a sneer. With dainty, almost timid gestures he began fingering the sandwiches; appraisingly he drew one of them apart and gazed down at the slim red slice of meat; then, with a critical air, he lifted the ham toward him, and sniffed at it anxiously. And all at once he uttered a cry of disgust, and shoved the food from him as though it were something loathsome.

Never had I admired the manners of the man from tomorrow, but it seemed to me that such boorishness passed all excusable limits.

"Why, what's the matter?" demanded Cloud, stepping forward to examine the rejected food. "Anything wrong with the sandwiches?"

"Anything wrong?" echoed Wormwood, as though he had been insulted. "What abominable filth have you offered me? Surely, I could not have been mistaken! It is flesh—the disguised burnt flesh of a fellow animal!"

"Why, it's only—it's only ham!" gasped Cloud, too amazed for words. "Surely, you're not—you're not a Hebrew, are you? Your religion doesn't forbid you to eat pork?" raged Cloud.

"Religion? What an idea! Who told you there is any religion left in the twenty-third century? No, I haven't any religion. I'm just an ordinary, sober, self-respecting citizen. Like all other right-thinking men, I detest cannibalism!"

"Cannibalism?" we all repeated, and stared at one another in astonishment, thinking that the man from tomorrow had queer ideas of a jest.

"What's wrong in saying I detest cannibalism?" Wormwood raged, while glaring at us with accusing eyes…

But all at once a light seemed to burst upon him. "Ah! I had forgotten! In the twentieth century, the whole civilized world was cannibalistic. It was before the Moral Awakening, when men first perceived the monstrousness of preying upon their fellow creatures. Of course! Of course! I should have remembered! After all, I shouldn't blame you for your barbarian habits—you really don't know any better."

"So people in your own age never eat meat?" I asked.

"Eat what? What was that word? Meat? How revolting! You mean, the flesh and blood of our brother mammals? Do you think we're tigers—or wolves? Can't you understand?—the twenty-third century is an enlightened era."

"Then no one ever—ever touches flesh?" Dr. Horn inquired, incredulously.

"Oh, I won't say no one ever does. Sometimes some degenerate does show an atavistic liking for the ancestral fare. There are hospitals, of course, for such pathological cases. But, fortunately, such cases are very rare."

"Well, I for one am thankful I don't live in the twenty-third century," I muttered, sure that my taste for beefsteak would have landed me in a sanitarium.

"Seeing that you're a vegetarian, Mr. Wormwood," declared Cloud, gloomily, "I'm afraid I haven't anything in the place for you. You came here on such short notice, you see. Guess I'd better go out to round up something—"

"In that case, I'll go with you," the man from tomorrow decided. "Being here now, whether I want to be or not, I might as well make the best of things and have a look at the twentieth century."

Cloud's face was darkened with sudden embarrassment. "But Mr. Wormwood, you can't go out on the street—in those clothes," he stammered, with a gesture toward the abbreviated costume of our visitor.

"What's the matter with my clothes?" demanded Wormwood, in an affronted manner. "You don't want me to go without them, do you?"

"Well, let's see now—let's see," faltered our host, with a troubled expression. "I have an extra suit—though it's even more of a rag than the one I'm wearing. Or maybe—if you'll stay here a while—I'll be able to borrow some money, and buy you a suit."

"What?" bawled the man from tomorrow. "Buy me a suit? Me, wear one of these twentieth century uniforms? Hide the beautiful body that nature has given me? Put a fence around my neck, and a hothouse about my chest! Check the circulation, accumulate the perspiration! Debar the sunlight and make myself miserable and unhealthy—and all for what? No, never. Never will I imprison myself in such irrational garb!"

"Really, Mr. Wormwood," I explained, in a halting manner, "really, it's necessary—if you want to appear on the street. Indeed, it's quite necessary—if you're to retain your self-respect."

"Self-respect?" cried our visitor, his thin fists clenched, his nostrils quivering with rage. "That's just the point! I have too much self-respect to make a monkey of myself!"

Whereupon, turning once more to Cloud, he shrilled, "Sir, I insist—I insist that you take me out on the street with you! I will go clad as I am now—and in no other way! I am hungry—and I ask you to give me food! I am curious to see this age—and I demand that you help me to see it!"

These words were uttered in such authoritative, determined tones that one might have thought Cloud a six-year-old and Wormwood his father. I was therefore delighted to observe with what courage the inventor resisted the insolence of his guest. "My dear friend," he maintained, "I have told you what I intend doing, and I will not go back on my word. I will not permit you to accompany me out of this house—not unless you are clothed more suitably. If you will but wait a while—"

"I will not wait!" flashed back the man from tomorrow. "Not one moment will I wait! Make ready to accompany me—or else take care!"

Into Wormwood's eyes there had come a passionate, fiery light—a blaze that frightened me I did not know why, so earnest and intense was it and so charged with suggestions of evil.

"Take care!" he repeated, with an angry vehemence. "You do not know with what you are meddling! I give you a final chance! Heed my request! Else you shall see—you shall see what the twenty-third century can do!"

Cloud trembled slightly; his lips flickered; he raised his hand fearfully before his face, as though to ward off some nameless peril. But, when he spoke, his tones were steady, and there was resolution in his glance. "You have heard my answer," he said.

Instantly the hand of Wormwood darted into the inner folds of his garment and emerged with a glittering pointed object smaller than a toy pistol. Before we had had time to observe its nature came a flash of green light and a low droning sound; and, to our consternation, Cloud uttered a groan and sank to the floor.

Thinking that he had been killed, Dr. Horn and I sprang to his side and bent over him frantically. So still and silent did he lie that for a moment we retained the impression that he was dead. But as we rubbed his hands and loosened his clothing, we observed with astonishment that there was no sign of a bullet wound. And, after a minute, we were reassured to see him open his eyes and move his lips in puzzled questioning.

"Have no fear for him," we heard the voice of the man from tomorrow, in slow, matter-of-fact tones. "He is not really hurt. But his entire body below the neck is paralyzed, and will remain paralyzed for twenty-four hours, after which he will recover. I simply wanted to teach him that it is bad policy to defy me. Fortunately, I happened to have a little phial of the inter-molecular G-rays in my pocket. Our hyperspace observatory is in a lonely place, you see, and I always keep some of the rays with me for possible use against marauders or wild beasts. Its effect, as our scientists discovered by experiments on volunteers, is to check the operations of the nervous system by an instantaneous action, like that of a powerful poison or drug."

Paying little heed to these words, Dr. Horn and I lifted the sufferer to the couch, upon which we laid him as gently as we could.

With a bewildered expression, he looked up at us; and, as he did so, his lips trembled into slow speech:

"I don't know what's come over me. I really don't know. I seemed to feel a stunning blow, then everything went black... It doesn't hurt any, but most of my body is as numb as if it wasn't there."

"Now you can see what comes of being reckless!" reprimanded the man from tomorrow, as he bent over the couch with a warning finger. "Consider yourself lucky! Had I used a stronger charge, you might have been paralyzed for a week."

Then, turning to Dr. Horn and myself with a commanding gesture, he continued, almost with military brusqueness:

"I trust you two men have also learned caution! You may profit from your friend's example! Come with me! I want you to show me the twentieth century you are so proud of!"

"Not now! Please, not now!" I protested, keeping one eye fastened upon Wormwood, while with the other I glanced at my watch. "God! It's almost nine o'clock! My wife will be nearly crazy that I haven't come home to supper!"

"Almost nine o'clock?" echoed Dr. Horn, with a groan.

"Why, I'd forgotten all about time! How will I ever explain to Alice? I was to have called to take her to the theatre!"

The man from tomorrow merely grinned. "You'll have to solve those little problems as best as you can," he decided, with a shrug.

"Come…are you ready? I'm getting anxious to see the twentieth century."

"But tomorrow! Won't tomorrow do just as well?" pleaded Dr. Horn, almost desperately. "I really must rush off to my fiancée—"

"And my wife—she'll never forgive me!" I chimed in, shuddering at the thought of many a difficult moment to come.

"Tomorrow—I promise you—tomorrow I'll be at your service!"

"Oh, these women—the way they did interfere in the twentieth century!" muttered Wormwood. "But, of course, I can't accept any such excuse. For the last time, I ask you, are you ready? If so, we'd better be getting along!"

By way of emphasizing these words, our visitor again drew forth the little pistol-like contrivance that had so effectively silenced Cloud's protest.

At the sight of this implement, we realized the futility of further arguments. Cursing the evil fortune that had brought us face to face with a man from tomorrow; groaning at the thought of the superior science that had subdued us and at the cruel advantage that our guest had taken of us; shaken with misgivings for the future and fearful lest we should end in jail or in a madhouse, we signified our submission and dolefully accompanied Wormwood out of the room and down the long stairs to the street.

As he passed through the doorway, we cast a last sad glance back at Cloud, who was gazing lugubriously at us from his helpless berth on the couch. "We can't leave him here like this!" I protested. "Who is to take care of him in our absence?"

But the man from tomorrow answered airily, "Oh, he won't need any care. The G-rays will induce pleasant sleep."

And then, as he forced Dr. Horn and me to walk one on each side of him, in the attentive manner of old friends, he burst into a low chuckle, he enthused:

"Do you know, I think after all I'm going to enjoy the twentieth century! It was really such a queer, period of history, when everybody did such funny things! I believe I'll like it better than a farce comedy!"

And he slapped his knee with a puny hand, and broke into the gayest laughter we had yet heard from his lips.

CHAPTER SIX
A Tour of Inspection

AS WE descended to the pavement in company with the man from tomorrow, Dr. Horn and I were relieved to find the street comparatively deserted. Before us, in garish multitudes, glared the long even rows of arc-lights; above us loomed the monotonously regular files of the six-story tenements; while the heavens, as usual, were obscured with the smoke and dust of the city.

"Ah, how glad I am to be out!" exclaimed the man from tomorrow, flinging his bare arms skyward as if in ecstasy. "What a strange scene! How unreal it all looks! It reminds me of some curious antique prints I have seen! And so this is how people lived before the Reign of Sanitation?"

"Reign of Sanitation?" I demanded.

"Exactly! You surely don't call it sanitary to live in brick cages without air or sunlight?" inquired our visitor, as we walked slowly down the street. "Do you notice the abominable reek in the air? If it weren't so historic, it would be insufferable!"

I sniffed the air appraisingly, but could notice nothing unusual.

"By the way, what city is this?" continued Wormwood. "New York, you say? I believe that was one of the seaboard cities of the United States in the Neurotic Age? Yes, to be sure! That was before the second Interoceanic War! New York used to be considered an important little place, I understand... Well, well, it's interesting to be walking on the site of ancient cities!"

As the man from tomorrow uttered these words, we set out together across a street—which came near to being the last street he crossed in this century. An automobile, moving at a reckless pace, shot suddenly around a corner; and our visitor whose gaze was cast upward at the top stories of the tenements, would certainly have been struck had not Dr. Horn flung out a saving hand and dragged him out of danger.

Shaken by this experience, we reached the pavement, where Wormwood began to ply us with indignant questions. "By all the constellations! What infernal machine was that? What do you mean by exposing visitors to diabolical attacks? Can't a man even cross the street without fear of martyrdom? Surely, you don't allow lunatics to go raging at large! Or was it a deliberate attempt to kill me? Never, never have I been treated with such lack of consideration!"

Doing our best to check the ravings of the man from tomorrow, we informed him that what he had seen was only a motor car.

"Motor car? Motor car? he repeated after us, by no means pacified. "I don't know what you mean!"

"Well, there's another one over there," explained Dr. Horn, pointing to a taxicab cruising along the street.

The cab driver, thinking that Dr. Horn was signaling to him, stopped short within arm's grasp—and so Wormwood had his first clear view of a modern automobile.

"Oh, now I see! So that's what they are!" he cried, with an air of sudden enlightenment. "Of course I should have known! Haven't I observed them often enough in museums? They're the carriages that used to clutter the streets of cities before the general adoption of air-transportation. They used to poison the atmosphere with carbon monoxide gas, so that it is estimated that, in the latter part of the Neurotic Age, a million persons a year fell dead from asphyxiation on city streets. Oh, yes, I understand all about them!"

So speaking, the man from tomorrow chuckled beneath his breath, as though enjoying some rare and secret joke.

"What cumbrous-looking affairs they are!" he continued, as one of the magnificent Reels-Royal Sedans went gliding past. "So grotesque and ponderous! I wonder that they're permitted by the Department of Public Esthetics! And what noises they make! They remind me of wild beasts in a menagerie! I see now why this is the Neurotic Age!"

I had already opened my mouth to reply—when a more important subject demanded our attention. Until the present moment, the freakish apparel of the man from tomorrow had aroused but little notice, since we had been walking in the obscurity of a side-street; but now all at once we had arrived at the corner of a brilliantly lighted avenue, where streams of people were drifting back and forth before the glaring shop windows.

"Ah!" exclaimed our companion, his eyes wide with wonder. "How odd! Just the place for me!"

And, despite my frantic efforts to restrain him, he started off down the avenue.

No one can imagine what I felt at that critical moment. Here was I, a respectable college professor, who all his life had never been known to depart from the path of sobriety! Yet now all at once, through no fault of my own, I must appear in public in company with a half-dressed clown, and be subjected to the jeers and taunts of the multitude! How could I be able to face my classes tomorrow if the facts were to become known?

At that thought, a terrible sinking sensation overcame me, and I was tempted once more to revolt. Necessity being the mother of recklessness, I conceived an idea; slouching a pace or two behind my new-made master, I toyed with some wild notion of dashing into a sheltering doorway and escaping.

But the man from tomorrow was quick to divine my strategy. "Step to my side, sir!" he commanded, with an angry glance in my direction. "And don't ever let me see you trying that again—not unless you'd enjoy being paralyzed…"

There being nothing else to do, I sighed and meekly obeyed orders, my short-lived hopes of freedom cast aside.

Already, although we had turned into the avenue but a moment ago, I was conscious of the attention we were receiving. Two painted-lipped girls paused at the corner, pointed to our companion and giggled; several passing men stopped short to peer at us before continuing on their way with loud guffaws; a small child, led by its mother's hand, burst into a tittering exclamation, "Oh, Mamma, look at the man in the funny nightgown!"

Feeling, that I should have liked to sink into the earth and disappear, I saw the bright lights of a momentary haven looming before us. "Alschuler's Restaurant" I read on an electric sign; and though I had little doubt but that it would prove an atrocious eating place, I was thankful to grasp at the temporary refuge it offered. "Come," I suggested to my lord and leader. "Let's all have a bite before seeing the town."

To this proposal the man from tomorrow replied with an appropriate, "Very good!" and immediately gave proof of his interest by the haste with which he sought the restaurant.

Fortunately, we were able to procure a private booth, although some of the customers boorishly left their tables to stare at us as we entered, and the head waiter peered at us so peculiarly that nothing, except the secret passage of a bit of paper, seemed able to prevent our immediate ejection.

It would be painful to dwell upon the details of that meal, which was probably the most embarrassing I ever attempted to consume. When the soup was brought on, the man from tomorrow took one sniff, and then shoved it from him with a disgusted expression. "Ugh! Some of that vile beast-flesh is in it!" When the salad arrived, saturated with French dressing, he sampled one lettuce leaf, and promptly called to the waiter, "Sir! Take this out, wash it off thoroughly, and then bring it back unadulterated!" When the fish appeared, he merely made a grimace of repulsion, looked away and offered us his portion. When the waiter asked whether he wished his coffee with his meal or later, he appeared puzzled and learned with evident surprise that coffee was a beverage. Afterwards, sampling the drink, he made a wry face and declared that it was "bitter enough for a medicine." And finally, having explored the bill of fare and found nothing to please him, he made a meal of bread and milk, with which he declared himself well satisfied.

During the repast, Dr. Horn and I made repeated attempts to reach the telephone booth, which was located at the further end of the restaurant; but our guest, thinking that we were planning to escape, resolutely checked all our efforts. "I don't know what you mean by telephone booths," he declared, suspiciously. "What is a telephone? In the twenty-third century, each man carries his own small radio set, enabling him to send messages home at any time."

It now appeared certain that I should not be able to communicate with my wife for hours yet. Restlessly tapping my knees in my nervousness and fidgeting in my chair like a three-year-old, I was barely able to touch my food, while I vainly tried to imagine the sort of reception I should receive when at last I reached home.

Dr. Horn, likewise, seemed occupied with solemn meditations. He too was hardly able to eat; his stern, intellectual face, normally thin and long, looked even longer and thinner than usual. Every now and then he would shake his head dolefully, and mutter, "This is going to put me in a terrible position with Alice. Do you think, Professor, she will believe my absence wasn't deliberate? How am I ever going to explain?"

"Better not explain at all," finally suggested the man from tomorrow, smiling a helpful smile. "You'd have to tell the truth, and I've found that truthful explanations cause trouble."

Having offered this advice, Wormwood announced himself finished with his bread and milk; and, permitting me to settle matters with the waiter, rose jauntily to leave.

It was only when we were again upon the street that our real troubles commenced. Disregarding the combined pleas of Dr. Horn and myself, the man from tomorrow remained inflexibly determined to haunt the brightest and most frequented thoroughfares. "How am I to see the twentieth century," he demanded, "if I am to confine myself to side streets!" And so, with the two of us trailing at his side, he sauntered merrily along the avenue; while, as if his appearance were not attracting sufficient attention, he filled the intervals between conversation by humming snatches of some queer tune—a jerky, unmelodious tune which I had never heard before, and which struck my ears as unpleasantly as would Chinese music.

"That is the work of Manowsky—one of the greatest of twenty-third century composers," he explained, in response to Dr. Horn's questions.

I wish that I could draw a veil over the moments that followed. I wish that I could erase from memory the shame and horror of that harassing interval, when I was shocked and humiliated as never before in this life. But alas…the recollection of those torments is ingrained too deeply ever to be blotted out. It returns to me even now in nightmares; it galls and scourges me, even though it has become no more than the figment of a bewildering adventure… But let me proceed. Let me record how people paused to stare and gape at us; how some smiled or snickered, and others openly mocked; how a crowd, led by some half-grown ragamuffins, began to form at our heels, hooting and howling, and roaring a ribald something about bathing costumes; how gradually the mob deepened, until we found ourselves in the center of a veritable multitude, which walled us about on all sides, as though we were a circus exhibition, until those on the outer edges of the throng had to struggle to get a glimpse of us.

How describe the feeling of mortification that was overwhelming me! How depict my horror when, amid the surging demons that had closed in about us, I thought I recognized the faces of two of my college students, who, I felt sure, would broadcast the news of my disgrace! Or how express my shocked anger and dismay at the raillery that was filling the air about us? "What is he? A living freak? A wild man from Madagascar…? New style in undershirts…! Say, did you get a glimpse at the bathing beauty!" While, from the borders of the crowd, a childish voice would be heard. "Look at the crazy man!" or "Oh, Ma, take me to see the circus!" Such exclamations, and others of a far more irritating type, all of them in lamentably bad taste and some of them too vulgar to repeat, were raining upon us in uproarious showers; and meantime the throng was growing at such a rate that, it seemed to me, it would soon constitute a menace to traffic.

At first the man from tomorrow stared at this curious rabble with a good-natured amusement. He seemed pleased to be the center of so much attention; he was grateful for what he termed the opportunity "of judging the twentieth century animal at first hand." He passed various, interested comments upon the looks and apparel of the spectators; he remarked calmly that most of the faces were of a degenerate type indicating the uneugenic nature of the age; he decided that, being burdened with an excess of clothes, they were all weighed down with repressions and complexes, which made them look "a little strained and inhuman."

"I wish I was back in my own age!" he sighed. "Any newspaper would pay a thousand tantrums for the story of my visit here!"

But gradually, as the crowd increased, Wormwood's interest in his observers diminished. They began hedging him in too closely; they began to take undesired familiarities, to press against him or to pat him in an intimate manner on the back or shoulders; they began to obscure his view of the streets and the buildings; they even presumed to pass jokes concerning his small stature, calling him a "dwarf," a "midget," and a "runt." And thus, perhaps without intending to, they irritated him beyond all measure.

Sudden and surprising was his transformation from smiling good humor to bristling defiance. "So? You think I'm small? You think I'm small, do you?" he roared, in a voice that could be heard above the din of the street traffic. "You pygmy creatures of a pygmy age! If any of you could come to my times, where men are measured by their brains, you would look tinier than fleas! Be gone, all of you! Cease annoying me! Can't you leave a Superman to go his way in peace?"

The only effect of these words was to produce renewed laughter. "The Superman! See the Superman! Make way for the Superman!" jeered the multitude, which, with hilarious mockery, commenced to press about their victim more tightly than ever.

"Begone!" repeated Wormwood, in the same thundering tones as before. "Begone, I advise you! Can't you understand English? This is my last warning! Leave me alone, or it will not be well with you!"

But the crowd, laughing more tumultuously than ever, ringed their entertainer about more closely still, and showed no intention of dispersing.

Then it was that a startling thing occurred. The hand of the man from tomorrow was seen to reach suddenly into his garment; a small pistol-like object appeared; there was a droning sound, a flash of greenish light, a second flash, then a third—and three successive members of the mob groaned and sank helplessly to the ground.

The laughter of the multitude had ceased. A wide gap was opened as the spectators, pale-faced and shuddering, gaped at the victims and withdrew as though Wormwood were the bearer of a plague. Confused cries issued from their midst; there was a movement of panic, and a stampeding of heavy forms; men shoved and pushed their fellows savagely in the effort to escape; the shriek of a woman and the moan of a wounded youth added to the confusion; while Wormwood, seizing my right arm and Dr. Horn's left, started off past the rabble and down the street as nonchalantly as though nothing in particular had occurred.

CHAPTER SEVEN
In the Toils of the Law

"I REALLY don't see what the excitement was all about," remarked the man from tomorrow, as he led Dr. Horn and myself slowly away. "What is there so strange about me? Have the people of this age never looked on bare arms or legs before? I didn't know there was anything unusual about my skin."

He paused, and regarded his exposed limbs quizzically; then hastily proceeded. "It isn't as if I were huge and ungainly, like most of the men of this age. The majority of your countrymen, I observe, are giants—over five and a half feet in height! And there are some monsters that must be six feet and even more! Now, in my own century, five feet and one inch is considered the proper height for a man. It has been this way ever since the Interoceanic wars, which reduced the average stature—"

How much longer Wormwood continued in this vein I do not know, for neither Dr. Horn or I were listening. Our attention was attracted toward a spot to our rear, where some interesting developments were in progress. We saw that we were by no means free of the mob, as we had thought. Despite the paralysis of three persons and the ensuing panic, there were still many who seemed unwilling to lose sight of us, and who trailed behind us in little slinking groups at a safe distance. In addition, the attention of fresh passers-by, who knew nothing of the events of a few moments ago, were gravitating toward us at such a rate that it would be only a matter of minutes before we were again the center of a rabble.

Accordingly, I made a hasty suggestion to the man from tomorrow. "Don't you think we'd better take a taxi? Otherwise, we'll have no end of trouble."

"Taxi?" he demanded. "What's that…? Oh, you mean one of those funny-looking little carts? The kind that race through the streets trying to murder honest people? No thank you! I have a perfect horror of dying in the twentieth century. However, maybe there happens to be an airport near? If you can charter a tri-plane—"

This was as far as the speaker could proceed. Emerging from the throng to our rear, I saw two blue-frocked club-wielding individuals, who sent a cold shiver down my spine. And, at the side of these representatives of law and order, a little man in plain clothes was running in screaming excitement. "That's them! There they are! Dangerous lunatics! The whole three of them! Killed five men! Grab them, before they get away!"

"Better watch out," I whispered to the man from tomorrow. "The police are after us."

"The police had better watch out!" he muttered, reaching into his pocket for the paralyzing rays.

"For God's sake, don't try anything like that!" warned Dr. Horn, in a voice of horror. "If you do—"

I dread to think what would have happened had the man from tomorrow carried out his intention and struck down the two officers of the law. Fortunately, Dr. Horn's words caused him to hesitate for just the fracture of a second; and that brief hesitation was all-important, since it gave one of the policemen time to steal forward and to clasp his arms about Wormwood's slender form.

In the officer's powerful grip, our companion was helpless as a babe; it was only a few seconds before the handcuffs had rattled about his wrists.

Reduced thus to impotence, he made up in rage for what he lacked in physical power. "Let me go! I'll have you punished! I'll report you to the Head Triumvirate! By all the stars in the firmament, what sort of an age is this? You no sooner get a man from an enlightened era, than you act as if he wants to steal your century! Let loose those disgraceful bonds from my hands, or I vow—as surely as I come from another dimension, I vow it—you will live to regret your impudence!"

Hearty laughter was his response. Someone tapped his head significantly; someone else, from deep in the rear, let forth a mocking howl. "The Superman! He still thinks he's the Superman! Listen to the Superman talk!" And renewed ripples of merriment sounded from the gathering swarms of spectators.

At this juncture, on an unfortunate impulse, it occurred to me to say something on behalf of the victim. Small as was my liking for the man from tomorrow, I thought that after all he was entitled to some consideration as the sole known visitor from another age; moreover, I feared that science would lose invaluable opportunities for investigation should we find no better lodging for him than a jail.

"Officer—hold one minute!" I cried. "Aren't you making a mistake? You don't understand. If you'll give me a chance to explain—"

"Explain! Explain! Let him explain to the judge!" someone burst forth, in hooting derision. "He's another of the gang!"

"And he too!" contributed a second member of the mob, designating Dr. Horn. "They're all in together! All three of them! I saw them working together the whole time!"

To my unspeakable shame and horror, the policemen accepted this distorted version of the affair. Never had any man better occasion to deplore the poor judgment of our officers of justice! With such speed that I hardly had time to realize what was happening, I felt a pair of cold steel fetters clattering about my wrists; I saw that Dr. Horn, too, was being seized and shackled;

and I heard my captor's voice thundering in my ear, "You'd both better come along as accessories before the crime!"

"But what have I done, sir?" I demanded; while, in my mortification, I must have blushed to the very tip of my fingers. "What have I done?"

The only heed my captor took was to mutter, grimly, "you've done enough to be pulled in! The rest you can tell in court!"

As his voice subsided, there came the dry, critical comment of the man from tomorrow, who, apparently, had forgotten his anger in assuming the role of an aloof observer. "How primitive. How primitive. What barbarian methods of punishment they employed in the twentieth century!"

The outburst of laughter that greeted these words was cut short by the bells of the patrol wagon, which was arriving in noisy haste. Imagine my rage and despair when I was ordered into this vehicle! Imagine my exasperation to hear the jeers of the mobs, and to see the ring of idiotic faces that gaped up at me in mockery! Yet, despite the tumult of my emotions, I had time for a glance at the man from tomorrow, who preceded me into the wagon with a grimace of utmost distaste. "Is this ride considered part of the punishment?" he asked, as we started to move along the avenue. "As an ingenious means of torture, it is far from bad!"

During the following minutes, instead of meditating upon the fate that awaited him, he busied himself with trivial chatter. Every time the wagon gave a jolt or a jerk, he would make a wry face and remark how uncomfortable it was to live in an age before the invention of automatic friction-destroyers. Every time we reached an intersection and had to wait for the traffic signals, he would declare that there were only two civilized ways to travel—in the air, and underground. Every time the horns of some passing motor dinned in his ears, he would wince as if he had been struck, and would observe that were he forced to remain with us for a few years, he would probably become as neurotic as our best citizens. Never once did the seriousness of his predicament—or of ours— seem to occur to him; but on and on he babbled, mistaking our best apartment houses for barracks or inquiring why the glare of the electric signs and the shop windows was not prohibited by law—until, in the end, I fervently wished that he had been gagged as well as handcuffed.

At last, fortunately his garrulousness was ended by our arrival at our destination. I had had visions of being led directly to a cell, where I would have to remain amid the ruffians and the vermin; yet, although I was to be spared this fate, it was not vastly preferable to being bundled out of the patrol and into one of those night courts, where the city's human wastage comes to trial.

As we entered the courtroom, I observed that it was fairly well crowded; and as the officers shoved my companions and myself to seats at one side, I was relieved to find that our coming caused much less attention than we had aroused elsewhere. Was it that freakish sights were mere commonplaces here?

A long, long period of waiting ensued. Even more than the ride in the patrol car, or the encounter with the mob, this constituted the real ordeal of the evening. No man could have been more nervous than I, as, still in handcuffs, I writhed and twisted between Dr. Horn and one of the policemen. With the feeling of one over whom a sword is dangling, I watched the judge decide the cases ahead of ours; nor was my apprehension relieved by the discovery that that official, a bespectacled man of about forty, whose features seemed vaguely familiar, was almost savagely severe in his decisions. First came a roisterer charged with creating a disturbance while drunk, and there followed the snapping judgment, "Thirty days!"; then came a painted woman of an all-too-recognizable type, upon whom the magistrate scowled while bellowing, "Sixty days this time, Maggie!"; then came a youth accused of precipitating a street brawl and resisting an officer, and we heard the roaring sentence, "A hundred dollars fine or a hundred days!" Case after case was disposed of in rapid order; and always, I observed, the judgment was "Guilty," while, as time went by, the penalties seemed to be growing constantly more severe. What should I do, I wondered, if I too were adjudged guilty? How face the humiliation of being sentenced by the night court? Vague thoughts of suicide came to me as I noticed several newspaper reporters scribbling within arm's length; and thoughts of worse than suicide harassed me as I considered the scandal if my arrest should become known at the University. "Savant spends night in jail," I read in imagination in the headlines. "Professor Howard taken in street raid." Well I knew how the heads of gossips would nod! How my students would whisper among themselves! How I should be called to the President's Office, or perhaps before the Board of Regents to explain. At the least, should I not have to resign my professorship? For who would now consider me a fitting moral guide for the young? It was hard, exceedingly hard, I reflected, to have worked for forty years to build myself a respectable position, and now all at once to be discredited and disgraced owing to a visitor from another dimension.

While such meditations absorbed me, the man from tomorrow was watching the court proceedings with the interest of a spectator at a play. He seemed to have forgotten his shackled hands; he seemed to be giving no thought to his impending sentence; he leaned far forward in his seat, and his blue eyes glittered with amusement as the judge decided case after case. "They should not have a judge in this court! They should have a psychiatrist!" he whispered to Dr. Horn, in tones loud enough for everyone to overhear, whereupon the magistrate stopped short in the middle of a sentence and glared at Wormwood with such stern rebuking eyes that I felt that the man from tomorrow had forfeited any chance he might have had for a lenient verdict.

At last, after ages and ages of suspense, our turn for trial arrived. Trembling in every limb and muscle, I stood between Wormwood and Dr. Horn before the bar of justice; while one of the officers, towering to our right, loudly proclaimed the charge.

"Disorderly conduct and indecent exposure!" he announced, designating the man from tomorrow. "In the other two cases, disorderly conduct and inciting to riot! When I first saw the defendants—"

And the officers went on to declare our various sins and derelictions in no uncertain language.

To my surprise, the judge paid no apparent heed.

Instead, his gaze was fastened upon me with a strange scrutiny. There was such a prying interest, such a puzzled questioning in his watery gray eyes, that I squirmed and writhed inwardly; I wondered whether he regarded me as a particularly interesting species of offender, an unusual example of the criminal type. What was my astonishment, accordingly, when a sudden smile broke out upon his face! And when, turning to one of my accusers, he bawled:

"Officer Murphy, haven't you made a mistake?"

Officer Murphy looked startled. "Why, Your Honor," he gasped, "what—what mistake could there be?"

"Unfetter that man at once!" commanded the magistrate. "And, after this, be more careful whom you lay your clumsy hands on!"

"Very well, Your Honor," acquiesced the bewildered agent of the law, as he mercifully freed me from my handcuffs.

Feeling like a hero in a fairy story, who has been saved in the nick of time by a guardian angel, I stared uncomprehendingly at the judge.

And now, surprise of surprises! The dignity of the bench was violated! The hand of His Honor shot down toward mine! "Glad to see you again, Professor!" he declared, heartily. And, while I gaped at him in a bewildered way, he leaned down to me, and whispered, "I didn't recognize you at first. Don't suppose you recognize me, either. No wonder! I was in one of your classes in physics, way back in nineteen nine. Science wasn't my long suit, but you let me through anyhow. It surely is a pleasure to see you once more!"

As I glanced about me at the leering spectators, at the grinning man from tomorrow and at my assistant glowering in handcuffs, I thought that I could have imagined more delightful circumstances for a reunion.

"I'm sure you're here by some stupid mistake, Professor," continued His Honor, in secretive tones. "Such things do happen, you know—the officers lose their heads now and then and pick on the wrong man. You'd better tell me all about it. No need to assure me you weren't willingly in such company as that."

With a disdainful gesture, the judge designated the man from tomorrow.

"No, not willingly—but he was in my company just the same," volunteered the man from tomorrow.

"Silence! Answer when you're spoken to!" thundered the judge. And then, turning to me, "What a strange, heavy sort of speech that man has! Shouldn't be surprised if he'd been drinking. Well, Professor, now let's hear your story."

For a moment I was silent. It occurred to me that the last thing I could state was the truth—were I to declare that our visitor was from the twenty-third century, would the judge not believe my mind enfeebled by age? And so I set about to invent a tale. If I faltered over the first few words, interspersing the syllables with hems and haws innumerable, the judge probably laid the blame to a natural embarrassment; for he smiled indulgently down upon me, and seemed to have no suspicion of my predicament.

Encouraged by his friendliness, I was not long in collecting my thoughts and launching forth upon a fluent narrative.

"Your Honor," I reported, "I greatly deplore the necessity of being seen in public along with this gentleman, Mr. Wormwood. No one could be less in favor than I of his unconventional apparel. The fact is, Your Honor, that he has been a subject for experimental study at the University by my assistant Dr. Horn and myself. You see him now—in his laboratory costume. He has not been, I fear, quite right in his head of late; he has some very strange ideas which I beg you not to heed. I will not say he has not—well, an excessive fondness for the flask. This evening, when he ran off down the street in his present undress, what could Dr. Horn and I do but follow him and attempt to bring him back? Unfortunately, his appearance called forth a mob, whose company he so enjoyed that it was impossible for us to do anything with him. It was in the effort to explain these matters to the officers that Dr. Horn and I were apprehended."

His Honor scowled severely in the direction of Officer Murphy. "Ever let me catch you making a mistake like this again, and I'll have you demoted!" his angry eyes appeared to say. But to me he declared, "I understand, Professor. I understand. Everything is explained."

"Thank you, Your Honor," I acknowledged, bowing.

"Oh, you think everything is explained, do you?" mocked the man from tomorrow, with a reckless disregard for the rules of court procedure. "Then will you please tell me how it was that I could paralyze three men?"

The judge rapped for order, and glared savagely at Wormwood. "For the last time, I ask you to be silent!" he roared. "Otherwise, I'll commit you for contempt!"

The man from tomorrow opened his mouth, but said no other word; yet there was amusement rather than fear in his glance.

Turning to the policeman, the magistrate inquired, "Officer Murphy, what was this nonsense about paralyzing three men?"

"Why, I really don't know, Your Honor," declared Officer Murphy. "That is, I don't know except what I heard."

"What was that?"

The policeman hesitated. "Well, it's this way, Your Honor. The man that summoned me said something about some queer sort of pistol being discharged with a blaze of green light. Five men—or maybe ten—fell down and couldn't move again. I have the witness here to tell about it himself."

Low titters of amusement were rippling around the courtroom, and the judge had to hammer again for order. "Officer Murphy," he cried, in tones of thunder, "you should know better than to repeat such a tale!"

"Well, I wasn't saying I believed it, Your Honor," apologized Officer Murphy, with a crestfallen look. "Just the same, the witness is here, if you want to hear him—"

"There is no need for such stories to be heard again!" bellowed the judge, bringing his clenched fist down before him with finality.

His face now assumed a thoughtful expression; and, with an inquiring air, he turned to me. "Well, Professor, what do you think we'd better do with this man...this Mr. Woodworm, or whatever you call him? The law about indecent exposure, of course, is clear enough. Still, I don't know that his looks are so much indecent as—well, unconventional. He hasn't done any real harm, and if you thought you could guarantee—"

"Why, yes, Your Honor," I caught up, seeing a sudden avenue of hope. "While I can't be absolutely responsible for him, I would do my best. His conduct may strike you as erratic, but I assure you he is not dangerous. If you would permit me, I should be glad to lodge him in my own house tonight, and would try to see—"

"Good!" approved the judge. "The very thing! You may take him home at once, Professor. Call a taxi, of course, so that there will be no more street scenes. By tomorrow, I trust, he will—er—have sufficiently recovered to appear fully clothed."

"I will do what I can," I promised, not attempting to relieve His Honor of the idea that the man from tomorrow was drunk.

"Excellent!" bawled the judge. "Case dismissed!" As we filed out of the courtroom, we could see that all eyes were fastened upon us with twinkling glances. It was with the utmost relief that Dr. Horn and I summoned a taxicab after we had been unshackled, and, at the risk of being paralyzed, pushed the man from tomorrow into it, and gave the driver my home address.

CHAPTER EIGHT
A Lodging for the Night

WHEN eventually I reached home, it lacked just a few minutes of midnight. I was greeted by a distracted wife, who fell into my arms with tears and lamentations, and mingled her sobs of relief with reproaches at my long absence. "Where under heaven were you?" she demanded, when her first paroxysms of emotion had subsided. "Oh, Ellery, where, where were you? Why didn't you let me hear from you? I thought you had been killed! Why, I must have called up every hospital in town! None of them could give me any news!"

"I have had a very unusual experience, my dear," was all I was able to say—when all at once her eyes fell upon the man from tomorrow.

"Gracious, Ellery, what have we here?" she exclaimed, in a nerve-wracked manner. "What have we here? Why, the poor man! What has happened to his clothes?"

"He, why—er—er—he has had a slight accident," I attempted to explain, not quite certain what to say. "You—you mustn't mind his looks. He's a traveler—from far away. He's a little mixed up about our customs. I've asked him to stay for the night. Dr. Horn and I have been taking charge of him. I just left Dr. Horn at the door."

"You—you don't mean to say he's going to stay here!" gasped my poor wife, overwhelmed at this news. And I am sure that had I not taken her consolingly into my arms, the tears would have come in torrents.

At this juncture the man from tomorrow, never slow in an emergency, did his best to come to my relief.

"You need not trouble, my dear lady," he said, waving his right arm in what I judge was considered the chivalrous manner in his age. "You need not trouble at all—I am not particular. If you but have a nice quiet corner on the roof—"

"What's that? Corner on the roof?" echoed my wife and I in one voice; while into her eyes there came a slightly frightened expression, as though she suspected that she was in the presence of a dangerous lunatic.

"Oh, well then, if you haven't any roof space," continued our guest, obligingly, "maybe you have a removal external platform—"

Observing the blank air with which we were regarding him, he stopped abruptly short; and then, after a puzzled moment, attempted to explain:

"Oh, I had forgotten! You haven't advanced to that stage yet. In my own century, most families have space on the roof—it's considered the healthiest way of sleeping. But some people, being too far from the top floor, put detachable sleeping platforms out of their windows."

"Ellery, what under heaven is the man talking about?" demanded my wife, turning to me in a bewildered way. And in her eyes there was a reproving fire, as though she would add, "My dear man, you always do invite such queer guests to the house!"

"Pay no heed to him," I counseled. "He isn't quite used to our ways yet... Shall I show the visitor to the spare room, Jane?"

"I guess you might as well," she sighed, in a voice that seemed to imply that the whole affair was beyond her comprehension. "Yes, I'm sure the room is all ready."

A moment later, I had led the man from tomorrow to his bedroom. Having entered it in a rather suspicious, hesitant manner, he glanced all about him from wall to wall and from floor to ceiling, as if to take in every speck and detail; and a frown gathered to his pallid features and gradually deepened.

"How hot the place is!" he declared, although both windows had been opened wide and the temperature of the May night could not have been much over sixty. "These twentieth century houses are quaint to look at, but terrible to live in! You are really sure I can't go up on the roof...? No? Then where are your cold air faucets? Oh, if that isn't intolerable! Cold air faucets aren't invented yet! Then tell me where I can find the wall remover."

"Wall remover?"

He stared at me in growing dismay. His pale, twisted features showed an expression of unmistakable pain; he stroked his bulbous forehead anxiously with his thin hand. "Why, don't you even know what a wall remover is? You mean to say that hasn't been invented, either! What an age! What an age! You simply don't seem to have any conveniences at all. I suppose you have nothing except the old-fashioned fixed walls, which aren't meant to be taken down till the building is destroyed."

"Well, what else should we have?"

"What else, indeed?" The man from tomorrow peered at me with a scornful amusement. "What would you think of a man who couldn't take off his clothes till he died? So I suppose you imagine you have to swelter all summer behind closed walls, which keep out the sunlight and air? What a strange notion! All walls in our times are made in removable divisions, with spring attachments, so that they may be neatly folded up upon the pressure of an electric button. That is one way of keeping houses cool in summer."

"Sorry, Mr. Wormwood, but we're still mere savages," I replied dryly, a little angered at his supercilious manner. "We have no folding walls. You will have to put up as well as you can with our antique accommodations."

"Oh, I'm not blaming you!" he was quick to declare. "It's not really your fault. You're merely the victim of the backwardness of the times."

"Maybe that's it. Well, goodnight," I said, yawning; for I was exceedingly tired, and was not anxious to prolong the conversation.

But the man from tomorrow would not let me leave until after I had answered innumerable questions, and had explained how to switch on and off the electric lights—appliances which, since they were obsolete in his own age, he looked upon with something of the interest of an antiquarian. When I closed the door behind me, he was amusing himself by turning them on and off with the delight of a child in a new toy.

After a troubled night's sleep, I arose fairly early the following morning, browsed about in a closet to find an old suit, and at length, armed with a respectable looking pair of gray trousers, a coat and various other articles of masculine apparel, knocked somewhat apprehensively at the room of the man from tomorrow.

I had to rap twice, and three times, before a drowsy voice called out, "Enter!" Then, pushing open the door, I was treated to a surprise. At the first glance, I noticed that the bed had not been slept upon—it had been dismantled as though by Vandals! All that I saw was the bare steel springs and frame; while ten feet beyond, near the open window, the mattress, sheets and blankets had all been piled together in a disordered mass, in the center of which the man from tomorrow was curled up like a caterpillar.

"Heaven preserve me!" I cried, hastily closing the door behind me. "What's come over you? If my wife were to see this, she'd go wild!"

"Why, what's wrong?" innocently inquired the man from tomorrow, as he arose in complete undress. "I was merely trying to make myself comfortable," It was too warm in the bed, so I moved to a cooler place."

"But look! Can't you see what you've done?" I stormed. "Is this the way to treat the bed coverings?"

But he was staring at me with such a lack of comprehension that my words stopped short in my throat.

"In my own age," he remarked, in a hurt manner, "a guest is expected to make himself comfortable in any way that suits him best."

Accepting this rebuke, I pointed to the mass of clothing that I held in my hand. "Here, Wormwood, better dress in these. After last night's experience, you can see how impractical it is to wear twenty-third century clothing in the twentieth century."

"Yes, I can see," he admitted, sadly, "that I must suffer the doom of all who are ahead of their times. I must be jeered at and laughed at. I must endure ridicule and abuse. I must become the butt of fools, and undergo the agonies of martyrdom. Ah, well! A man must sacrifice something when he undertakes to reform his ancestors."

"You can keep your twenty-third century costume as a curiosity," I continued, pointing to the discarded garment. "But if you're to live in the twentieth century, you must do as the twentieth century does."

"If I did as the twentieth century does, I wouldn't really be living at all," he rejoined, dolefully. "However, I can see that there is a certain practical logic to your remarks. If one were a dweller among the donkeys, I suppose, one wouldn't be respected unless one knew how to bray. Very well, then! I must compromise with my ideals, and look as commonplace as the citizens of this age. Bring on the clothes! I'll try as many of them as I can stand, but more than that I won't promise you!"

Now began a battle royal. Although the man from tomorrow seemed to have capitulated, he was far from having made a total surrender. How I pleaded and argued with him! How I struggled before he could be induced to don a pair of trousers! How many appeals passed over him in vain before he would consent to wear a shirt! And yet this represented the utmost limits of my conquest the fruits of half an hour of such nerve-racking work as I had never put in before a college class! Resolutely, despite all my efforts, he refused even to try on a pair of shoes or socks, being better content with the thin little sandals of the twenty-third century; he refused the use of underwear; he refused a tie and collar, declaring that he saw no conceivable use for them; he declined absolutely to put on a coat, maintaining that it would subserve neither the purposes of beauty nor of comfort. I cannot say that he was exactly what might be called "presentable" as he was finally arrayed, for my clothes were vastly too big for him and fitted him like bags, and—though I hesitated to admit it even to myself—it occurred to me that he had looked less unattractive in his native costume. However, most of the exposed parts of his skin had now been covered, and he might therefore appear in civilized society without shocking the delicate susceptibilities of the age.

"At last you look like a modern man!" I informed him, sighing with relief at his transformation. Whereupon he regarded himself with a wry expression, did a turn or two about the room in the tentative manner of a young lady trying on a new costume, and then remarked, gloomily, "Well, I suppose I'll get used to it in time. I suppose I'll have to get used to it. But it's a good thing my own people can't see me now. How Maranna and the rest of them would laugh! They'd suspect I had some disease and wanted to hide my skin. I might be arrested for indecent concealment."

Having thus expressed his views, the man from tomorrow drew up his lips into an expression of grim resignation, and soberly concluded, "I guess I'm ready for you now. All prepared to see the twentieth century by daylight. Come, shall we start?"

CHAPTER NINE
Romance and Discovery

AS THE man from tomorrow and I were coming down the stairs, we heard the sound of voices in excited disputation.

"No, Roscoe," I could make out the stubborn tones of a woman, "you can't get me to believe it. I've come here just to give you your chance to prove it all, it's such a nice little fairy story!"

"But, Alice, you just wait till you see him!" pleaded a masculine voice. "Just wait!" Professor Howard will bear me out! I'll swear to you—"

"No need for swearing!" I interrupted, as the man from tomorrow and I reached the bottom of the stairs, and I nodded to Dr. Horn and his fiancée, who were awaiting us in the sitting room. "What is the argument all about?"

"Alice won't accept my word—about why I couldn't keep my appointment last night—though I ran over the first thing this morning to explain!" testified Dr. Horn, in a flustered manner. "Maybe you can convince her, Professor."

"Maybe I can," I concurred. "But first let me introduce our friend. Miss Whitcomb—Mr. Wormwood."

The man from tomorrow swung low with a flourish, like the courtier of a medieval king. One hand was placed significantly over his heart; the other was lifted wide in a gallant gesture, which brought a titter to the lips of Miss Whitcomb.

"It does me honor, my dear lady," said our guest, apparently not noticing the girl's amusement, "to make the acquaintance of such a delightful representative of her sex."

Thereupon he flung forth both hands, and took Miss Whitcomb's reluctant ones in his.

While I had no doubt that this was to be considered the courteous manner of address in the twenty-third century. I was a little alarmed at the effusiveness of the man from tomorrow. I was particularly alarmed when I saw with what admiring eyes he was staring at the young lady. Miss Whitcomb, with her tall, well built form, her clear complexion, blue eyes and finely modeled features, was far from an unattractive person, and there were many men who would not have been immune to her charms; yet never before had I seen anyone show his feelings so soon or so openly and unreservedly.

"Miss Whitcomb," continued the man from tomorrow, with irrepressible fluency, "I have been more than a little bewildered at this curious century of yours. Many of your habits are so peculiar that I fear I shall never get quite used to them, and naturally I am feeling just a little homesick for my own age. But ladies like you will help me to forget. Yes, I might even say that, through my good fortune in meeting you, this generation is redeemed in my estimation."

Having made this speech, the man from tomorrow executed another of his chivalrous bows; while the rest of us gazed at him open-mouthed, not knowing whether to believe his exaggerated language as serious or in jest.

"By the way, Miss Whitcomb," proceeded our guest, in a brisker, more business-like manner, "do you expect to be at home this evening? If so, and if you are doing nothing in particular, it will give me pleasure—"

It was now Dr. Horn's turn to speak. The scowl that darkened his features did not indicate that he enjoyed the turn that matters had taken. "Miss Whitcomb is engaged this evening!" he snapped, cutting short the man from tomorrow. "She and I have an important appointment. Come, Alice, shall we be going?"

But Wormwood, unperturbed, continued suavely. "Dr. Horn, I put my question to the young lady, and so, of course, I shall expect my answer from no one else. I do not know how such things are managed in this century, but in my own times a full-grown woman is usually considered competent to decide her own affairs."

From the manner in which Dr. Horn glowered at our visitor, I feared that it would not have taken much to bring them to blows.

But Miss Whitcomb, although it seemed to me that she shrank from her new acquaintance, answered in a pleasant enough voice, "I thank you very much, Mr. Wormwood. It is very good of you. But I am engaged for this evening."

"Well, I suppose that can't be helped," conceded the man from tomorrow. "However, there are other evenings coming. From present indications, my stay among you will be a prolonged one. Perhaps we shall still see much of one another."

"Perhaps," she replied, without enthusiasm.

"Come, let's be going!" Dr. Horn brusquely repeated. "Goodbye, Professor. See you on the Campus."

"Goodbye, Mr. Wormwood," said Miss Whitcomb, in low, restrained tones.

"Goodbye, my dear lady," returned Wormwood, bowing once more. "Our acquaintance thus far, I regret, has been unpleasantly short. But then, you remember the words of the poet:

> " 'A moment's meeting in an April mood
> Is worth ten years of Arctic solitude.' "

"No, I'm afraid I don't remember," she confessed.

"Really!" The man from tomorrow looked surprised. "Oh, but of course, I should have recalled! They were written by Jensen-Thayer, who wasn't born till 2050! Too bad you've never read him. He was a great poet."

"Come! We've got to be going!" reiterated Dr. Horn, in more surly tones than ever. And, taking Miss Whitcomb's arm, he retreated without so much as a backward glance at the man from tomorrow.

Over the breakfast table—at which our guest refused to eat more than an orange and a plate of prunes—I undertook to refer tactfully to the liberties he had taken with Miss Whitcomb.

"I know nothing about the customs of your age," I said, "but in our age that sort of thing isn't done. No, it simply isn't done. In the first place, Miss Whitcomb is not at liberty to make dates with young men. She is engaged to become another man's wife. Her wedding to Dr. Horn has been announced—"

"But what has that to do with it?" interrupted the man from tomorrow, with a puzzled air. "I never can make out the ways of this century—you have such singular ideas! Now I wasn't proposing to the girl. For that matter, though, I don't see why I shouldn't, if she cares enough for me. I was merely suggesting a bit of friendly intercourse, and I don't see any reason why Dr. Horn should object. Just because she's engaged to him, should she deny herself the charms of all other masculine society?"

"But Miss Whitcomb," I returned, slightly irritated, "is a fine, high-minded young lady, and wouldn't want any other masculine society."

The eyes of the man from tomorrow opened wide with amazement. His thin lips made a gaping oval of surprise. "Oh, so that's it!" he ejaculated. "Well, I do remember reading some bad reports of my forefathers! So the masculine society of this age is so unfit—"

"Nothing of the kind!" I denied, wondering where he had gotten such an idea.

But, disregarding my words, he went on to explain. "Well, fortunately, I'm not a man of this age. So you needn't fear. My intentions are honorable. No young lady has cause for alarm—"

"I wasn't questioning that," I assured him. "Just the same, Wormwood, if you want to get along in the twentieth century, you'll have to change your tactics. Even if Miss Whitcomb wasn't engaged, do you think she'd have made an appointment with you on such short acquaintance?"

"Why not?" he demanded. "How could we make our short acquaintance longer without arranging to meet again?"

I opened my mouth to reply to this ridiculous question; but, not being able to think of a satisfactory answer, I decided that it was unworthy of attention.

Several seconds passed in silence while I bent over my soft-boiled eggs and my companion watched me quizzically. Finally, resolving upon a different line of tack, I inquired, "Even from your own point of view, Wormwood, I shouldn't think you'd want to become too familiar with the girls of this century. Didn't you say something about being engaged to a Miss Maranna?"

"Yes, of course! But how far away Maranna is!" sighed the man from tomorrow, with a wistful expression. "I don't think I'd be disloyal to her—not in our own century. But, surely, it would be unreasonable of her to expect me to remain in perpetual bachelorhood three hundred years before she was born. No, Maranna would have more understanding than that. She always was of a logical disposition, being the daughter of a mathematician and a female judge by a eugenic union."

The conversation having taken a sentimental turn, my guest lapsed into a melancholy mood; and his eyes, burning with a soft, sad light, seemed to be fixed on things far away and still unborn.

A few minutes later, upon rising from the breakfast table, I consulted my watch and found that it was almost time to leave for the Campus. How to provide my visitor with something to occupy him for the rest of the day was now a problem; but I solved the difficulty—so I thought—by leading him into the library, where more than two thousand choice volumes were stacked almost to the ceiling.

"No doubt you will be able to entertain yourself for a few hours here," I suggested. "I shall see you sometime this afternoon. Meanwhile, if you need anything, just call for Mrs. Howard."

"Oh, I'm sure I'll not need anything," he assured me. "My requirements, as you have found, are of the simplest." And then, with manifest curiosity, he began devoting himself to the bookcases.

"Strange bindings, these!" he remarked, taking out a typical cloth-bound tome. "Interesting to see, but how flimsy! Probably this was made before binding in flexible tinalfer came into vogue. That is to say, a tin, aluminum and iron alloy, of exceeding lightness, and guaranteed to be indestructible. Well, well, well! I suppose the old bindings did well enough in their way. Now let's see, what authors have you? I suppose you have editions of Rubinbower, Bellovitz, and De la Chaine?"

"Rubinbower, Bellovitz, and De la Chaine?" I repeated, in bewilderment.

"Oh, I'm always forgetting!" was the annoyed response. "It didn't occur to me—they haven't been born yet. Well, let's see what books you do have. Though it seems hard to imagine any library without the epics of Rubinbower or the satires of De la Chaine!"

A minute passed while Wormwood scrutinized the contents of my case with a disapproving air.

"Strange!" he finally announced. "I don't recollect any of these names! The study of literature used to be one of my hobbies, too…Theodore Dreiser, James Branch Cabell, Anatole France, Bernard Shaw. Who were they? You know, I can't place any of them. To come to think of it, of course, that's not surprising—the twentieth century was such a decadent period in literature. Its writers were such second-raters! No one reads them much nowadays—that is to say, in the twenty-third century—unless he's preparing some erudite work on 'Literature Decline, Its Causes and Effects,' or 'Fads and Foibles in Literature, with Special Reference to the Poetasters of the Neurotic Age.' "

"From the way you speak," I replied indignantly, "I suppose you've read a good deal of twentieth century literature?"

"Why, no, no—can't say that I have," Wormwood admitted, haltingly. "My taste has always inclined toward the classics."

"Then read before you criticize!" I advised, supplying him with copies of Rudyard Kipling, H. G. Wells, Romain Rolland, and other leading modern authors. And with that, and a few words of final advice, I bade him a hasty farewell.

As I left the room, he was drawing a volume from the case with an expression of delighted recognition. "Ah! John Milton! And Shakespeare, too! I'm glad to see copies of our great predecessors. Strange, how little your age seems to have profited by their example!"

During the twenty minutes' journey to the Campus, my mind was occupied with matters more weighty by far than Wormwood's opinions of contemporary literature. What to do with him was the problem that was troubling me, for I had neither the inclination nor the ability to lodge such a guest indefinitely at my home. But where else was he to go? Surely, even were he well supplied with money—and it was all too evident that he had not a penny—he would be less capable than a child of caring for himself in this century; while, on the other hand, his paralyzing rays would make him a public menace. Again, he was doubtless the possessor of much knowledge that our age could not acquire through normal means for generations yet, and the loss to science would be inestimable were he to keep this precious information to himself; hence it seemed to me that I had no more the right, than I had the desire, to detain him long at my house, or to withhold from the world the incredible facts of his origin. All in all, it appeared to me, the best course would be to take some of my colleagues into my confidence, to invite them to my home to interview the man from tomorrow, and to seek their advice as to our visitor's future.

In order not to take my associates too much by surprise, I decided not to begin by explaining what had occurred. I merely informed them, in a purposely mysterious manner, that an event of the first scientific importance had occurred, and that there would be a meeting to discuss it at my house that evening; and I begged them to disregard all other engagements in order to be present. Partly because of my assurance that phenomenal revelations were in store, and partly because of the pulsating earnestness which, I am sure, I could not wholly conceal, I had little difficulty in prevailing upon my fellow faculty members; and it was not long before I was able to look forward to seeing six or eight distinguished scientists at my home in the evening.

After leaving the University in the afternoon, I turned my footsteps toward the lodgings of Mr. Cloud. When I had last seen him, he had been in a state of paralysis; and, despite the assurance of the man from tomorrow that the inventor would be well again within twenty-four hours, it occurred to me that he might possibly be in need of assistance. I was therefore relieved to find him almost recovered. It is true that, when I arrived, he had difficulty in opening the door to let me in; that his muscles still worked stiffly and the numbness had not quite left his limbs. But the effect of the paralysis was passing, and it should not be long, he thought, before he was his normal self again.

"I'm glad you came, Professor," said he, his face brightening with a welcoming smile as I entered. "It's been pretty lonesome lying here all by myself. Was any man ever so unfortunate before, I wonder? Here our visitor from the twenty-third century not only ruins the work of years by his arrival, but has the poor manners to paralyze the author of his being!"

"Very naturally, he feels a grudge against you for bringing him into this century," I declared, as I took a seat on the threadbare couch. "But don't worry, Mr. Cloud, you're not the only victim." And, as briefly as possible, I described my own adventures with the man from tomorrow.

The inventor listened to my recital with an interested air, and then remarked, "The question now is this, Professor: how are we to get our visitor back to his rightful century? Personally, I don't see any way. The apparatus that got him here is shattered, and I haven't any funds to rebuild it—even if that would be of any avail. I'm afraid he's going to prove an infernal nuisance to our century. I dread to think how many people he will paralyze."

"I've been considering all that, Mr. Cloud," I admitted, reflectively. "And that brings us back to your invention. If we could make some interested person see what a work of genius it is, maybe we could procure the funds to build you a new laboratory. I'll tell you what—" Here I hesitated for a moment, since a fresh idea had come to me. "I'll tell you what, Mr. Cloud. Suppose you get ready and come with me now. There's going to be a meeting of scientists at my home this evening. That should give you your opportunity. You'll explain about your Dimension Machine, and I'll do my best to substantiate your claims. If my colleagues become sufficiently interested, no doubt something will be done for you. What do you say?"

"Good!" ejaculated Cloud, taking my hand heartily. "It's mighty decent of you, Professor!"

But, almost instantly, the light died from his face. "There's just one objection," he mumbled. "Would I— would I have to meet Mr. Wormwood again?"

"I'm afraid that would be necessary."

For a moment Cloud was silent. "You know, I hate to come within range of those paralyzing rays," he assured me, with the air of a martyr. "But I suppose I must take the chance. I'll try to remember it's all in the interests of science. I'll be ready in just a second, Professor."

Although the inventor still walked a little feebly and stiffly, we found that the effect of the paralysis had vanished once he attempted to use his limbs actively. Within a few minutes, we were on the way to my home, while my mind was occupied with surmises and misgivings as to the behavior of the man from tomorrow during my absence.

CHAPTER TEN
Adventure and Conflict

WHEN Cloud and I were within a block or two of my home, our attention was attracted by the sounds of loud disputation, in which the shouts and yells of excited humans were mingled with the snarls and howling of a dog. At one of the street corners, a crowd of boys and men had gathered, jeering and clamoring by fits and starts; while in their midst, in the intervals between the hoots and catcalls, the voices of two embattled men could be heard.

At first my companion and I had no idea what the fight was all about, nor could we make out who the combatants were. "Doubtless it's only some street ruffians," I remarked, and would have gone quietly home and taken no further notice of the affair— had not Cloud insisted on drawing me near the scene of the disturbance.

And it was not a minute before I became interested in ways I had scarcely expected.

"You insignificant little flyspeck!" we heard the voice of some unseen contestant. "Go home to your mother, and leave real men alone! What do you mean by breaking into my affairs? Is it my dog, or yours? Say just another word, and I'll wipe the sidewalk with you!"

"Say just another word, and I'll paralyze you!" rang forth the reply, in tones that were startlingly familiar. "You despicable puppy! The muzzle should have been on you, and not on the dog!"

Hoots and yells of glee greeted these words, accompanied by a renewed uproar of barking.

Excitedly Cloud and I pushed forward. "Stop! Stop!" I cried, forgetting my professional dignity in the agitation of the moment, while in furious haste I broke through the crowd. "Stop! Just one minute!"

There, in the center of the mob, were two well-known figures! One of them was my neighbor, Philip Preston, the son of Judge Preston; the other was the man from tomorrow! Both of them were wild-eyed with rage; both of them, with flushed faces, dilated nostrils, and clenched and quivering fists, seemed ready to commit murder. Certainly, had I not arrived in the nick of time, either the man from tomorrow would have been badly mauled, or else Preston would have been paralyzed!

"If you think it's your dog—" the judge's son was saying, as I strode into the thick of the combat, and, interposing myself between the two antagonists, halted the hostilities and demanded what was the matter.

Both of the opponents, though appearing to resent my intrusion, attempted to answer at once. But it was the man from tomorrow who, being quicker and more fluent of speech, managed to make himself heard.

"What was the matter?" he shrilled, to the accompaniment of an undertone of derisive laughter from the mob. "This two-legged brute, who goes by the name of a man, had the cruelty to clamp down the jaws of his dog with a leather strap, which he calls a muzzle! I saw the poor animal nosing against the trees and walls, trying his pitiful best to remove the encumbrance—and so what could I do but act like a man and take it off for him?"

"Yes, but it was my dog! And my muzzle, too!" shrieked Preston, while, with brandished fists, he edged forward, as though, despite my interference, he would force his way to his foe and pummel him. "What business is it of yours, I'd like to know? You broke the muzzle when I asked for it, and then tried to keep me from getting the animal back!"

"You weren't fit to get it back!" cried the man from tomorrow, while the crowd still shrieked and gibbered with glee. "Who are you to command the immortal soul of a dumb beast? Any man of honor would have done as I did!"

And once more the throng howled and roared.

"Listen here, Wormwood," I said, managing for the first time to put in a word of explanation, "I don't think you quite understand. This gentleman here—Mr. Preston—isn't cruel. He's merely obeying a city ordinance requiring dogs to be muzzled. He had to do as he did—according to the law."

"According to the law!" echoed Wormwood, in bewilderment. "What sort of law would that be? No, no, I won't believe it! No law could be so cruel! That the poor, dumb animals, who haven't even a word in the making of the laws, should be treated so heartlessly—incredible! Why, it's punishment without representation!"

"We don't consider it punishment," I insisted, although I could see how incredulously the man from tomorrow was smiling. And then, perceiving that there was nothing to be gained from further argumentation I turned to Preston and promised, "I'll make up to you for the broken muzzle." And to Wormwood I added, "Better come along with me now. I want to speak to you."

Flinging a final bolt at his adversary, "Lucky for you, you didn't get paralyzed", the man from tomorrow slouched into place behind Cloud and myself, and, heedless of the grins and mockery of the mob, began calmly to inquire where I had been and why I had remained away so long.

"I've had some interesting times since you left," he confided. "Of course, I couldn't remain very long in your library, reading those musty antique books, especially since so few of the really good writers were to be found there. And so I decided to go out and inspect the twentieth century in my own way. Unluckily, I didn't know where to go, and most of the time I got lost in the slums. There was one street of tenements that interested me particularly. I asked someone its name, and had a good long laugh to myself, it was so inappropriate."

"What was it called?" I inquired, with visions of Mulberry Street.

"Park Avenue."

"Park Avenue! You don't mean to say—"

But the man from tomorrow, not seeming to hear me, continued garrulously. "By the glorious stars, I don't see how anyone can bear to live in such a place! The buildings were all eight or ten stories high, and there isn't a bit of greenery. The motor cars on the streets were thick as packs of wolves, and the air was so badly poisoned I got a headache. Nowhere was there a sign of trace of beauty, or of an open space, or even of a restful spot for the eyes. It was all delightful enough from the historical point of view, but, by the Everlasting, how I do pity those poor souls that have to live there!"

"Poor souls!" I echoed. "Why, they're our richest citizens!"

The man from tomorrow stared at me in the gaping, unbelieving manner that had come to be almost habitual with him.

"Now why don't you tell me something reasonable?" he asked. "What motive could your richest citizens have for living in the slums? What conceivable motive? Unless, of course..." Here the speaker smiled as if sudden comprehension had come to him. "...unless, of course, they wish to do penance for the sin of possessing more than they need."

"Not at all!" I denied. "You know nothing whatever of the matter! They are so far from doing penance that they are the envy of millions!"

The man from tomorrow looked more bewildered than ever; but once more he struggled to adjust his intellect to the demands of this staggering problem.

"Then the only explanation I can see," he ruminated, "is that the dwellers there, while rich in pocket, are so poor at heart that they do not miss the wide spaces, the open skies, the green trees, the grasses and the waters."

By this time we had reached my house; and, after entering and being greeted by my wife, we made ourselves comfortable in the sitting room.

"Don't you have any big buildings in your own time?" asked Cloud, by way of continuing the conversation.

"Unfortunately, we do," Wormwood acknowledged, sadly. "The increase in population has made that evil necessary. But our laws provide that for every square foot that is built upon, two square feet must be reserved for streets, gardens and recreation grounds. There are some reformers who believe the ratio should be three to one, or even four to one. While such ideas are generally considered impractical, no self-respecting community would think of returning to the cramped conditions of the Anthill Age."

"The Anthill Age?" Cloud demanded.

"Oh, that's another name for the Neurotic Age."

A moment passed in silence; then, hoping to give a different turn to the conversation, I inquired, "Well, Wormwood, was Park Avenue the only street you inspected?"

"By no means! I discovered others that looked even more poverty-ridden. I will admit that this was highly venturesome of me, for I had to cross at many intersections, and every time I did so, I had to screw up my courage in the manner of a swimmer diving into a shark-infested sea. Of course, I never knew whether or not I was to arrive on the other side. But by the grace of good fortune and much agile dodging, I escaped all those terrific four-wheeled engines that came thundering toward me like bloodthirsty goblins; and thus, at the risk of my life, I did manage to see something of this century. I was particularly interested in your shop windows, which had such curious displays that they reminded me of museums. For example, there were windows full of little brown finger-shaped objects; and upon going into one of the shops and asking the clerk what they were for, he looked at me as if he thought I were out of my mind, and said, 'For smoking, of course!' That made me laugh outright, for the idea seemed simply too delicious for words. Just the same, he was not joking; only a minute afterwards, I saw a man put a light to one of those silly, brown affairs and stick it into his mouth with such a serious air, that I had to laugh again."

The man from tomorrow paused long enough to smile whimsically; then lightly continued:

"After that, I saw lots of other amusing things. First there was a store with the sign, 'Finest Drugs' and upon looking into the window, what did I see but a pile of books! Then there was another store with a whole array of nauseating-looking articles—all green and pink and red and yellow and other disgusting colors— and I saw a sign 'Choice Confectionery,' suggesting that these unnatural things were meant to eat! After that, I was ready to find stores containing blue potatoes or purple loaves of bread, and was rather surprised not to come across any. But what I did see next was amazing enough—a shop with a lot of pretty little trinkets, such as we give our children to play with—pearls, rubies, sapphires, diamonds and the like! I was astonished to discover that they were being sold for real money! 'Well, well, well, how the world has changed!' I thought. And I was filled with pity for the men of the twentieth century, who didn't know any better than to waste their time on baubles.

"So thinking, I passed on into a big, broad street, very twisted and irregular, which I judged to be one of the central thoroughfares of the town. There were enormous signs strung everywhere high up on the buildings; and, naturally, I looked at these with great interest, for I supposed that they would embody uplifting thoughts from the great poets and philosophers, such as one finds above the cities of the twenty-third century. But alas! What a grand disappointment! Could the authors of the twentieth century—decadent as they were—be responsible for such sentiments? I asked myself. The more I gazed, the more perplexed I became; for I did not see anything that made sense. 'Sixty-six varieties—sold everywhere,' I remember reading; and 'Buy Squirmley's Peppered Chewing Gum.' By the way, what is 'chewing gum?' Then there was something about 'Rough-Edge Tires.' Another reference which, somehow, I didn't quite catch; and after that I read about a woman named Dolly Dolores, who was to appear in a play called 'The Devil of Deep Gulch.' By this time I decided that I had seen enough, and so I started back. I had kept careful track of the way, and had not much trouble about returning—although once I was nearly run down by one of those man-eating cars. The driver never knew how near he came to being paralyzed! But nothing else of interest happened till I got near your house, when I saw that brute of a man abusing the dog."

Having completed this recitation, the man from tomorrow yawned, and wearily announced, "Heavens, but I am tired! This tour of the twentieth century has been about all I have been able to stand!"

And then, without so much as asking permission, he stretched himself out at full length on my wife's best sofa, and was soon contentedly snoring.

CHAPTER ELEVEN
The Examiners Assemble

OF the scientists whom I had invited to my home that evening, all except one had arrived by the appointed hour. Truly, they made a notable gathering—there was Professor Milton Rushmore, the well known anthropologist; there was Professor Charles Warrington, my colleague in the Physics Department; there was Professor Hilbert Carroway, renowned for his textbooks on physiology; there was Dr. Virgil Stoner, a psychologist whose reputation was nationwide; there was Professor Rhys Thornwell, the chemist; and there were one or two others of equal distinction. To my regret, Dr. Horn was not to be present, since he could not be induced to break his appointment with Miss Whitcomb; and this was most unfortunate, and was greatly to enhance the difficulties of my task.

When finally my visitors had all convened in the library and sat smoking and chatting together, I was conscious of an atmosphere of suspense and unspoken questioning which secretly troubled me, for as yet none of my colleagues had any suspicion of the reason for our meeting, and I was not sure how best to make the revelation. I solved the difficulty, however, by calling in Mr. Cloud, who was waiting in an adjoining room in company with the man from tomorrow; and, having introduced the inventor as a still unrecognized scientific genius, I bade him tell his story of the Dimension Machine. This he did with fluency and gusto, beginning with his early struggles, dwelling at length upon his years of investigation and adversity, and ending with an account of the success of the Dimension Machine and with the views it had provided of the remote past and future. Regardless of the stares of perplexity and doubt on the faces of his auditors, Cloud had boldly described how scraps and debris from past ages had been deposited in the Dimension Machine, and was preparing to tell of the arrival of our visitor from the twenty-third century—when all at once the door was flung open and the man from tomorrow stood framed in the entrance.

"I beg pardon," he startled us all by saying, as he nodded in my direction. "Your radio-vizor is ringing!"

"Radio-vizor!" I gasped; and then instantly I understood—the telephone was sounding in the hall!

I excused myself, and dashed to the instrument. "Hello... No...no! Wrong number!" one might have heard me snap, followed by a "Damn it" under my breath. Then, returning to the library, I was further irritated to find the man from tomorrow in conversation with my guests, who were regarding him with smiles and twinkles of amusement.

"My name is John Wormwood," he was saying. "What is your name? Professor Rushmore? I didn't catch the first name. Oh, Milton Rushmore. This is a great honor, Milton, I assure you. I hope we shall see much more of each other..."

Breaking in upon the man from tomorrow, I demanded, "What's the matter, Wormwood? Don't you how to address Professor Milton properly?"

"Why what's wrong?" inquired Wormwood, with a blank expression. "Didn't he say that Milton was his name? In my in own century—"

The storm of laughter, that burst upon us, cut short these words; and it was after several minutes had passed, that someone had a chance to ask, "What was it that you were saying, Mr. Wormwood, about a radio something—"

"A radio-visor? It's an improvement on an old-fashioned talking instrument—a tele—tele—no, not teleplane. I just can't recollect the term. In my excitement just now, I had forgotten that radio-vizors weren't invented until after the Neurotic Age."

At these words, renewed merriment convulsed my visitors. When the outburst had subsided, I saw that they were staring at Wormwood in that curiously indulgent manner that we reserve for children, and for those who are not quite right in the head.

"Your jests sound exceedingly clever, sir," declared Professor Rushmore, patronizingly, "but I must admit that I don't exactly get them."

"That's only to be expected, since I was quite serious," declared Wormwood, simply.

The fresh laughter that greeted these words was such as few serious men could have hoped to evoke.

It was only too apparent that matters were going from bad to worse. If the conversation continued in this vein, would not my colleagues think that I had summoned them to a vaudeville show instead of a serious scientific discussion? And so I found an immediate explanation necessary. "Do not pay any heed to Mr. Wormwood," I pleaded. "What he says is all sensible enough, but before you listen you must understand more about him. And that is what I have called you here tonight to consider. The facts, I believe, are the most extraordinary in the history of science. Had they not been demonstrated to me beyond all question, I would not insult your intelligence by presenting an account of them. So prepare yourselves for a revelation. Prepare for an epoch-making announcement. Mr. Wormwood is not a man of your own age. He owes his presence here to Mr. Cloud's Dimension Machine. He was born in the twenty-third century."

I came to an emphatic halt, and the silence that fell upon us was sepulchral. All eyes were fastened upon me with a fixed, inquiring scrutiny; but the faces of the listeners, it seemed to me, were drawn up into hard, hostile lines, as though they had no sympathy with what I had been saying—as though they were neither ready nor willing to accept it.

But after a moment, when the silence was becoming almost too heavy to bear, aid came to me from an unexpected quarter.

"You're all a lot of hard-baked doubters, aren't you?" suddenly demanded the man from tomorrow. "You don't believe one word, I suppose? You can't imagine that I came from another century?"

There was a momentary pause of embarrassment; then the booming voice of Dr. Virgil Stoner was heard.

"Well now, Mr. Wormwood, isn't that a good deal to imagine? I pride myself we're not exactly without imagination, any of us; but, at the same time, we're not gullible peasants. When we hear such a—er—remarkable story, we require proof."

"Proof?" flung back the man from tomorrow, disdainfully. "If it's proof that you're seeking, haven't you got it already? Why, can't you take just one glance at me, and decide for yourself? Do I look like one of you? Can't you see the marks of a superior century written all over me?"

And the man from tomorrow strutted back and forth like a cock displaying himself before the hens.

Amused smiles played once more upon several faces; but Dr. Stoner was obdurate.

"Well, I guess I'm blind," he admitted. "I can't see the marks of any superiority at all."

He paused, gravely wrinkled up his brow, and continued. "I trust that you won't mind, Mr. Wormwood, if I talk to you a little frankly. Have you ever visited a psychiatrist? I should say that a psychoanalyst would be able to help you. Possibly some childhood repression, working through the channels of the subconscious, has produced this delusion of a future birth—"

"Delusion?" cried the man from tomorrow, quick as always to anger. "I tell you the only delusion is your own! Your mind is so stuffed and padded with out-of-date notions, that when you see the glimmer of a new idea you call it a delusion! If a bat were made to see the sunlight, no doubt he would call that a delusion too!"

Filled with a perfect frenzy of indignation, the man from tomorrow paced the room with clenched fists; and the angry fires that darted from his eyes did not bode well for Dr. Stoner.

In one or two faces there was still an amused glitter; but most of my visitors were looking grave and even a little anxious, as though Wormwood were not merely a madman, but a dangerous madman.

It was Professor Thornwell who broke the embarrassing silence that followed. "Mr. Wormwood, you still haven't offered us any definite proof. Surely, it's not unreasonable to ask for some convincing evidence."

"There's no such thing as convincing evidence—for those that don't want to be convinced!" proclaimed the man from tomorrow.

With these words, he did another whirl about the room I then, taking counsel with himself, he decided, "Very well! I'll give you a chance! Just wait here a minute, and we'll see! We'll see!"

Before I had any idea what he was about, he had gone darting out of the room.

"Here! Where are you going?" I called out, with some vague notion of rushing after him. But he did not answer and, thinking it best to leave him to his own devices, I sank back into my seat with a sigh, and awaited developments.

"A curious individual!" remarked Dr. Stoner, thoughtfully. "A most curious individual! How I should like to psychoanalyze him! One thing is apparent from his remark about his superiority—which is that he has an inferiority complex. Aside from that, I can't be certain just what the trouble is. Perhaps his case is one of incipient, dementia praecox; and then again it may turn out to be the manic-depressive type. I should say that the hysterical symptoms indicate a form of psychosis in which—"

Unfortunately for Dr. Stoner, the man from tomorrow returned at this point; and so the psychologist was never to complete his diagnosis.

In Wormwood's hands was an object that I recognized only too well—the garment he had worn upon his arrival from his own century.

"See! Look at this closely!" he requested, thrusting the article into Professor Thornwell's hands. "Tell me whether anything like this was produced in the Neurotic Age!"

Like a group of schoolgirls examining a new dress, all had arisen in fluttering excitement, and, with staccato exclamations, were crowding around Professor Thornwell.

"Why, I—I don't know that I have seen anything just like it," gasped the chemist. "I—I don't know what it's made of."

"You will observe that it is not cloth," pointed out the man from tomorrow. "Note carefully—there are no threads."

"No, there are no threads. It is not cloth," conceded Thornwell, struggling with his surprise. "I'll be blest I've ever seen anything to match it!"

"How light it is!" someone else was commenting. "And how smooth and flexible! How strangely it shimmers! It's like silk to the touch, and yet it isn't silk."

"No, it certainly isn't," agreed the man from tomorrow. "It's a product of synthetic chemistry—made up of silicon, aluminum, and one or two other ingredients. The formula wasn't discovered until 2190. Ever since that time, it's been the backbone of the garment industry. It's cheaper than cotton, and it never wears out."

"By heaven!" ejaculated Thornwell. "I wonder if you'd let me take it with me. I'd like to analyze it—examine it in the laboratory."

"Go ahead!" Wormwood acquiesced, with a shrug. "But don't imagine that you people, at this early date, have the equipment to duplicate it."

Pleased that Wormwood had thought of so effective a method of substantiating my story, I lifted my voice with perhaps just a faint note of triumph.

"Well now, my friends, I wonder whether you're convinced? Do you agree that our visitor was not born in our own age?"

But not yet had the truth prevailed! Once again that unconquerable skeptic, Dr. Stoner, insisted on objecting!

"By no means, Howard! Why should I agree?" he demanded. "Even a child wouldn't be deceived by such arguments! Just because you show me a new kind of cloth, does that prove that its maker is not a man of our own century! Suppose it's a new invention, which hasn't been put on the market yet? All in all, that's a far more likely theory, it seems to me. I still cling to my original contention. Mr. Wormwood should seek the services of some good psychiatrist—"

"Oh, should I?" caught up the man from tomorrow, whose eyes were darting irate lightnings at Dr. Stoner. "Because your own mind is impenetrable, I should have my mind examined? Well, let that be! So you still want more proof? What would you say if I were to give it to you?"

There was such force and determination in these words, and the speaker came to such an emphatic halt, that for the moment Stoner seemed at a loss for a reply.

"So you still want more proof?" repeated the man from tomorrow, in slower, more significant tones. "If you ask it, I promise you that you shall not ask in vain!"

"Of course I ask it!" asserted Dr. Stoner. "Why not—"

Before the psychologist could complete his sentence, Wormwood had reached into his trouser pocket and drawn forth the little pistol-shaped contrivance. There came the ominous droning sound that I had already heard twice before, and the flash of green light—and Stoner groaned, staggered, and fell...

Several minutes later, after the commotion had begun to subside and the paralyzed psychologist had been lifted to the couch, one might have heard the clear, unimpassioned tones of the man from tomorrow:

"Sorry, my friend. I was sorry to have to do that. But don't worry—you will be all right again within twenty-four hours. Surely, you will not mind the momentary inconvenience—it is all in the interest of science. Perhaps now you have the proof you were looking for."

Dr. Stoner muttered beneath his breath, but made no audible reply.

"Maybe there are some of you who are still looking for proof," continued Wormwood, blandly. "Maybe some of you hold that the paralyzing rays also are a twentieth century invention, which has still to be put on the market. If, therefore, you be seeking a still more convincing demonstration—"

But apparently no further demonstration was to be necessary. My colleagues one and all cast apprehensive glances in the direction of the man from tomorrow, and announced themselves fully persuaded. I observed that none of them demanded a more thorough acquaintanceship with the rays, and that their attitude toward our visitor had grown much more polite, not to say respectful. In fact, several of them were edging toward the door, and one or two went so far as to reach for their hats, when I, in the most reassuring tones I could command, sought to pacify them:

"Be seated, gentlemen! You are none of you in any danger. Mr. Wormwood will not repeat his little performance—that I guarantee."

"No, gentlemen," confirmed Wormwood. "There is no need to repeat the performance—since you are all convinced."

Reluctantly, and with tremors of hesitation, my visitors returned to their seats; and while Stoner, after momentarily regaining consciousness, lapsed back into slumber, the rest of us launched into a questionnaire regarding the twenty-third century.

CHAPTER TWELVE

The Inquisition Continues

SEATED around the room in a grave-eyed group, my visitors peered at the man from tomorrow as though he was an animal from some other world. Cigars and cigarettes once more went the rounds, and there was an undercurrent of whispered conversation; but the center of attention was Wormwood, who was kept busy answering queries.

"What year were you born in?" inquired Professor Warrington, by way of opening the attack; while he and several of his colleagues drew forth notebooks and pencils.

"In the second year of the Decade of the Great Epic," stated the man from tomorrow.

We merely stared at him, as though he was speaking in some unknown tongue. But, seeing how blank every one looked, he went on to explain:

"Pardon me! I had forgotten what century it was!

No doubt you haven't yet adopted the practice of giving each decade a name, after some notable work which it has bequeathed to the world. My birth decade, you see, took its name from the immortal poem of Geoffrey La Platte, who was then at the superb height of his powers. Expressed in your prosaic speech, my birth may he said to have occurred about the year 2195."

Rapidly the pencils of the examiners made their way across the paper, while Professor Carroway flung the next question:

"What is your age, sir?"

"My age?" The man from tomorrow looked surprised. "Why, haven't you guessed it? I have reached the Epoch of Ascendance."

"The Epoch of Ascendance?"

The man from tomorrow looked more surprised than ever. "I see that you don't even know what that means. Well, then, let me explain. We count age by important periods or epochs, not by years. First there is the Epoch of Infancy; then of Childhood; then of Adolescence; then of Ascendance, which in the case of most men of intellect lasts as long as they live, no matter how long that may be; though, in the case of a few unfortunates, it gives place to a fifth Epoch, the Epoch of Decadence. Heaven spare me from ever falling into that doom!"

Once more the pencils were racing across the page; and this time it was Professor Rushmore who continued the questionnaire:

"What is your lineage, sir? Your parents? Your family tree? Your ancestors?"

"My lineage is of the best," proclaimed the man from tomorrow, tapping his thin chest proudly. "I am born of a eugenic union. My father was rated perfect in ninety-eight points out of a hundred in the intelligence examinations before the National Academy. My mother received an equal rating for imaginative range and emotional depth. And so, you see, I had an excellent all-around start in life."

"I'm afraid I don't see," persisted Professor Rushmore. "Who were your father and mother? What did they do for a living? What sort of people did they spring from?"

"They sprang from the best, of course. Their parents, too, were eugenically selected. As for their living, they got that in the same way as everyone else—from the State. My father was a teacher of rhetoric in one of the Regional Universities of Arts and Letters. It was from him that I inherited my love of literature. My mother was a concert musician, who gave public performances on the peraltimo."

"The what?" we all gasped.

"The peraltimo! You mean to say you haven't heard of that, either? Now really? That makes it difficult for me. There are so many things you've never heard of. The peraltimo is the most popular instrument of our times. It produces all manner of harmonious sounds by the manipulation of the radio waves. It is like a whole symphony orchestra, yet only one person controls it. Well, well, well! So the peraltimo is unknown to you! That certainly is news..."

Into the eyes of the man from tomorrow, as he uttered these words, there crept a faintly contemptuous gleam, as though he were saying to himself, "Thank heaven! I was born in an enlightened era!"

"All that is very interesting, Mr. Wormwood, but aren't we getting away from our subject?" demanded Professor Rushmore, whose scowling face proclaimed him still on the trail of a single idea. "We were talking about your lineage. Now who made up your line of descent before your father and mother—"

"Before my father and mother?" shouted the witness. "Didn't I tell you my grandparents also had eugenic-qualifications? Otherwise, do you suppose I could be what I am today?"

The man from tomorrow paused, and, puffing out his chest pompously, resumed. "Beyond the third generation, I've never really troubled very much to inquire. Why should I? Naturally, since the course of evolution is onward and upward, my remote forebears must have been inferior to me!"

Peering at the frail, undersized figure of the man from tomorrow, with his bulging forehead and irregularly placed nose and chin, we could not help smiling a bit. My lips had already parted to utter something biting and sarcastic, when we were interrupted by the mumblings of Dr. Stoner, who had been lying quietly on the couch. Opening his eyes, he muttered something inaudible, stared at us pathetically, and then passed again into unconsciousness.

"Poor fellow!" murmured Cloud. "It's hit him pretty hard! He must be more susceptible to the paralysis than I was—I didn't sleep nearly so much. But, sleep or no sleep, it's an experience one doesn't care to have repeated."

Meanwhile the man from tomorrow, peering into space with staring eyes, seemed unaware of Cloud's remarks. "Do you know," he cried in wavering tones, as though some appalling thought had just occurred to him, "do you know— it comes over me, maybe you and I are all related in a distant way! What if some of you are my great-great-great-great grandfathers?"

Hearty laughter greeted this suggestion; but the solemn face of the man from tomorrow showed that the words had been spoken in deadly earnestness.

"No way of disproving it!" he sighed. "No way at all!" Indeed, it is only too likely! All of us have so many ancestors ten generations back! However, it's what I am now that counts, not what I come from!"

Though all of us were still smiling a bit, I am afraid that we were approaching the limits of our good humor; for the supercilious manner of the man from tomorrow was becoming galling in the extreme.

"Oh, you mustn't take personal offense, any of you," he resumed, as if reading our thoughts. "You're not responsible for your times. Really, I must say you're about the most tolerable set of men I've seen in this century. If only you were less ridiculously dressed, you might appear even in the twenty-third century without being noticed."

The speaker paused; but we all sat tense and silent, with ears alert and staring eyes.

"Of course, I couldn't say as much for most of your contemporaries," he added. "Now for example this morning, when I strolled along the streets, I took particular note of the passing faces. Never was the need of eugenic breeding so apparent to me before! Why, most of the men and women were of the type that would be marked 'Class D' or 'Culls' by our sociologists—the class forbidden to mate or rear children. What features they had! What features! It almost gives me nausea to think of them! Bloated and blotted! Purple-veined and distorted! Red nosed and baggy-chinned! Fat as hogs or bony as vultures! Eyes dead as stone, or rapacious as carrion-birds! Lips ghastly with crimson paint, and cheeks deathly white as chalk. No trace of spirit left in any of them, no rapture, no loveliness, no hint of green fields, of blue skies, of dawn or sunset, but only the drabness and foulness of the clay! Faugh! When I remember them, I think of the caricature that one of our artists once made, in which the souls of beasts were seen masquerading behind the clothes and forms of men!"

The passion with which Wormwood uttered these words was such that we all remained without speech.

It was a minute or two before any of us had anything more to say; then at last Professor Warrington saw fit to continue the questionnaire:

"You were telling us some facts about yourself, Mr. Wormwood. Maybe you would enlighten us a little further—we're more interested in hearing about your times than about ours. What did you say your profession was?"

"My profession," declared the man from tomorrow, with dignity, "is that of a Physical Researcher."

"A Physical what?"

"A Physical Researcher. In our times, the two important types of scientists are the Physical Researchers and the Psychical Researchers. As the means to a well-rounded education, I have of course studied extensively in both fields—but, my preferences running toward the Physical, I began to conduct investigations into Hyperspace before I had completed my Adolescent Epoch, and in due time, as I have already told our host, was promoted to the charge of a Hyperspace Observatory."

"I see. I see," declared Professor Warrington, although, from his puzzled manner, I feared that he did not see at all. And now, I wonder, would you mind if I were to ask a very personal question?"

"Go ahead," encouraged the man from tomorrow. "I have no secrets to hide."

"Well then, just for the sake of comparing your times with ours, maybe you would tell us how much salary you earned?"

"The same as everyone, of course! A thousand tantrums a year!"

"How much is that?"

The man from tomorrow hesitated. "I really don't know what, to say. It is a thousand tantrums, that's all—which is estimated as the amount necessary to keep a single person in comfort for a year. Hence it is the amount that everyone receives for his specialized services to the government."

"And is that all that anyone may earn?"

"By no means. If you make anything extra for outside activities or especially meritorious services, you are free to devote the surplus to some public work."

"Can't you use it for yourself?"

"Oh, yes, I suppose you could—if you wanted to. But who would want to? Except, of course, some egocentric individuals of a type, which, fortunately, is very rare. To be able to make some distinctive contribution to the public welfare is considered such an honor that there is a tremendous competition to achieve it. It is regarded as the ultimate mark of success."

The speeding pencils of several listeners noted down these remarks. But before they had finished, Professor Rushmore made himself heard again:

"You said something about being a single person, Mr. Wormwood. Then I take it that you have never been married?"

"Never—what?" demanded the man from tomorrow, screwing up his eyes in perplexed inquiry.

"Never married!"

The perplexity of the man from tomorrow only deepened. "I didn't quite catch that word. Would you mind repeating it?" he requested.

"I asked if you were never married."

"Married? Married? I—I really don't know," he admitted, with a hopeless nod in Rushmore's direction. "Is it anything that's done to one by way of chastisement?"

At this we all burst into laughter, in which Wormwood did not share.

"The word, I fear, is not one to be found in our vocabulary," he concluded. "Possibly it is no more than twentieth century slang?"

"On the contrary, it is the most serious word in English," announced Professor Rushmore, severely. "It means—well, when a man and woman became husband and wife."

Instantly a light came into Wormwood's face. "Oh, why didn't you say so? You want to know if I am mated. Why, no, I'm ashamed to say—no, I'm not, though I've advanced well into the Epoch of Ascendance. Don't imagine, though, that I haven't been passed by the Eugenics Commission. I was pronounced Double A mental type. But until lately I was so preoccupied with my work that I had no thought to give to my duties to society. It was only recently, when I met Maranna, that I decided to be mated. The event was to have taken place—well, it was to have taken place very, very soon."

The words of the man from tomorrow trailed to a doleful conclusion. His blue eyes were dimmed and flooded; his twisted features, furrowed into tight and pathetic lines, looked even more twisted than usual. "I—I had forgotten again," he muttered, brokenly, "The event is not to take place for more than three hundred years yet!"

Such was the strength of his grief that he had to turn from us, clenching his fists and biting savagely into his lips.

I thought that the questionnaire had now proceeded far enough. It was time to get down to the real business of the evening—time to decide what was to be done with the man from tomorrow; time to ask ourselves what aid could be given to Mr. Cloud and his invention. Without further delay, accordingly, I mentioned both these matters, beginning with the affair of Cloud and the Dimension Machine; and, after half-an-hour's discussion, I was gratified to be able to accept Professor Warrington's suggestion that Cloud be recommended as this year's recipient of the annual Enderby Award for Scientific Research, and that meanwhile we make up a small collection to reestablish him in his laboratory.

Turning to the problem of the man from tomorrow, we had even more of an enigma to solve; he appeared so clearly out of place in this century, that almost anything that we proposed seemed likely to be the wrong thing. One of my visitors advised that Wormwood be lodged in a downtown hotel, but this idea I emphatically vetoed, for I foresaw that he would be ejected if not jailed within twenty-four hours; another favored a boarding house, but this again seemed needlessly cruel, since Wormwood, not being a meat-eater, would probably have starved; a third suggested that we find him a home with some quiet private family; but here once more I objected, since I did not believe the family existed which would be able to endure his ways.

Finally, after we had debated for more than an hour and no solution seemed forthcoming, Professor Warrington offered the saving proposal:

"Why not bring him as our guest to the Faculty Club? We can all go partners on his expenses, and will probably be more than repaid by the scientific information he will offer us. Besides, since we will have him directly under our eyes, he will not be apt to make any very serious blunders through ignorance of modern ways."

"Just the idea, Warrington!" ejaculated Professor Carroway, enthusiastically. "I think that solves the problem!"

"Yes, that solves it!" agreed Professor Rushmore and Professor Thornwell in one voice.

And thus the matter, apparently, was settled.

But the man from tomorrow had still to be heard. "Your offer, no doubt, is very kind, and I thank you for it," he declared, coolly. "Just the same, how do you know that I will enjoy living in this Faculty Club of yours? What if it should have only the primitive housing accommodations common in your age? I am already getting used to my present quarters, and the effect of a change might be disastrous to one of my susceptibilities. I believe, therefore, that I shall remain where I am."

Here, indeed, was an unlooked-for obstacle! Now that we had nicely disposed of the man from tomorrow, was he to persist in rejecting the new arrangements? Already I had seen enough of his eccentricities to know that this was far from unlikely; and I shuddered as I thought of the possibility that he would remain beneath my roof. Already my domestic peace had been profoundly enough disturbed! Already my wife had complained sufficiently as to how the man from tomorrow had attempted to admit air by removing the window sashes from their frames, and how he had faded her precious Tavelyn rugs by letting in the sunlight!

Reflecting that, were he to remain with us much longer, it would be time for me to leave, I addressed Wormwood with considerable asperity. "No doubt you do not realize, sir, when you are being well treated. No doubt it honors me to have the representative of a superior century in my home. I will admit that I should feel grateful. But I do not mind informing you—and you may paralyze me, if you wish, for my truthfulness I—that never before has my house been so violently disturbed as since your arrival!"

"Thank you," responded Wormwood, with a bow. "Now, at last, everything is clear to me. I appreciate your frankness in pointing out the facts, and value your friendship all the more in consequence. Now would you mind telling me, just what advantages would I have in this Faculty Club of yours?"

"The greatest advantages this century can offer," stated my colleague Warrington, coming calmly to the rescue. "I should arrange that for you. I promise Mr. Wormwood, you would have the freedom of the Campus. You would be able to visit the classes and lecture rooms at will. You would see how a twentieth century University functions. You would acquire an education in present-day habits, standards and thoughts. In other words, you would equip yourself for life in the twentieth century."

"Good!" exclaimed the man from tomorrow, with enthusiasm. "Why didn't you explain before? That is the very thing I have been wanting! Of course, I accept only too gladly!"

Thereupon it was agreed that I was to escort Wormwood to his new home on the following morning; and then, while I thanked my friends for their cooperation and promised to care for Dr. Stoner till he revived from his paralysis, the meeting quietly adjourned.

CHAPTER THIRTEEN
A Nerve-Racking Expedition

BEFORE accompanying the man from tomorrow to the University, I risked another quarrel for the sake of his appearance.

Hitherto, as I have stated, he had worn no clothes other than a shirt, sandals and trousers—certainly not enough, I thought, to enable him to make a respectable entry at college! And so, after heated argumentation and long persuasion, I induced him to wear an old coat of mine that, while not matching the rest of his apparel, appeared considerably better than no coat at all. Despite all my pleas, he remained adamantine in refusing the use of collar and cravat; nor could I induce him to don a pair of shoes. I did, however, persuade him to accept an old pair of tennis slippers, which I found in the attic; and at the same time he consented reluctantly to wear socks, although without the assistance of garters.

"See how bit by bit my freedom is being checked and curbed!" he complained, when finally he was arrayed in his new outfit. "Alas! You people of the twentieth century give so much thought to what a man wears. In the twenty-third century, we pay heed only to what a man is."

"Clothes make the man," I dogmatized, forced to take refuge in platitudes.

"Clothes make the scarecrow!" he flung back, vehemently. "A well-clad doll may out-dress an emperor!"

Seeing no point in pursuing the discussion, I merely shrugged, and suggested, "Well, Wormwood, let's be going. We'll have to set out early if I'm to show you around before my classes begin."

"I'm all ready," declared the man from tomorrow.

Before leaving, he bade an effusive farewell to my wife, whose face shone with undisguised relief; then, scoffingly refusing the hat that I put out for him, he joined me bareheaded in my journey toward the Campus.

The greater part of the journey was to be made by subway; and though not a long trip, as subway expeditions go, it seemed long enough by the time we had reached our destination.

As we descended the stairway at one of the express stations, I noticed that my companion was holding up his nose and sniffing the air in a peculiar manner. His steps hesitated and faltered; he drew back as if uncertain whether or not to proceed. "Aren't you making a mistake?" he inquired. "Surely, you don't want to endanger your health in this pestiferous basement!"

"It isn't a basement!" I assured him. "It's a subway!"

"Subway? Subway?" he returned; and again he sniffed the air appraisingly. "You don't say so? Why, I should never have guessed it. The air doesn't seem to be ozonized at all!"

"Ozonized?"

"Unozonized subways," he continued, as he still hesitated halfway down the stairs, "have been forbidden by all modern Boards of Health, regardless of the protests of the Gravediggers' Union and the Undertakers' Association. So do you really expect me to venture down there? Remember, I haven't acquired the immunity that springs from long practice."

"Come, come, Wormwood, don't be foolish," I appealed, as I half coaxed him, half dragged him down the stairs.

But his pale features were crossed with an expression of fear, and he still drew back. "No doubt you haven't even any Solar Energizers, with their life giving sun-like rays," he continued, irrepressibly. "No, I'm sure you haven't. They weren't invented before the Decade of the Ultra-Violet Beam. Ah, well, since I can't wait that long, I shall have to take my chances now, I suppose!"

Still sniffing, he allowed me to accompany him down the stairs, to deposit his fare for him, and to push him through the turnstile.

Then all at once a disturbing incident occurred. Some hurried strap-hanger, emerging from a local train and tearing across the platform toward the closing doors of an express, apparently neglected to see Wormwood in his haste, and ran into him with such speed, that the two of them fell together in a sprawling heap. Fortunately, my companion was not badly injured, for he had the good luck to come down on top of another passenger; but never before had I seen any man quite so infuriated. There was murder glaring in his eyes; his hand, which flashed into his pocket to draw forth a concealed weapon, would surely have been guilty of a paralyzing deed—had not his intended victim wriggled through the almost closed door of the express train barely in time to avert his wrath.

"The ruffian! Brigand! Assassin! By the stars, what does this mean?" the man from tomorrow demanded, as he picked himself up and mournfully rubbed a bruised shin. "Do the police usually allow lunatics at large?"

"The man is not a lunatic," I corrected. "And not a ruffian, either. "Probably nothing but an overworked business man."

"He looked much more like a maniac to me!" insisted Wormwood. "So then? Is this a typical subway rider? And typical subway manners?"

"Yes, quite typical," I was forced to admit.

The man from tomorrow said nothing in reply, but I saw that he was edging toward the stairway, and probably would have made his escape had the crowds not been descending so impetuously that he feared to be knocked over again.

"Heaven preserve me!" he muttered, mopping his brow. "What a headache I have! It's like being in jail—once you get in, there's no way out till your sentence is up!"

He was now gasping so heavily for breath, that, in any other place, his efforts would have attracted attention. I was just a little concerned about him but, attributing the trouble to the after-effects of his fall, I tried to dismiss it from my mind. "Our train will be here in a minute," I said—and, just at that moment, it came shooting down the track, with a flashing of green lights and a thundering and grinding of wheels and brakes.

The man from tomorrow flung both hands to his ears. "Just listen to it! Just listen to it!" he moaned. "What a commotion!"

His succeeding words were drowned out by the uproar of the train, but I thought I could make out something about "unmuffled noises" and "disgrace of not having a Friction Silencer."

Firmly grasping his arm, lest he again attempt to escape, I guided him into the car, which, as usual at this time of the morning, was jammed almost to the doors. He was now panting rather piteously; and though, as I had swayed beside him on the platform, I consoled myself by reflecting that the ride would take only a few minutes, I did wonder whether it would not have been wiser to have traveled by taxicab.

Within a minute, I had my answer. All at once the man from tomorrow gave a gulp and a groan; every trace of color left his face; his eyes closed, and his knees sagged beneath him. Had I not reached out and grasped him, he would have fallen; even as it was, I was able to support him only by a staggering effort; while he hung in my hands, limp and loose, as a sack of beans.

Now what frantic thoughts and visions assailed me! What if the man from tomorrow should die? What if the subway had been too much for his frail constitution? Smitten by fiery pangs of conscience, I accused myself in unsparing terms; I told myself that I had had no right to expose my charge to an unfamiliar and deadly mode of travel. Surely, it would be a pitiable thing if he, our only recorded visitor from a future century, should perish prematurely, a victim of the haste and bustle of our age!

Shaken by such fears, I found myself in the center of an excited crowd, which had cleared a space for the stricken man on the floor of the car. "Air! Air! Give him air!" I cried, seeing how closely the spectators were swarming about him. But they pressed in around him more closely than ever, while gibbering like silly children. "What's happened? What's happened? Is he drunk? Fainted? What's the matter? What's the matter?" Some idiot even had the audacity to murmur into my ear, "Never fear, sir. Your son will be all right." And all the while Wormwood, lying motionless with a placid expression, looked more like a corpse than a living man.

Bending down to him, I loosened his clothing—although, for that matter, it seemed to me plentifully loose already; I fanned him with my hands, I rubbed his limbs, and then, accepting a flask passed me by some obliging person, I pressed a forbidden stimulant anxiously to Wormwood's lips.

Immediately, as though at some magical stroke, a tremor passed through his body; his hands began to twitch and flutter; his lips quivered, and gave expression to a faint groan; his eyes opened—and he looked up at us in a dazed, blank way.

"Maranna!" he mumbled, like one not quite in possession of his senses. "Maranna! Where have you gone?"

And then, as his wits gradually returned and he was able to sway upward to a sitting posture, he put his hands to his eyes, and demanded, gloomily, "Oh, why did you do it? Why did you wake me up? I thought I was back in the twenty-third century—back again with Maranna! Her arms were about me—we were so happy together! Oh, why, why did I have to return here?"

Several of the spectators smiled or tittered; but, thinking Wormwood delirious, they made little comment. Two or three of us joined forces to help him to his feet; and then, since we had just arrived at our station, I thanked my assistants, and did my best to escort my companion out of the car and up the stairs to the street.

At first he walked with such slow and wavering footsteps that I feared he was about to collapse again; but once we had gotten out of the subway and into the comparatively pure air of the street, he heaved a mighty sigh and drew a long breath, then threw out his chest and exclaimed, "I guess I'm better now! My head still aches, but that will pass in time. Do you know, that subway had me pretty nearly asphyxiated!"

Much to my relief, he had now recovered sufficiently to walk the block or two to the Campus. It is true that he looked unusually bloodless and pale; yet it was clear to me that the danger was over for the present. But inwardly I vowed that never again would I enter the subway with him.

In silence we reached the University grounds and passed the main buildings, including administration offices, dormitories and lecture halls. Then, looking up at the eight and ten story buildings that housed one of our country's foremost educational institutions, the man from tomorrow suddenly demanded:

"Well, when do we get to the University?"

I looked at him in astonishment, trying to detect a glitter in his eyes. But there was no evidence that he was joking.

"How much further to the University?" he repeated, a little irritated at my silence.

"What makes you think it's any further?" I returned. "You're already on the Campus."

It was now his turn to be surprised. "This…the Campus?" he inquired, slowly. "No, no, you don't mean it! Why, this is nothing but a part of the city!"

"Well, the University is a part of the city."

"But—but it's impossible!" he blurted out, in an unbelieving way. "Where are your green fields? Where are your groves, your brooklets and meadow-flowers? Where are your shady dells for classrooms, your hills and woodland paths for thoughtful strolls? Why, this isn't a University! It's nothing but a pile of buildings! Looks more like a factory to me!"

"Maybe that's what it is," I acknowledged. "At any rate, it is a factory where we turn out trained minds.

"Trained minds cannot be made like trained monkeys!" snapped the man from tomorrow.

Then, more soberly, he remarked, "Really, I can't understand what you do with all these buildings—except maybe to use them as storage places for books and laboratory equipment. How can you expect to educate a man between walls? Don't you understand the cramping results of such repression? Why, psychologists have long ago pointed out what happens when we damn up the nature-impulses. I believe it was Harrington who, way back in the twenty-first century, demonstrated that, if the young mind is not brought into contact with the open, it will develop an Artificiality Bias, which will dry up the juices of mental spontaneity and deaden it to civilizing influences—and, in particular, to the imaginative and poetic instincts. Ever since Harrington's enunciation of this fundamental truth, no man has been regarded as really educated unless he has spent several years in contact with the out-of-doors."

In reply to this harangue, I could do nothing but grunt.

By this time, fortunately, we had arrived at the Faculty Club. It was a relief to be able to enter; to be able to attend to such mundane matters as to introduce Wormwood to the clerk and to list his name on the register before having him shown up to his room. Yet a further difficulty now intervened; disdaining the elevator, which, it seemed, was without "pneumatic jerk-eliminators," the man from tomorrow declared that he had had sufficient experience with twentieth century modes of transportation, and insisted on walking up to his quarters on the fourth floor.

As I puffed and panted at his side up the long wearisome flights, I reflected that it was fortunate that he had not been assigned to lodgings on the twelfth story.

CHAPTER FOURTEEN
The Man from Tomorrow Looks at Science

AFTER the man from tomorrow had been installed n in his new room—which, he declared, would have suited him perfectly had it but possessed removable walls—he announced himself ready to set out with me to inspect the University. Not knowing exactly what to do with him, since it was almost time for me to lecture in the Freshman Course on "Tendencies in Modern Physics," I suggested that he accompany me and join the audience. This he eagerly consented to do, stating that it would be interesting to learn how far the science of the Neurotic Age had advanced. And so off we trotted together, and within a few minutes had reached the lecture room. He was astonished at the vastness of the hall, with its long sloping rows of seats that accommodated hundreds of students; at first, indeed, he mistook the place for a theatre, and would not believe that he was in a classroom. "What is the use of lecturing to so many persons all at once?" was his bewildered inquiry. "How enter into any personal discussions? And, without personal discussions, who would not prefer a book to a lecture?"

"Better wait and find out," was all I could advise.

Fortunately, it was almost time for the lecture to begin, so that I was under no necessity of continuing the discussion. Mounting to the platform, I looked briefly over my notes, while the students pressed into the room by the drove, and the man from tomorrow seated himself expectantly in the center of the front row.

The subject that I had chosen was, "Recent Theories as to the Nature of the Physical Universe." The choice was an appropriate one, I thought; I knew that the man from tomorrow would be critical of all that I said, and I could think of no more impressive subject of discussion than the revelations of those great modern physicists who had revolutionized our ideas of space and matter. And so I discoursed energetically upon recent investigations into the atom and the electron; while, during the latter half of the hour, I turned to one of the foremost of all the moderns, Einstein, and briefly outlined his contributions.

This was, of course, a great deal of territory to cover in an hour's lecture; but, though there were necessarily vast gaps and omissions, I thought that I had succeeded at least in conveying some idea of the essentials of the subject.

From time to time, during the course of my talk, I glanced down at the man from tomorrow, whose eyes were glued upon me in rapt attention. At first I observed an expression of puzzled questioning on his face; but after a while, when I had advanced to the heart of my subject, I noticed that the puzzled look gave place to a faint smile, which gradually deepened and broadened and never left him during the entire period.

Irritated at the thought that Wormwood was secretly laughing at me, I lost no time about seeking the cause when the lecture was over. "Do you think you were attending a vaudeville?" I inquired, rather sharply. "Do you find modern physical knowledge altogether ridiculous? Is it really so exceedingly amusing to you?"

"Well, how could it help being just a little amusing?" he returned. "Remember, Physical Research is my especial field. And when I hear you mention some of the beginners, such as Michelson and Einstein, is it strange if I find it entertaining? Not that these men were not accomplished enough in their way—one must judge them in the light of their times. They are not without historic importance, due to the fact that they paved the way for the Astro-Physical demonstrations of Hylitz and the Psycho-Physical Cosmo-Conception of Van der Street."

"Who was Van der Street?" I asked.

But Wormwood continued, without seeming to hear me:

"Now what strikes me as strange—I might say elementary in your beliefs—is their one-sidedness. It is curious that, having identified energy and matter as, at root, one and the same thing, you haven't gone a step further and realized how the third great factor in the universe is to be linked to the other two. By that I mean, of course, the factor of spirit. It was the renowned Japanese psychologist, Hikomo Kiakawi, who, late in the twenty-second century, demonstrated that the energy of our minds is at heart one with the energy of matter, and that the whole universe, as in the conception of the great idealistic philosophers, can thus be reduced to nothing but spirit. This belief, the basis of twenty third century Physical Research, is regarded as rudimentary by the scientists of my own times, and no Physical Researchers would think of disregarding the established facts. Naturally, therefore, your own views impressed me—well, shall I say somewhat as you might be impressed by old Ptolemy's ideas of astronomy?"

As he concluded these remarks, the man from tomorrow broke into a smile that was dangerously close to laughter; while I, helpless before his superior knowledge, could only stare and nod, and secretly wish that he would keep his information to himself.

A few minutes later, hoping to get rid of him for a while—for I could think of nothing more maddening than to have him at my side all day—I hastily introduced him to some of my fellow professors, and was relieved to see him go ambling away at the side of Dr. Ambrose, of the Department of Astronomy.

For an hour or two, consequently, I was mercifully able to forget all about him. But alas! My good fortune was Dr. Ambrose's ill luck; that very noon the astronomer waylaid me as I was leaving my office to go to lunch, and the things he had to say were neither kindly nor polite.

"Sacred heavens, Howard!" he burst out, grasping my arm in a manner that struck me as almost pugnacious, "who was that lunatic you let loose on me? What asylum did he come from? Did you mean it as a practical joke? If so, it was a cruel one—"

"Sorry, Ambrose," I said, consolingly. "Sorry, I forgot to tell you he's a traveler from far away." And briefly I explained the facts.

"Well, that seems to account for things," declared Ambrose, somewhat mollified. "I never did see a man with such preposterous ideas. Let me tell you what happened. First of all, trying to be pleasant to him, I described our modern astronomical progress, and mentioned the 200-inch refracting telescope, the largest in the world, that is being made with such long-drawn-out labor and at such prodigious expense. What do you suppose? The man looked actually scornful. He said it was all right for practice work; would do for freshmen classes and the like. But he wanted to know if we didn't have any 800-inch or 1000-inch refractors. Upon receiving a negative answer, he looked a little contemptuous, and said that our science had a long way to go yet. Then he wanted to know whether we had discovered the fifth planet beyond Neptune, a speck smaller than the earth, which he described as revolving at a distance of 9,200,000,000 miles from the sun. Also, he wanted to know whether we had never seen the moving shadows on Mars, which he claimed were believed to be either airships or gigantic winged animals. But they couldn't be seen except through instruments that brought Mars within twenty-five miles."

"That's really interesting! Very interesting!" I commented. "Maybe he knows whether or not Mars is inhabited..."

But Dr. Ambrose, disregarding my remarks, hastily went on to explain. "Naturally, I listened to him as one listens to a drunken man; I thought he was suffering from insane delusions. I wasn't particularly pleased when he followed me to my classroom, and took a seat under my very nose; and I wouldn't have permitted him to stay, if he hadn't been so insistent on remaining. Well, I can assure you, I wish I had thrown him out. I have been teaching a good many years, but never before have I been so insulted! The conduct of this Mr. Wormwood was outrageous! Do you want me to go on?"

"I'm listening," I said; while, with a sinking sensation I wondered how many persons the man from tomorrow had paralyzed.

Dr. Ambrose hesitated; stroked his beard angrily; and, with one fist clenched, continued. "It was in the midst of the lecture. I had been discussing the nebular hypothesis. After briefly describing the views of Laplace, I came down to modern conceptions, mentioning the beliefs of Moulton and Chamberlain and other recent investigators. All at once, when I had paused for breath, I heard a voice, in the strange, heavy accentuation of your friend, 'But all that, sir, is discarded theory! Modern research has shed new light on the subject!'

"Can you imagine my embarrassment? My students, of course, began to titter and giggle, finding the interruption, I am sure, more interesting than the lecture. And meanwhile that damnably insolent fellow, who seems to think that he knows everything under the sun, continued to speak, as though he were delivering the lecture, and not I! He made quite a talk, I can assure you! I tried constantly to interrupt him, but it was no use—he went right on and on and on. I forget all that he said, except that he mentioned dozens of names I'd never heard of before, and became excited about something that he called the Star-Swarm Theory of Solar Evolution—the details of which I couldn't quite make out, although I understood him as saying that most reputable scientists accepted it. This, of course, made me angrier than ever—was he trying to imply that I was not a reputable scientist? You can take my word, it was a relief when he at last took his seat; but, from the way my students were snickering and laughing, it was clear that they wouldn't have minded if he'd kept right on till the end of the hour."

"Really, I'm surprised that he didn't," I said, happy in the knowledge that, after all, no one had been paralyzed. "Modesty is not exactly Mr. Wormwood's leading merit."

"Well, he's your friend, not mine...Now just a word of advice, Howard," was Ambrose's parting shot, as his great gaunt form made ready to go shuffling off down the aisle. "Don't introduce this Wormwood too promiscuously—not if you don't want to become the most unpopular man on the Campus!"

In defiance of this suggestion, which, unquestionably, had much good, sound sense behind it, a plan was soon to be launched to make the man from tomorrow much more widely known. That very noon the idea was proposed to me by Dr. Horn and Professor Warrington, with whom I chanced to have lunch.

"Horn and I have been talking about Mr. Wormwood," began the latter gravely. "After all, it is a notable thing to have a visitor from another century, and so we have been thinking that it would be only fair to give a public reception in his honor. Besides, there are many of our colleagues who would like to make his acquaintance—and I cannot think of any better way than to give a dinner, let us say, at the Faculty Club, to which as many as possible would be invited."

"No doubt there is something to be said for the idea," I responded, not exactly enthusiastically. "In the case of an ordinary visitor, it would be the courteous thing. But I—well, to be quite frank, I'm not quite sure that Mr. Wormwood would know how to act at a public reception."

"Nonsense!" denied Warrington, impatiently. "The man doesn't lack intelligence!"

"No—not intelligence. What he lacks is—well, a knowledge of our ways. I should therefore advise that, if you do hold a reception, you wait a while yet."

"On the contrary," dissented Warrington, becoming so excited that he upset his water glass and drenched his mashed potatoes, "we were figuring on holding it as early as possible. You see, the facts about this Wormwood are bound to get out sooner or later— sooner rather than later, I'm afraid—and if we wait too long we'll lose all the credit of discovering him. That's the reason for this reception, at which the facts about him are to be made known."

"Yes, that's it exactly!" reiterated Dr. Horn. "Think what a feather it will be in our caps! Think what luster it will shed upon our University! Why, it will make us world famous! A man from another century—what other institution of learning could boast such a contribution!"

"What other institution, indeed?" Warrington took up the argument. "Why, man, haven't you considered the increased endowments it will bring us—the funds from wealthy stock brokers, oil magnates, and other patrons of the arts! I don't want to be over-enthusiastic, but I predict that it would do us almost as much good as a championship football team!"

"Well, perhaps not quite that much good," denied the conservative Dr. Horn. "But as much as could be expected from any scientific achievement!"

"After all," I reminded my friends, "you must remember that neither we nor the University have really anything to do with Wormwood's being here. It is Mr. Cloud that deserves the credit."

Professor Warrington looked annoyed, and absently fumbled at a crust of bread, which he broke into crumbs and discarded. "Yes, yes, of course, we'll, not deny him his bit of praise," he declared, hastily. "Still, the real making of Mr. Wormwood rests with us. That is why the reception will be indispensable."

Personally, I still did not consider the reception indispensable— a fact of which I tried my best to convince my friends. But I was outvoted two to one; and, what was worse, I was powerless to prevent them from proceeding with their plans. The most that I would vouchsafe them was my consent to be present at the party; and they, well pleased with this concession, which I had granted reluctantly beneath the compulsion of their combined attack, assured me that they would lose no time about proceeding with their scheme, and that it would not be more than a week before the man from tomorrow shone in the limelight of recognition.

CHAPTER FIFTEEN
The Guest of Honor

WHEN a committee headed by Dr. Horn visited the man from tomorrow to inform him that he was to be the guest of honor at a public reception, he received his callers most graciously, although, it is said, his attitude was that of one who knowingly receives no more than his due.

"Certainly, you may count upon my presence," he assured the members of the delegation. "I am to be the guest of honor, you say? Well, it shall give me pleasure to honor you."

Thereupon he bowed low in his courteous twenty-third century fashion; and then, when someone opened his mouth to speak, he hastily added, "No, no, don't mention it. It's perfectly all right— no need for thanks. I too am honored, I assure you. Now when, did you say, is this notable event to take place?"

The proposed date was stated; after which Dr. Horn made bold to request, "We shall of course expect a little after-dinner talk from you, Mr. Wormwood. Nothing very long—a few minutes, at most. I thought it best to notify you in advance."

"That was most considerate," declared Wormwood, with another bow. "Naturally, I would have prepared a talk anyhow. There is so much I have been wanting to say, and this should give me the opportunity to say it."

"The pleasure will be all ours," returned Dr. Horn, as the committee prepared to leave.

Even after Wormwood had accepted the invitation, there remained one or two knotty problems to be solved. The reception was to be a formal affair—and would it net therefore be impossible for the guest of honor to appear in the highly informal apparel he had previously worn? It was not without misgivings that Professor Warrington put the question to me; yet I, profiting from past experience, resolutely refused to have anything to do with the matter, leaving it to Warrington and two of his associates to visit the man from tomorrow and induce him to wear a borrowed full-dress suit. I do not know exactly what transpired at this meeting, but I do know that it lasted for over an hour, and that when at length the three professors returned they were red-faced and scowling.

"Whew!" burst forth Warrington, as he flung himself down into a chair and fervidly mopped his brow. "That was worse than driving nails into steel plate! You ought to have heard how he harangued upon the savagery of twentieth century dress! Said it subserved neither comfort, beauty nor health! It represented a form of slavery for the benefit of the garment makers and sellers! Ye gods! What an imbecile!"

"Well, did you show him his error?" I inquired.

"Show him his error? How could I? It would be as easy to reason with a block of wood. He remained unconvinced till the end. But, thank heaven! He did make one concession. He agreed to wear a suit for a single evening, provided we never asked him to humiliate himself again. Humiliate himself! Think of it! That's the expression he used! Never once occurred to him to thank us for renting the suit at our own expense!"

"Thought we should thank him instead! His air was that of a martyr!" put in another member of the visiting committee. "You should have seen his grim, resigned expression; you would have thought he was being crucified! Even so, I don't believe he would have agreed, if it hadn't been, as he said, that he wanted to try every variety of twentieth century experience, even the most deadly, so as to be able to form a fair estimate of our times."

Although Wormwood may not have taken to the idea of wearing formal dress, it is certain that he did regard his prospective speech as of high importance. During the entire day preceding the reception, he was not to be seen about the Campus; he did not visit the classrooms nor spend his hours reading at the University library, as had been his wont ever since his installation at the Faculty Club; he immured himself in his room, where he remained throughout the day; he gave orders that no one be permitted to see him, and was scarcely heard from except when, every hour or two, he sent down to the clerk for a new supply of letter paper. It was remarked that the man from tomorrow must have a voluminous correspondence; however, it was noted that he asked for no stamps. But it was not until the following day that the mystery was solved, when one of the chamber maids found the waste basket full of discarded letter paper, on which various queer notations had been recorded and crossed out in a big, heavy hand: "My friends of the twentieth century, the pleasure that I bring you today—" Or, "Fellow guests and diners, as the poet Gandolini remarked, in the first part of that great lyric cycle, which took the twenty-second century by storm—" Or again, "My kind hosts and hostesses, on this occasion I think sadly of another party I attended, in the Decade of the Lunar Flight, three hundred years to come—"

It speaks well for Wormwood's powers of concealment that, until after the reception, no one suspected what prodigies of creation he had undertaken. It is true that, when he made his appearance that evening, he was looking noticeably worn, and was even paler than usual; but we attributed this to the strain and excitement of the event, no less than to the inconvenience of his formal attire. All in all, he did not appear to be at his best; something seemed to have gone out of him as he faced us in his immaculately white starched shirt and swallow-tail coat; it was as if his very personality had been starched as well. There was little vim and spontaneity about him; the light in his eyes was grave and subdued, the expression on his well-razored features was just a little shamefaced, and his hands were fumbling constantly at his collar, as though he still could not reconcile himself to its use.

"You know, I feel just as if I'm choking," he said to me, drawing me into a corner apart from the other guests. "Really, I never thought I'd descend to this. How do I keep my self-respect if I'm to put my limbs into a cage? This halter of mine"—once more he tugged impatiently at his collar—"strikes me as the symbol of the sameness, the artificiality, the obstructing conventionality of twentieth century life."

"Oh, come, come, it isn't so bad as all that," I reprimanded, weary of the incessant complaints of the man from tomorrow. "One must endure something for the sake of society... Tell me, how do you like the arrangements made in your honor?"

Approvingly I pointed to the decorated hall, with its ferns and palm leaves and its softly glowing red and orange lights.

"Oh, it's all very interesting!" he acknowledged. "Quite quaint and interesting! To be sure, it's insufferably hot, since you haven't arrived at the modern practice of holding receptions in the open air. Again, I can never get used to those electric lights of yours. They are so hard on the eyes; they seem so unnatural. Now with inter-atomic lighting—"

At this point, much to my relief, we were interrupted by the approach of a small group of guests who, escorted by Professor Warrington, were anxious to be introduced to the man from tomorrow.

"Mr. Wormwood, meet Dr. Small. Mr. Wormwood, meet the Reverend Grislow," said Professor Warrington; and Wormwood, bowing graciously, shook both hands of each of the gentlemen in turn, after the practice of his own century. "I am flattered at the opportunity of making your acquaintance," he assured them, in the formal phraseology of three hundred years from now.

Then, turning to the Reverend Grislow, he remarked, "Pardon me, sir but I did not quite get your name. That is to say, not the first name."

"I did not mention his first name," interposed Professor Warrington, with a scowl. "I said he was the Reverend Grislow."

"The Reverend Grislow?" repeated the man from tomorrow, questioningly. "Reverend Grislow? Reverend, you say? I take it then, sir, that this is some title of distinction, conferred on you by the State in reward for some unselfish or benevolent deed."

"Why, why—not—not exactly," faltered Grislow, a little taken aback. "I am called Reverend—well, like all other wearers of the cloth, I am called Reverend because, you see, sir, I am a minister of the Gospel."

"No, I don't see," declared the irrepressible Wormwood. "Wearers of what cloth? And what is a minister of the Gospel?"

It was Professor Warrington who, leaping into the breach during the embarrassing silence that ensued, explained that a minister was a man of religion, a preacher, a leader in piety. And the Reverend Grislow finished by stating that he taught the religion of Christ, and "shepherded his little flock in the ways of righteousness."

The bewildered expression on the face of the man from tomorrow only deepened at this explanation.

"Man of religion! Leader in piety! Shepherding your little flock in ways of righteousness!" he echoed. "What does all this mean? Must a righteous man be led to do the needful thing? Does a pious person require a leader?"

"Oh, dear me, I see we haven't put matters properly at all!" murmured Grislow, greatly annoyed. "I see you've got a very wrong idea. What I really lead people in is their beliefs. They follow me in the doctrines I preach—"

"Follow you in the doctrines you preach?" thundered the man from tomorrow, not allowing Grislow time to finish. "If that isn't abominable! So the people of this century accept their beliefs like their clothes! All you have to do is to provide the pattern and the donkeys follow it! I see now! I see lots of things I could not understand before! I never could quite picture the state of mind of my ancestors before the Era of Emancipation put an end to group religion! But now it's all plain as day! There wasn't any state of mind! There was only blank obedience to a dogma!"

The Reverend Grislow opened his mouth to reply; but it seemed to me that he wore a wilted, hopeless expression, and was relieved to be able to slink away when the approach of several other guests offered him a chance to escape.

The man from tomorrow now entered into a discussion with Professor Handley, of the Department of Paleontology, and waxed eloquent regarding the twenty-third century discoveries of reptilian fossils. But suddenly, in the midst of the exposition of a new theory as to the extinction of the dinosaurs, all the ardor of his discourse deserted him; he stopped short, faltered, grew red in the face, and continued as if he no longer felt any interest in the Age of Saurians. I noticed that his eyes were fastened upon a certain point halfway across the room, where several newcomers had just appeared, and where Dr. Horn was engaged in a voluble discourse with Miss Whitcomb. Had not Professor Handley been bent upon pursuing the question of dinosaurian extinction; had he not followed with some fluent remarks upon the racial term of life of the Brontosaurus, the Tyrannosaurus and other ancient monsters, I believe that the man from tomorrow would have made his immediate departure to the side of Dr. Horn's fiancée. As it was, Wormwood had to content himself with casting hungry glances in her direction, which she apparently neither noticed nor returned; while, by the time the paleontologist had thoroughly considered the problem of the Brontosaurus in all its various aspects and diverged into the kindred theme of the Pterodactyls, the moment had arrived for us all to take our places at the tables, and the man from tomorrow had lost all immediate opportunity for converse with his fair friend.

As the guest of honor, Wormwood was of course seated near the head of the table. To his left sat the Chairman, Professor Warrington; to his right was Professor Handley, who seemed delighted at the opportunity of continuing the discussion he had so interestingly begun; across from him was Mr. Cloud, for whom we had borrowed a suit for the occasion, and who looked somewhat stiff and seedy in his unaccustomed finery; while I was placed at Mr. Cloud's right, and next to me was Dr. Horn, at whose side Miss Whitcomb sat just out of reach of Wormwood's conversation, although by no means out of range of his admiring eyes. I shall not even attempt a list of the other men and women whose presence graced that splendid affair; I shall only state that, in addition to the President of the University and some of our leading Faculty Members, there was a United States Senator, a Federal Judge, and the editor of a leading newspaper; while two scientists of international repute, who chanced to be in town on a brief stay, had consented to attend the function. Possibly the man from tomorrow did not realize it, but a more brilliant group could not have been gathered to honor him had he been a visiting Crown Prince.

Instead of appearing pleased, however, he twitched nervously in his seat, and continued to pull and fumble at his collar throughout the greater part of the dinner; while on his face there was a bored expression that seemed to say, "Heavens! How soon will this be over?" He did not seem impressed when the Chairman proposed a toast to "Our guest of honor and the twenty-third century." He looked as if he were about to yawn all during the Chairman's address, in which the circumstances of his arrival were described and his character and attainments were eulogized; while his eyes continued to seek out those of Miss Whitcomb with such brazenness that after a while the girl began to blush and made an obvious effort to avoid looking in his direction.

None the less, most of the guests seemed to be enjoying themselves; from all sides I heard the remark that never before, despite many sumptuous repasts, had so perfect a banquet been served at the Faculty Club. Surely, the chef had outdone himself! Fearing the criticism of posterity, as represented by our guest of honor, he had evidently spared no effort to produce masterpieces of the culinary art. But alas! All his exertions might have been spared, so far as the chief object of his attentions was concerned. For the man from tomorrow seemed incapable of appreciating masterpieces. When the caviar was brought on, he merely sniffed, made a wry face, and shoved the plate from him. "What is this foul-smelling concoction?" he asked, with his usual frankness. When the chicken soup appeared, he found a single whiff sufficient; when the oyster patties arrived, he tested one with an appraising fork, then suddenly elevated his nostrils, as if they had been assaulted by something vile and ordered the waiter to remove the dish at once. The fish and the roast left him with an expression of disgust that would have had to be seen in order to be appreciated; the potatoes he came near to sampling, when he discovered that they had been placed in contact with the gravy; the green peas he rejected for a similar reason; and the dessert—an elaborate bit of French pastry—he refused with some mumbled comment about "sickening sweetness." During the entire evening, the only things which I saw him consume were two radishes and a leaf of lettuce!

His abstemiousness was not unobserved by other persons. "You don't eat much, I see, Mr. Wormwood," remarked Professor Handley, toward the conclusion of the meal. "Evidently you're not very hungry tonight."

"Not very hungry?" was Wormwood's surprising response, uttered with just a trace of indignation. "What makes you think so? Why, I'm ravenous as a wolf! I haven't had one good square meal yet this century! Oh, how I long for a good old-fashioned bean-feast! I've been losing weight steadily—I've gone down four pounds, and I've only been here a week!"

The man from tomorrow sighed; and immediately afterwards, being asked by the waiter whether he preferred tea or coffee, he mumbled, "Water, please!" Then, thrusting his untouched plate from him, he sighed once more, motioned the waiter back, and instructed, "Please, sir, no ice in the water!"

A few minutes later, when the guests were idling over their coffee and cigars, the outstanding event of the evening occurred— the after-dinner talk of the man from tomorrow. Chairman Warrington paved the way for his appearance by stating that he "would no doubt want to describe his impressions of the present century." And Wormwood, rising amid profuse applause and bowing elaborately, did not have to be asked a second time.

"Ladies and gentlemen of the twentieth century," he began, in a rapid, heavy voice, "I want to begin by thanking you all, and particularly those of you whose friendship I have had the pleasure of making: Dr. Horn here; and Mr. Cloud; and Professor Howard; and Mrs. Howard, who, I regret to say, does not appear to be present today; and the Chairman, Professor Warrington; and Professor Carroway; and last, but not least"—here his eyes chanced to fall upon a fair feminine form across from him—"last but not least, the charming Alice—the charming Alice Whitcomb, who has shown me that not all the bewitching ladies were born in the twenty-third century."

The speaker paused long enough to wave gallantly in the direction of Miss Whitcomb, whose face had turned a flaming crimson, and who looked as if she would have liked to disappear beneath the table. Meanwhile one or two of the guests began to titter; someone else burst noisily into applause; while Dr. Horn, glaring sullenly at Wormwood, clenched his fists as though preparing for a hand-to-hand encounter.

Apparently not noticing the amusement that glowed from every face, the man from tomorrow proceeded:

"Our Chairman, I am surprised to say, has accurately divined the subject of this evening's talk. He is correct in conjecturing that I want to describe my impressions of the twentieth century. This, of course, is a subject so broad that it could be dealt with at the length of many volumes. But such extensive treatment not being possible tonight, I must confine myself to certain minor aspects of the theme. My topic, ladies and gentlemen, is 'A Defense of the Twentieth Century.' For I believe that the twentieth century is worthy of defense. It makes me angry to remember the attacks that have been launched against it in my own times. Thus far I have had only a casual glimpse, yet I have seen enough to know that it is not so bad as it is represented to be. It is not true, as historians have recorded, that it was altogether an era of smoke and dust, of panicky striving that reached no goal, of senseless self-absorption, of delirious amusements, of pomp and vanity, of rags and gilded folly. Even less is it true that the age is one of unbridled superstition; indeed, the only superstition I have come across thus far is that certain bits of printed paper, which you seem to value above all else, can procure anything you wish beneath the sun. This naive faith, which, so far as I have been able to observe, is shared by the more cultured classes no less than by the uncultured, is really less vicious than one might imagine; I assure you that I have been heartily amused by it. However, I am ready to concede to each age the right to its own foibles and eccentricities. Do not primitive people believe in the power of moon-gods and wind-gods? Did not the ancients conduct their human sacrifices? Did not the Dark Ages have their illusions and bloody wars?"

As the man from tomorrow proceeded, he had been waxing more and more oratorical; and his arms, out-flung in eloquent gesticulations, had been performing such loops and spirals about the table, that I feared he would upset a decanter of water or a cup of hot coffee. Probably due to the effect of the unwonted exertion, he gasped and sputtered a little; and his hands, reaching more than once toward his collar, testified plainly to the source of the trouble. Finally, just as he had reached the most impressive point in his address, his patience seemed to attain its limits; up flew his hands once more, and, to my utter consternation, there came a ripping noise as the offending collar was torn out of place. There followed something that sounded like an oath—no one could make out the exact words, but perhaps it was twenty-third century slang; then the discarded article was tossed unceremoniously on to one of the chairs, and the speaker was ready to continue.

It is needless to describe how the audience stared and started; how the faces of the men were crossed with smiles and laughter; how some of the women turned away their eyes, and others wore an expression of shocked righteousness; while I for my own part, feeling that the worst was yet to come, sat peering at Wormwood's shirt with fascinated gaze, and was mightily relieved to see that it remained in place.

Meanwhile the man from tomorrow, apparently unaware that anything unusual had occurred, resumed his address with unperturbed eloquence:

"I was discussing, ladies and gentlemen, the superstitions of the twentieth century. I might add that that age had a right to be more superstitious than it actually was, considering how little was then known as to the nature of the universe. You must recall that the fundamental problems of science and philosophy were still as far from solution as in the day of Aristotle; that the nature of life was not understood, that its origin was unknown and its goal and meaning still matters of dispute, while scientists could not even say positively what energy it is that controls the universe, nor whether any man has lived before this life or is to live again. In an atmosphere moldy with such ignorance, superstition is bound to thrive; and therefore should not blame the men of the twentieth century if they were more deeply steeped in darkness than the dwellers of an emancipated age."

With a resounding thump, the man from tomorrow brought his fist down upon the table. Observing that several persons at the other end of the room were engaged in a whispered conversation and were apparently paying no attention to him, he pointed in the direction of the errant ones, and thundered, "If the gentlemen over yonder will have the courtesy to permit me, I still have a few more remarks to make!"

The gentlemen in question—who were none other than United States Senator Parkinson and Federal Judge Wilbert—dropped into silence, to the accompaniment of low, amused murmurs from all parts of the room.

Sonorously the man from tomorrow resumed. "The message, which I bring to you today, my friends, is a message of consolation. However gloomy the signs appear; however deeply you may seem to be sunken in the mire of the abyss, remember that there is still hope for the present century. The Neurotic Age will not last forever; the Era of Enlightenment lies ahead. The pseudo-knowledge of your times will give place to true knowledge; the pseudo-science in which you place trust will be supplanted by true science; the savagery of your social customs will be tamed and overcome; the glory of a real civilization will yet over-spread your land. Remember, if there were no darkness, we could not appreciate the light! Even though, in your own lives, you may not see it come to pass, you will know that it is being prepared for posterity.

"And now, my friends, by way of conclusion, I cannot think of anything more fitting than to quote briefly from one of my own contemporaries, the renowned poet Stanislaus Starvinowski, who summarizes my thoughts as ably as I could express them myself:

" 'Our era is the ripened fruit,
Of which past times were but the root.
Yet roots are needed, though they grow
Sunless in earth and mud below.' "

With a final emphatic gesticulation, the man from tomorrow took his seat. There was a momentary silence; then a low trickling of applause greeted him, about as faint and unenthusiastic as I have ever heard. But the man from tomorrow, mopping his brow and loosening the upper buttons of his shirt, looked as pleased as he was tired; while his eyes, fixed on a certain point across the table, restlessly sought and sought for an approving glance from a particular young lady, who seemed quite unaware of his interest and devoted herself to an energetic discussion with the gentleman to her right.

CHAPTER SIXTEEN
An Affair of the Heart

AFTER dinner the tables were cleared away, and an hour or two of dancing ensued. In this pastime, I observed, the man from tomorrow took no part; he remained standing at one end of the room, engaged in almost incessant conversation with various persons anxious for his opinion on this or that aspect of twentieth century life.

"What's the matter, Mr. Wormwood?" I finally heard Dr. Small inquire. "Don't you dance?"

"Dance?" returned Wormwood, apparently surprised at this question. "Of course not! My occupation is that of a Physical Researcher!"

This reply must have impressed Dr. Small queerly, for he immediately flung another question, to which the man from tomorrow made emphatic response:

"Naturally, I'm not expected to dance. My field of work is science, not esthetics. You see, among our people the only ones that continue to dance beyond the Adolescent Epoch are those that take it up as an art, a life-work, giving public performances in the old Greek fashion, and striving to excel by their grace and beauty."

"But you do have dances—that is to say, our kind of dances?" persisted Dr. Small.

"Oh, yes, indeed! They are considered a suitable form of recreation for those in the Adolescent Epoch. As preliminaries to matrimony they have been found quite satisfactory; they are better than a public meeting bureau for the two sexes. Then, again, the particular variety of chatter that they encourage is well adapted to those in the Adolescent Epoch; they are excellent for persons who wish to shine by means of their feet rather than by their heads. Accordingly, those in the Epoch of Ascendance would as soon think of going to dances, as they would think of playing with dolls, tops or rattles!"

"I don't quite see how you make that out," Dr. Small dissented. "In our day, many grownups find real pleasure in dances."

"Perhaps that's because they are mentally still in the Adolescent Epoch," decided Wormwood, with a thoughtful expression.

Unfortunately, he did not see fit to continue the discussion, for at that moment he caught a glimpse of the tall form of Miss Whitcomb as she and a partner ambled gracefully across the further end of the hall. "Pardon—pardon me," he said, with a sudden air of excitement, and started to make his way through the crowd in her direction.

Curious to learn what would happen, I followed him, and was amused to observe his surprise and disappointment when, having reached his destination, he stopped short and let his eyes rove in vain in all directions. Evidently Miss Whitcomb had seen his coming! She was nowhere in sight!

"Just give me time! I'll find her yet!" I thought I heard the man from tomorrow muttering beneath his breath; or maybe it was only that he was mumbling a curse in the vernacular of the twenty-third century. At all events, I noticed how his eyes continued to search and search the audience, like those of a mother seeking a lost child—but all to no avail. His intended quarry must have been wary in the extreme, for it was not until the end of the evening, when the guests were preparing to leave, that his efforts were greeted with success.

Then, when Miss Whitcomb had momentarily left Dr. Horn's side and had slipped away to get her coat, I saw the man from tomorrow intercept her as she was about to enter the Ladies' Rest Room.

"Alice—Alice Whitcomb!" I heard him call. "Just one minute, please!"

"Well?" she demanded, coldly, looking up at him in a flustered way, for he had barred her path and there was no possibility of eluding him.

"Alice, why do you always treat me so cruelly?" he asked, with an affronted air. "What have I done to you? Have I offended in any way? I assure you, there is no one, in this century, whom I have less desire to offend."

"What do you want of me?" she gasped, looking up at him with an expression that seemed to add, "And what right, sir, have you to be calling me 'Alice?'"

"All evening I have been trying to get a word with you," he continued. "But somehow you always kept out of sight. Why? I ask you. Why, when one smile from you would suffice to crown the whole evening with success?"

"Mr. Wormwood, I must be hurrying along," she pleaded, and tried to pass him. But he, blocking her path, fervently continued. While with one hand he gesticulated violently, and, with the other, beat nervously at his half-unbared chest:

"It is not much that I ask, Alice. Only that we meet in more propitious circumstances. Otherwise, how are we to get to know one another? Tell me, will you not be in the lobby of the Faculty Club tomorrow—say, tomorrow at five? I will be waiting for you there. Remember the time. Five o'clock. Are you listening?"

"Yes!" she cried, in desperation; and then, breaking past her admirer, she dashed into the haven of the rest room.

The man from tomorrow, turning away, threw out his chest and smiled like one who has made a conquest.

"I have just arranged an appointment with a delightful young lady," he said, coming face to face with me, unconscious that I had overheard the conversation. "She is to meet me tomorrow at five o'clock at the Faculty Club."

Since the matter had been settled, it seemed useless for me to argue or comment; I merely grunted, and slipped away. Yet there was something in the beaming hopefulness of the man from tomorrow that made me feel just a little sorry for him, as for a child who seeks some bright plaything in vain. During the following day, the thought of him was frequently in my mind; and it may have been my curiosity on his account that turned my footsteps toward the Faculty Club shortly before six o'clock. I did not really intend to look for him; none the less, I could not have avoided him had I tried, for he was sitting near the entrance, his eyes fixed patiently upon the great clock above the doorway. "Waiting for someone, Wormwood?" I could not forbear to inquire; and he looked up at me with a start, and mumbled, "Yes. She seems to be late. Wonder what can be keeping her. Do you suppose she could have gotten the wrong time?"

"Not unlikely," I said, and passed on into the reading room, where I occupied myself for over half an hour.

When I came back, the man from tomorrow was still sitting in the same position, his eyes still fastened upon the clock; but over his face a pained, almost hopeless expression had settled.

This time he did not even seem to see me as I passed, and I did not pause to speak to him. As yet I did not realize how deeply he had taken the matter to heart; nor was the true state of affairs to become apparent to me until after several days.

It was on the following afternoon that Wormwood made an unconscious revelation. He and I, in company with Professor Warrington, were walking together just outside the Campus, when suddenly, without a word of apology, he broke away from us and rushed toward a tall woman examining the shop windows across the street. "Alice!" he cried, loudly enough for every one in the street to hear. Alice! Alice Whitcomb!"

In a startled manner, the woman turned about, revealing a face old enough to be that of Miss Whitcomb's mother. And Wormwood stopped short, gasped, muttered something half-intelligible, and returned to us with a sheepish expression.

"Do you know," he declared, ruefully, "she looked almost exactly like Alice. I could have sworn it was she."

During the next day or two, the man from tomorrow made no further reference to the subject; but that it was weighing upon his mind was evident. He had the harried look of one gnawed by some secret trouble; he had become nervous, irritable, absent-minded; his eyes frequently wore a far-away brooding expression, as though they were fixed upon something desired and withdrawn, something forbidden and unattainable. Suddenly a new side of his character had been revealed; he seemed less remote from us, and more human than before; it was as if, by his foolhardy passion, he had established a new bond of fellowship with us.

Just to what depth—or heights—that passion could reach, was revealed to me before the end of the week, when I found Dr. Horn and Professor Carroway chuckling together over an ink-marked document which, I immediately judged, was not of an academic nature.

"What do you think? Our friend Wormwood has been playing the ardent romantic!" laughed Carroway, as I approached. "We've just been looking over one of his efforts. It certainly is a masterpiece of the epistolary art!"

"Masterpiece is the word!" agreed Dr. Horn. "But it wasn't meant for our profane gaze! Alice showed it to me last night—and I insisted on her letting me take it. Heavens, but we did have a hilarious time over it!"

"Come, let's see," I demanded.

Shamelessly they passed me the paper, which bore the heading of the Faculty Club; and shamelessly I read, in the handwriting of the man from tomorrow:

"Chivalrous Lady: I take the liberty of addressing you in this fashion, because I feel sure that one endowed with your grace of form and spirit must possess that full measure of chivalry, which we of the twenty-third century ascribe to the Superior Sex. It is to your charity that I appeal, for even if you find it impossible to cast your eyes upon my unworthiness, still your gallant heart will not permit you to see me miserably drooping for lack of you. Already I have made repeated efforts to knock upon those doors that have so cruelly been closed upon me. At the reception the other night I had the happiness to make an appointment with you. But alas...some indisposition must have forbidden you to keep the date. Then in desperation I wrote to you, begging you to fix an hour for some new appointment. Three days have gone by, and no answer has come. I have been watching every post; I can no longer bear the suspense. So I entreat you—listen to one of the weaker sex, a poor imploring man, who casts aside the last veil of modesty to unbare his heart before you—I entreat you, chivalrous lady, do not scorn my plea, but mention a rendezvous, so that I may greet you and heal my bleeding wounds in the consolation of your assuaging presence.

"I pray you do not deny me this boon, which I desire above all else in this century. For should you display that heartlessness so unnatural in one of your charm, there will remain only one course for me. Life in this generation will no longer have any value; I shall not continue to struggle through this sorry mockery of an existence. Within twenty-four hours, if I do not have your answer—a mercifully kind answer, O benevolent lady!—I shall seek the vial of release! I shall turn the poison darts against my own breast; I shall paralyze myself! And, until you relent, I shall remain paralyzed! Existence on any other terms is impossible!

"In conclusion, I bow before you, and humbly kiss your garment. Yours, in rapture and supplication,

"John."

It may have been hard-hearted of me, but I was smiling just a little by the time I had come to the end of this missive. "Evidently the style in love-letters will change a little by the twenty-third century," I remarked. "You don't think, do you, there's any danger of Wormwood carrying out his threat?"

Dr. Horn laughed shortly. "Oh, I don't suppose it would do him any harm to be paralyzed for a while. You know, when you come to think of it, isn't it an infernal nerve of his, troubling Alice with all this sort of bosh? The poor girl was quite upset about it at first, although in the end, after I'd pointed out how funny it really was, she almost cried with laughing. Considering all things, I do wish Wormwood would paralyze himself for a few days. That might give him time to cool off."

Afraid that our visitor would actually carry out his threat, I observed him with more than usual interest during the next day or two. I had already seen enough of the paralyzing rays to feel sure that I could recognize their effects—but I am certain that no sign of paralysis was to be noted in the man from tomorrow. Perhaps it was that, like other great lovers, he was mightier with words than with deeds; or perhaps there was so much to occupy his mind and engage his energies that he could not afford the luxury of paralysis.

Personally, I am inclined to the latter theory; for, at about this time, Wormwood was coming prominently into public attention, and there were such endless varieties of things for him to do and see and such endless processions of visitors that the detail of an unsuccessful love affair was likely to be shoved on to a back have received.

It was immediately following the reception that Wormwood was launched upon his public career. This was as we had expected; we knew that some of the attending scientists, as well as the newspaper editor, were certain to prepare reports for the press. Nor did any of them appear anxious to waste time; within twenty-four hours, the nation was taken by storm by the announcement that a traveler had descended upon us from another century!

It will be recalled what a gasp of universal surprise, not to say incredulity, this bit of news produced; how men turned to one another with doubtful stares and eager questionings; how some loudly acclaimed the tidings, while others received them scornfully or suspiciously or denied the possibility of the alleged events. "What? A man from the twenty-third century!" raged an editorial in one of our leading papers. "Surely, human gullibility must have no limits if claims so patently preposterous are to be accepted seriously. The next thing we know, we will be holding receptions for the proverbial man from Mars, if not for a visitor from the star Vega or Arcturus; or else we will be recovering Alexander the Great or Cleopatra from the dust of the centuries! A pox upon all such silly notions! The unfortunate, the incredible thing about the present claims is not, we regret to say, their own wild extravagance, but the fact that they are sponsored by men in whose scientific judgment the public has come to have confidence—Professor Ellery Howard, Professor Charles Warrington, and others of equal reputation. Surely, it must have taken an unconsciously clever imposter to dupe these eminent scientists!"

Other papers took a milder tone, yet stated their conviction that the supposed event would turn out to be a hoax; still others expressed themselves as in doubt, or refrained from passing judgment. But the prevailing attitude was one of skepticism; and those bold few who unhesitatingly proclaimed that Wormwood had dropped upon us out of another dimension, were either denounced as dupes or cranks or credulous fools or else were accused of deliberate fraud, and consequently became the objects of persecution. I, although I had always prided myself on standing high in the esteem of the community, could not fail to note a changed attitude—not only in the way certain of my former acquaintances would now avoid me, but in the slightly deferential manner of others, almost the patronizing air, as though they would say, "Poor old fellow; he used to be pretty clear-headed. Too bad what age has done to his brain!"

In my resentment at the attitude of the ignorant, many of whom, knowing nothing whatever of researches into the Fourth Dimension, denied the very possibility of its existence, I sought out the man from tomorrow and begged him to demonstrate publicly that he had really arrived from the twenty-third century.

But he was less concerned than I might have expected about establishing his identity. "If the geese won't believe I come from the future," he asked, "does that alter the fact? And if it doesn't alter the fact, are their beliefs of any importance? No doubt the minds of the masses are not fitted to receive the truth; for, as I have observed, this is a rational age—far too rational to see clearly."

"But really, Wormwood, something must be done," I persisted. "This may be a rational age, but it isn't in the least an unbelieving age. A man sits in a booth, and sees and talks with another man miles away—and no one denies that it has happened. Another man enters a boat in the Bay of Naples, and, by means of radio waves, turns on some electric lights in Australia—and, again, no one denies that it has happened. Compared with such marvels, the arrival of a visitor from a future century seems an everyday affair. Yet the world denies that he has come—and how convince it?"

"I'm sorry to say I don't know," returned the man from tomorrow, twiddling his fingers indifferently. "In my age, the opinions of fools are not regarded as of sufficient importance to engage the attention of wise men. What do you expect me to do? Paralyze all the investigators? I wouldn't mind trying with a few of the more skeptical; but the paralyzing rays, you see, would give out in time—"

"Surely, Wormwood, you can do something by means of your superior knowledge!" I interrupted. "See here—this thought occurs to me. Maybe you can look upon what is the past to your age but the future to ours, and recall some important historical occurrences that are about to take place. Then you might publicly predict them. After they had occurred, it would be evident enough you couldn't have drawn upon any ordinary source of knowledge."

"Now that idea isn't half bad," he answered, meditatively. "The trouble is that my historical knowledge of the twentieth century is so limited. Being more concerned with modern history, I devoted only a few months at college to the Neurotic Age... Well, anyhow, let's see, let's see. The year 1930! When I come to think of it, it seems so far back! What was there important occurring in that year? Any notable event at all?"

Wrinkling his brow into furrows of perplexity, the man from tomorrow sank into silence, and for a moment had nothing to say. "The year 1930," he at length repeated to himself, in a mumbled undertone. "1930. No, I can't remember anything. I can't remember." And he remained absorbed in a brown study, while once more he muttered, "I can't remember. No, no, I can't remember a thing."

Several minutes passed, and I had almost given up hope—when all at once his face brightened and he exclaimed, "Ah! Now I have it! It comes upon me like a flash! Just what we were taught in college! 1930 was memorable for two things! Yes, I'm sure it was 1930, and not 2030. Sometime in that year there was a riot in Kadore, India! And there was a volcanic eruption somewhere in the South Seas—in the Mandala Islands, I believe. Both of these events were of far reaching consequences—otherwise, I wouldn't have recalled them."

"Good! Good!" I cried, enthusiastically, almost as though I saw cause for rejoicing in riots and volcanic eruptions. "The very thing, Wormwood! You're perfectly certain of your dates, are you?"

"Yes, I'm certain enough," testified the man from tomorrow. "But there is just one trouble. I don't remember in what month these things happened. Maybe they have occurred already."

"No, no," I assured him; hastily. "They haven't occurred. But they may happen today or tomorrow. We'd better lose no time! You don't mind my making your prediction public?"

"Well, I don't see what I'm risking," he said, with a disdainful shrug; while I, barely taking time to thank him, rushed to the nearest telephone booth.

A moment later, having been connected with the office of the *Daily Leader*, I requested that a reporter be sent to me immediately.

CHAPTER SEVENTEEN
The Beginnings of Fame

IN ACCORDANCE with the recommendations of my colleagues and myself, the Endersby Award for Scientific Research for the current year was granted to James Richard Cloud. This Award, far from representing a mere barren honor, carried with it a considerable financial payment—a sum so substantial, indeed, that the inventor was able to repair the losses he had suffered upon the arrival of the man from tomorrow and to resume his investigations into the Fourth Dimension. In many ways, he was much better off than before; he no longer went about in rags; he had removed to a less dingy section of town and had installed himself in a more spacious laboratory; While by degrees he was rebuilding the Dimension Machine and was preparing for new glimpses into the unknown.

"Better watch out, Cloud," I suggested one day, when I visited him at his new quarters and found him laboring at the rods and gleaming mirrors of his remade machine. "I'd advise you to make your invention accident-proof. You see what one mischance has done—and what if there was to be another? I dread to think of the possibility that a man from the twenty-eighth century—"

"Never fear! Never fear!" he cut me short while he bent down to screw a steel bar into place. "Accidents like that don't happen twice. Besides, I'm equipping the machine with a safety shutter preventing deposits from other ages. And I'm adding a few other interesting attachments. Can you guess what I'm working toward?"

"How should I guess?" I inquired, with a shrug.

He looked up at me, his blue eyes a-glitter with a fiery eagerness.

"I'm trying to invent a Dimension Bridge!" he announced, and then returned to his screw and rod. "I want to make it possible for a man to step out across the void to another dimension. Of course, there are technical difficulties in the way. It's important, for example, to have a Direction Gauge, so that one will know just where one will arrive."

"Yes, but what is the use?" I asked. "Who wants to step out upon another dimension?"

"Oh, no one has to unless he wishes," returned Cloud, pausing to reach into the toolbox for a pair of pliers. "It's like aviation—the timid are not compelled by law to take a chance. But I imagine it would be an exhilarating sport to go gliding for a while through the seventh century—or the thirty-seventh! Don't believe, either, that I'm not near to success—another month or two may be all I need. The great obstacle is in the perfection of the Recall Coils; for, after one has left this dimension, it might be annoying not to be able to return… Well, before long I'll probably figure something out. I'm not worrying about it."

"Better not," I advised; for, from the severe, thoughtful manner in which Cloud wrinkled up his brow, it seemed to me that he was anything but unworried.

Not heeding me, he continued energetically to turn his screws and wield his pliers. Probably he was as far as I from realizing what a vast and sinister importance his invention was one day to have!

While Cloud was occupied with his ambitious projects, the man from tomorrow was advancing by leaps and jumps toward fame and fortune. At my solicitation, the newspapers had circulated his predictions concerning the riot in Kadore, India, and the volcanic eruption in the Mandala Islands. The forecasts were regarded as of such news-value, that they were published not in one paper but in many; indeed, there was scarcely a journal throughout the country that did not announce and comment upon them. It was generally agreed that, if the prophesized events actually were to occur, the claims of Wormwood as to his origin would be verified; but, with almost equal unanimity, it was assumed that the events would not occur. "Pooh!" exclaimed one of the editorials that I chanced to read. "Are we back in the days of witches and fortune-tellers? Are we to believe that unborn moments can be read like an open book? The very questions make one shudder for the intelligence of the age. One fears that a back-wash of medieval superstition has overtaken us…"

I must confess that, in the face of such attacks, I trembled just a little. What if the man from tomorrow had been confused about his dates? What if the occurrences he had foretold were not to take place until 1950 or 1960? Was it wise to have staked all on a single throw? Could we not have foreseen that, if his memory had misled him, he would be utterly discredited and the facts of his origin would never be believed?

But I might have spared my worries. It was only a week before, with triumphant suddenness, the first of Wormwood's predictions was vindicated. One morning the newspapers told in headlines of an insurrection in the remote village of Kadore in India, where the British troops had been opposed by the sympathizers of Gandhi, and several hundred persons had been killed in an affray that seemed likely to kindle all India…

"Wormwood, you are redeemed! You are saved! Now everyone will believe in you!" I cried, as I rushed to the Faculty Club with the paper containing the news of the outbreak. "See! Everything is as you predicted! No one will any longer be able to doubt your story!"

The man from tomorrow took up the paper without enthusiasm and let his eyes range along the columns.

"Yes, I knew it would all happen," he declared. "It was inevitable. You can't change the past. But that doesn't mean that people won't challenge my story. It's evident that you don't know the extent of human incredulity, which is as childishly unreasoning as credulity itself, and a thousand times more stubborn."

I fear that I showed my own incredulity by the unbelieving smile with which I heard these words. Yet Wormwood's remarks, as I was surprised to learn, were by no means unjustified. While some commentators were impressed, and while numbers of previously neutral critics were swept into acceptance of our claims, still the more determined doubters continued to doubt as resolutely as ever. "What has our supposed visitor from the future proved?" demanded the New York *Star*, a typical spokesman of the dissenting opinion. "One would have to be addle-headed to be convinced by so flimsy and spurious a demonstration. To begin with, how is one to know that mere coincidence will not explain the event in India, which Mr. Wormwood apparently foretold? Yet one is not even forced to take refuge in this simple and plausible explanation. There is another way of accounting for the facts; and a way that, in our view, is even more difficult to assail. The origin of Mr. Wormwood is admittedly unknown, while certain observers report that he has a cast of countenance not inconsistent with the view that he hails from the Far East. May he not, therefore, be a Hindu political exile in disguise? And may his foreknowledge of the impending riot not have been due to the fact that he was in touch with the conspirators? To our way of thinking, this is a much saner explanation than that he has sprung, wizard-like, from some remote century."

This editorial, which was frequently copied and commended, was believed by many persons to have disposed of the problem of the man from tomorrow! The sponsors of the *Star's* point of view, who no doubt imagined themselves to be hardheaded reasoning men, were willing to accept the theory of Wormwood's eastern origin without inquiry, and without troubling about the detail of proof. It was therefore unfortunate for their complacency that they were due to be disillusioned—for all at once there occurred an event which shook and shattered their whole delicately spun web of belief.

Only a week or two after the Indian riot, disquieting reports commenced to issue from the Mandala Islands. The great crater of Krauriporo, which had been silent for more than a century, began to show signs of activity; there were earth tremors of rapidly growing intensity; there were clouds of smoke and fire above the peak; there were rumblings from within the mountain, and violent electrical displays about the summit. "Surely, it is but a momentary outbreak," reported the astonished commentators. "After a little while, the flames will die down; the tremors will subside; there will be no real eruption."

Almost before the ink had dried upon these predictions, there came that terrific manifestation that startled and horrified the world. The slumbering genie of the lava awoke with cataclysmic violence; the crest of the crater blew into the sea with an explosion that could be heard for hundreds of miles—and suddenly the fairest of the Mandala Islands had been blackened and depopulated.

Let me not enter into the details of the disaster, which from the point of view of our story, is of importance only in so far as it confirmed Wormwood's prophecy. Was not the victory ours at last? I wondered, with a vague, triumphant thrill. How would the doubters explain the facts? Certainly, they would not claim that Wormwood had conspired to make the volcano erupt!

But my optimism merely showed how limited was my imagination. Those who had determined to remain unconvinced were still unconvinced. In particular, many of our so-called intellectuals prided themselves upon the logic of their dissent, and upon their discovery of flaws in the proof. "After all, has anything really extraordinary occurred?" remarked one of our leading journals of opinion. "Once more the explanation of coincidence is not to be discarded; but there is another solution that seems even more adequately to meet too facts. Preceding each volcanic eruption, there are probably long-continued disturbances within the earth—disturbances which could be measured and even located with definiteness if one had seismograph instruments of sufficient sensitiveness. It is true that no instruments of such sensitiveness are now known; but their existence is not inconceivable; indeed, we hold it more than likely that Mr. Wormwood has devised such a machine, and, with its aid, was able to prognosticate the approaching event in the Mandala Islands. It will be noted that he did not foretell the exact date of the occurrence, nor the particular island that was to witness the eruption; and these facts, we submit, are to be taken in confirmation of our theory. We regret to say that Mr. Wormwood is apparently wasting his talents; one with his incomparable powers of pretense should turn not to science, but to politics."

This opinion, of course, was an extreme one; fortunately, it did not find any general reflection except in the upper or reasoning circles of society. While the incredulity of the professional thinking men continued unabated, those individuals who had no reputation for intelligence to forfeit were now almost universally convinced that Wormwood was no less than what he claimed to be. Let the erudite journals scoff as they would! Let the lips of savants twist in ironic denial. Let sophisticated writers spill their ink in ridicule and scorn! Let pedants rant, and religious authorities rave and fume, claiming that the arrival of a man from another century would undermine the sanctity of the Church! Their plaints were mere foam against the great waters of popular belief that was rolling in, and rolling in, and daily gathering force and volume. Newspapers began to print long articles about the man from tomorrow; magazines began to describe him, or to record the experiences of those who had seen him; the radio began to vibrate with accounts of his appearance and manners; callers began to shower upon him by the scores and the hundreds, until his life was made miserable dodging them, and he saw only those whom he could not avoid.

Now all at once astonishing offers were deluging him, delivered in person and by the mail—offers that he appear in vaudeville, offers that he speak over the radio, offers that he address fashionable societies and clubs, offers that he be seen in the talking pictures! Almost over night he had become a celebrity, a public curiosity; he was to be as well known as any star of the diamond or heroine of the screen! Hence it seemed to be thought that he had no role in life except to offer amusement, notoriety, or profit to those who thronged to inspect or exploit him.

It would be futile if not impossible to attempt to describe all the curious adventures that befell the man from tomorrow during those throbbing days, and his still more curious reactions to the ideas and proposals of his visitors. There was so much that was noteworthy in Wormwood's conduct that whole chapters would not exhaust the subject; and I would accordingly feel it a great loss to pass on without mentioning at least one or two of his experiences.

In the beginning—and, indeed, throughout his entire public career—he was frequently sought by newspaper reporters. I had the good fortune to witness one of his encounters with the representatives of the press; an encounter that occurred during the early days of his notoriety, before he had learned to bar his doors whenever an enterprising young journalist appeared, and to let it be known that he was "indefinitely absent." On this occasion, Wormwood received his visitor willingly and graciously enough, and went so far as to consent to have his picture taken. When I arrived, the photographer was just leaving with a satisfied grin; while the reporter, seated opposite Wormwood with pad and pencil, was beginning a questionnaire.

"Mind waiting a few minutes?" Wormwood nodded to me; and I, not being in a great hurry, sat down to observe the course of events.

"Now what our readers want is a good human-interest story," said the reporter, a keen-eyed, cynical-faced man of about thirty-five, whose manner of speech reminded me of a machine-gun. "They would like to know any interesting little facts about you and your manner of life. They want to get down to the real facts. They want to know what you are like as a man... Cigarette, Mr. Wormwood?"

The reporter snapped open his cigarette case; but Wormwood recoiled as though a live snake had been offered him.

"Ah, I see that you don't care much about cigarettes," the interviewer rattled on. "Prefer cigars? No? Or a pipe? Perhaps I'd better draw a picture of you coiled up with a pipe—"

"What's a pipe?" demanded Wormwood.

The reporter stared. "Don't even know what a pipe is? This will make a first-rate story! Pristine ignorance of the twenty-third century! Now, Mr. Wormwood, maybe you can tell me what's your favorite hobby...? What beverage do you prefer...? What do you eat for breakfast...? Do you indulge in any sports or pastimes...? How much exercise do you take...?"

Beneath this storm of inquiries, Wormwood had suddenly turned flaming red. His fists began to clench; he arose with unexpected violence; his words came forth in an irate torrent. "See here, sir, do you think I am still in my Adolescent Epoch? Do you imagine that the only interesting thing about me is what I eat and drink? What purpose have you in coming here to insult me with all this petty chatter?"

"But it isn't petty chatter, sir," protested the interviewer. "Why, if you knew anything of modern papers, you'd realize that all this is of the very blood and sinew of journalism—the sort of thing everybody wants to know about—the sort of thing we can feature—"

The man from tomorrow impatiently covered the distance from door to window, and back again from window to door. "Well, that only goes to confirm what I've been suspecting all along," he mumbled. "In the twentieth century, the Adolescent Epoch seems to last for life."

"At least," ventured the reporter, veering to a new line of approach, "maybe you can answer a few very simple queries. Do you require eight hours of sleep, or can you get along with six...? Do you prefer tea to coffee...? Do you bathe daily...? Do you indulge in alcoholic stimulants...? Do you—"

"See here," interrupted Wormwood, his clenched fists upraised as though ready to do violence upon the person of his interviewer, "aren't you forgetting yourself? Are you a journalist, or are you a doctor?"

The reporter winced, and retreated for safety to the further corner of the room; while impetuously the man from tomorrow continued. "Of all the infernal impudence! To inquire into the private details of my life! What business is that of yours? Or of the public? What difference can it make which of your vile brews I prefer to drink, or how much of this hysterical age I sleep away? In my own times, only one's physician would dare to ask such questions!"

"No offense meant, Mr. Wormwood. No offense meant at all," apologized the interviewer.

He paused, as if at a loss for words; then, with a determined expression, glided back to his chair, and continued:

"Now surely, Mr. Wormwood, you don't want to be unreasonable. You don't mind letting me know a few of your opinions on general questions—nothing personal this time—nothing personal at all, I assure you. What, for example, is your view as to the Eighteenth Amendment?"

"The Eighteenth Amendment?" repeated the man from tomorrow, slowly. "The Eighteenth Amendment? Just which amendment was that? The one prohibiting slavery? No, possibly the one abolishing tariffs? Or forbidding armies and navies? I'm really not well up on Constitutional history—you see, there are one hundred and fourteen amendments in my own times—"

The reporter mentioned that the Eighteenth Amendment had to do with the liquor question.

At this information, Wormwood looked puzzled. "I really can't remember that there ever was such an Amendment," he declared. "What can the liquor question have to do with the law? Now in my own day, the most popular drink is Nectojuice, which is made with unfermented fruits and water. Here and there, other beverages do survive from the Neurotic Age; one still occasionally finds a pathological case of alcoholic poisoning, which is dealt with, of course, by the hospitals for the insane."

The interviewer recorded this information; then, with lightning rapidity, flung his next questions:

"What is your view of woman's suffrage...? Have you any ideas regarding Cubism in art...? Do you approve of freedom in sex relations...? Is it your opinion that the modern home is breaking up...? What have you to say on the unemployment situation...? And on prison reform...? Do you think the stock market is likely to improve...?"

As these questions were hurled at him, Wormwood's face was contorted by turns with surprise, disgust and perplexity; while the angry light was flashing back to his eyes.

"Sir," he exclaimed, "you are asking the ridiculous! I refuse to answer your questions! What do you suppose I am? A walking encyclopedia? How am I to be intelligently informed on such a wide variety of themes? Why do you not go to specialists?"

The reporter looked just a trifle annoyed. None the less, he attempted calmly to explain:

"You miss the point of this interview, Mr. Wormwood. I am not looking for expert opinions on any subject. I am merely looking for your opinion. Our readers will want to know what you think about these various things. That will be what will give the article its value—"

"Why, in the name of all things reasonable," thundered Wormwood, "will opinions based on ignorance be valuable? Do you want me to parade my misinformation? By the constellation of Orion you must take me for an idiot! There is only one field I will be questioned on! That is my specialty, Physical Research! I will not sputter for the amusement of fools!"

"But, Mr. Wormwood, don't you see," protested the reporter, desperately, "people are not interested in your specialty. They are interested only in what you think upon living, breathing topics— why girls leave home, the length of the new Paris skirts, the prospects that the Tigers will pull down the pennant this year and all that sort of thing."

"Well, I don't care what animals will pull down the pennant!" raged the man from tomorrow. "I have heard enough from you, sir! Your trivialities have outraged me sufficiently! Now get out! Get out before I have you thrown out! And when you get back to the imbecile paper that you represent, tell them that if ever they send another—"

"Oh, very well, sir, very well," conceded the reporter, hurriedly slipping his notebook into his pocket. "You don't need to get so testy about it. I'm merely doing what I'm required to do—and it's nothing out of the way. You ought to hear the questions I ask some men. I'd advise you, sir, if you want to see the interview in print, to look in Sunday's paper—"

"What? You're not going to print the interview, are you?" growled the man from tomorrow, as he started threateningly toward his foe. But the reporter, with a muttered oath, had already squeezed through the doorway and made his escape.

CHAPTER EIGHTEEN
Further Fruits of Renown

ON THE following Sunday morning, as I was preparing to enter the breakfast room, I was told that a visitor was waiting to see me. Surprised that I should have a caller at such an early hour, I looked into the sitting room—and there, impatiently pacing the floor, I observed the man from tomorrow.

Scarcely taking time to greet me, he thrust into my hand a newspaper he had been firmly clutching.

"See! Just look at this!" he stormed. "See what they've done to me! The thieves! The scandalmongers! I'll sue them! They want to ruin me! They want to kill my reputation! They should be prohibited by law—"

While Wormwood's wordy tempest went on and on, I took the paper from his hand. It was a copy of one of our most reputable journals, the *Sunday Universe*. Prominently placed on the front page of the "Special Feature Section" there was an article headed, "Man from Twenty-Third Century Finds Present Day Manners Queer; Gives Exclusive Interview to *Universe* Reporter." And, beneath this heading, there was a photograph two columns wide of a man whose features seemed vaguely familiar to me, although, I must confess, I would not have been able to identify him had it not been for the caption.

"Tell me now, does that look like me?" demanded the man from tomorrow, pointing to the flat blur of the photographed face. "Do you see any resemblance at all? Look at those small expressionless eyes! Look at that dough-like lump of a head! Actually, do I look anything like that at all?"

"Well, yes, I think I can notice some slight resemblance," testified Mrs. Howard, who had entered the room to shake hands with our visitor.

The man from tomorrow cast her a look that was like a sword-thrust; then suavely observed, "Really, my lady, you are to be congratulated upon your imagination."

Although I regarded this remark as not exactly in order, it required careful scrutiny to convince me that someone else's photograph had not been substituted for Wormwood's.

"What do you think? This libel of a picture is not even the worst!" sighed the man from tomorrow after Mrs. Howard had left the room. "It's nothing at all by comparison with what follows! Just you read it, and tell me if I haven't grounds for action! You heard what I said to that reporter. Now see what he has put into print!"

Without another word, I turned to the paper and read aloud:

"Evidently styles in men will change before the twenty-third century, if John Wormwood, the only known visitor from the future, is to be taken as a fair average sample of his times. A weakened little man of puny physique, with features more badly twisted than those of a professional pugilist, he has reminded more than one visitor of some strange species of monkey from the Brazilian jungles. Yet the grotesqueness of his features is atoned for by the brilliance of his mind and the amiability of his disposition. The *Universe* reporter, calling upon him at his quarters at the Faculty Club of Gotham University, was received most cordially and passed a pleasant hour chatting and listening to his opinions, which he was most voluble in offering.

" 'The manners of your present age,' Mr. Wormwood began, as he sat puffing away at a cigarette—"

"Now right there is where I object!" broke in the man from tomorrow, indignantly. "Maybe my looks are as bad as the paper says—though I'll never believe it—but I'll leave it to you, have I ever yet puffed away at one of those obnoxious little smoking stems?"

"Not so far as I know," I acknowledged. "But you shouldn't take what the paper says too seriously, Wormwood. After all, no one will hold it against you."

Having offered this admonition, I continued reading aloud:

" 'The manners of the present age,' Mr. Wormwood began, as he sat puffing away at a cigarette, 'impress me as so queer that I can never get used to them. Take, for example, the styles in women's clothes. In my own age, all women wear hats a yard wide, and skirts down to their ankles. Or take the matter of food. For breakfast, in the twenty-third century, I always ate a beefsteak or roast pork—' "

"Now just listen to that, will you!" fumed my visitor as he again paced the floor, while his hands nervously clasped and unclasped. "Would I ever say anything like that? All men and women in my age were dressed just as I was when I came here! And no one ate beefsteak! We had passed the cannibal stage! Oh, I tell you, it is ungodly!"

"Come, come," was my admonition, "no one nowadays will think less of you for eating beefsteaks!"

Then, passing down the column, I read:

"Mr. Wormwood was especially garrulous in stating his opinions on current events. After expressing his gratification at being heard in such an outstanding organ as the *Universe*, he declared himself in favor of the Eighteenth Amendment, and denied that it would ever be modified or repealed. He spoke approvingly of the policies of the Hoover administration, and said that he thought our country had entered an era of prosperity, justifying a lower income tax. Regarding the baseball prospects for the season, he said that he doubted whether the Tigers could again win the World's Championship. He also had many enlightening comments to make on the topic of world peace, the latest Supreme Court appointee, and the situation in China—"

"By all the stars in heaven, don't read any more!" broke in the man from tomorrow, snatching the paper from my grasp and crumbling it. "I can't bear it! I simply can't bear it! The unspeakable rascal! To invent such lies! Oh, I wish I could have had that reporter with me again—just for one minute! I'd paralyze him so that he wouldn't be seen for a month!"

"And what would that gain for you?" I muttered. "Well...what are you going to do about it?"

"What am I going to do? I'll write to the editor! I'll tell him his reporter is a scoundrel and a fraud! I'll demand a public retraction! He has insulted not only me, but the whole twenty-third century! I shall insist on his printing the truth—all the truth, and nothing but the truth! I'll write to the editor this very minute!"

Still in a frenzy, the man from tomorrow asked whether I had any writing materials handy; and, upon being supplied with ink and paper, sat down to pen his letter. He did not inform me precisely what he wrote; but I know that the task absorbed him for more than two hours, and that sheet after sheet was filled with his heavy scrawl. "No need to read this to you now," he said, when finally he displayed the thick envelope that embodied the fruits of his labors. "You'll see it when it appears in print. Do you suppose I'd better send it by Special Delivery?"

The following morning, and the morning after that, and for many mornings thenceforth, I glanced with anxious scrutiny into the correspondence columns of the *Universe*. But alas...the letter must have been mis-addressed, or perhaps the editor had more important material to print; for although I never missed a day and am sure that I could not have overlooked the article, I saw no communication above the signature of John Wormwood.

Fortunately, there were so many other things to occupy the attention of the man from tomorrow that he was soon able to forget his grievance against the *Universe*. His correspondence alone was enough to engage him for hours a day; indeed, it was becoming a problem to open and read, even without answering, the multitudinous letters that came to his door. Now that he was famous, he was being showered with the after-fruits of fame; and admirers and detractors and importunate individuals of every guild and species were addressing themselves to him at a great waste of stationery and stamps. It is impossible to estimate his daily average in letters and advertisements, but I believe it could not have been much greater had he conducted a mail order house. At all events, I know how surprised I was one day when, paying him an unexpected call, I saw a veritable mountain of unopened envelopes in one corner of the room, rising imposingly almost to the height of the table.

"What's the matter, Wormwood?" I gasped, while my eyes were glued upon this surprising spectacle. "Don't you intend to read your mail?"

"Oh, yes, I intend to read it—when I get time," he declared, with a yawn. "But it's been coming in so fast I can't keep up with it. I ought to have an automatic mail sifter and examiner. If most of it's of the same low quality as I've seen already, it's a shame to waste time and eyesight upon it."

"Why, what's wrong with it?" I demanded. "What's wrong? Just pick up a few of these at random, and read them—you'll soon find out! Go on... Don't hesitate," he urged, as he snatched a handful of letters and thrust them at me. "I don't mind. There's nothing private about them, anyhow."

Prompted by a rising curiosity, I tore open one of the envelopes, and read:

"Mr. John Wormwood:

Dear Sir: Let us congratulate you on your brilliant predictions, whereby you foretold the Indian riot and the Mandala eruption.

Since only one with an astrological training could attain such results, it is clear that you are deeply versed in the reading of the stars. We therefore take pleasure in forwarding you an invitation to join the International Association of Astrology—"

"International Association of Astrology!" groaned Wormwood. "Astrology, did you say? What an insult! Does anyone in the twentieth century still have faith in such superstition?"

Reluctantly I was forced to confess that some unscientific persons did retain such a faith.

"Impossible," he muttered. "It's like believing in witches and sorcery. Well, Professor, read on…"

I slit open a second envelope, and read the following, which was written in pencil in a sprawling, uncultivated hand:

"Dear Sir: Since you are such a wonderful fortuneteller, maybe you can help me out. My uncle Jim left on a sea voyage seventeen years ago, and said he wouldn't come back without making his fortune. My mother and me has been waiting ever since, but still haven't heard from him. We have tried lots of other palm-readers and fortune-tellers, but one said he was dead, and another said he was busy making a million in Africa. Maybe sir you could please tell me which is right and greatly oblige. Yours truly—"

"Aladdin and his genie come back to earth!" laughed Wormwood. "That's about the fiftieth of the same kind. They must think I'm a magician! Seem to believe I can do anything from locating a pet cat to directing them to their true love…"

"Now let's see what a third one has to say," I suggested, finding the letters more interesting than I had expected.

This time I selected a neatly typed envelope purporting to be from the "Distinguished Americans Publishing Company." The contents, immaculately embodied on imposingly printed paper, were as follows:

"Dear Mr. Wormwood: Your name has been recommended to us for inclusion in our forthcoming issue of *One Thousand Distinguished Americans,* which is due shortly to be off the press. We should be pleased to receive from you a biography of not more than one hundred words, recording the outstanding facts of your life. A printed form to guide you is enclosed. For this service we ordinarily require the nominal fee of twenty-five dollars, which will entitle you to two copies of the volume. Additional copies may be obtained at a reduction of ten per cent below the catalogue price.

"The accompanying circular contains testimonials from leading clergymen, authors, stage stars, theatrical producers, educators, and football champions. Trusting that we shall have the pleasure of including your name, we remain, etc."

"Well, Wormwood, there's an opportunity for you!" I remarked, dryly. "Let me congratulate you! You're now one of our thousand most distinguished citizens!"

"Not unless I pay the fee!" he snapped. "And that leaves me out! Want to read some more of the letters?"

Obedient to this invitation, I ripped open a few more envelopes and let my eyes race along the contents. I shall not weary the reader by mentioning the results in detail; but it is only fair to say that most of them maintained the same standard as those already perused. There was an invitation for Wormwood to take a correspondence course in astrology; there was a letter from an amorous young lady, who professed herself greatly taken with his photograph, and requested an appointment; there was a vigorous protest from the Secretary of the Anti-Dry League, deploring his stand on the Eighteenth Amendment; there was a letter from an enterprising business college, which evidently believing that he spoke a foreign tongue, promised to teach him English in fifteen lessons; there was an appeal for funds for the Foreign Mission Society, and three requests for his autograph from admiring ladies; there was a threat from an anonymous party, who demanded a payment of one thousand dollars under penalty of exposing him; there was an invitation to lecture at a prominent Church on "Why I Favor Prohibition," and a letter from the local Republican Club commending him for his endorsement of the Hoover policies and suggesting that he join that organization. These, together with several "confidential" offers by Real Estate companies and some advertisements of rugs, radios, and Skub's "Fine Meat Products," were all that I had any desire to glance through.

It would be needless to describe how the man from tomorrow sneered at each of the letters in turn, and how he refused to answer any of them, stating that "their unwarrantable vulgarity did not justify any response." Annoying as many of the letters were, they were less irritating than some of the offers made him in person—a fact which I had the opportunity to verify two or three days later, when I again paid Wormwood a call. And before I had reached his room on this occasion, I surmised that something was wrong. As I passed along the corridor, I was startled by the sound of voices raised in loud disputation; while clearly over all when I was about to rap at my friend's door, I heard his well-known tones shrilling in anger. "Get out now! Get out quick! Wait another moment, and I'll—I'll paralyze you!"

Realizing that I was barely in time to rescue some unwary victim, I did not hesitate for a second. Flinging open the door without formality, I found myself face to face with a red-cheeked Wormwood—and with a tall, insolent-eyed individual, who looked as if he could have crushed the man from tomorrow at a blow.

As I burst into the room, Wormwood was just snapping out the little pistol-like instrument containing the paralyzing rays. Another second, and there would have come the droning sound and the greenish flash—and the smitten man would have toppled to the floor.

At the risk of being paralyzed myself, I thrust myself between the man from tomorrow and his foe. "Go!" I commanded the imperiled one. "Go! Better be quick!"

"Just let me at him! I'll paralyze him!" snarled Wormwood, as he tried to force his way to his adversary.

The stranger, taking the hint, was already gliding toward the half-open door.

"Keep us in mind, Mr. Wormwood! Any time you're still interested, that offer remains good!" he called out over his shoulder—and then, warned by the sudden elevation of the pistol-like machine, he darted into the corridor and disappeared.

"The rogue! The scoundrel! Why did I let him escape?" muttered the man from tomorrow, with a regretful look; while, with clenched fists, he distractedly paced the floor. "Oh! The infernal schemer! Anyone who offers *his* trade deserves to be paralyzed!"

"What trade is that?" I demanded. "What is he, a counterfeiter? A gangster? He didn't try to blackmail you, did he? Or to offer you a bribe?"

"Yes, that was just it!" raged the man from tomorrow. "He offered me a bribe! And what a bribe! He must have thought me without self-respect! Must have thought I was as dishonest as he!"

I seated myself quietly on the couch, and waited for Wormwood to continue.

But it was several minutes before, growing more calm, he came to me, and still standing continued with, "What do you think he wanted me to do? What, except to sign my name to a damnable lie? To take money for falsifying myself—for falsifying my century! To let him have my photograph and use it—where do you suppose?"

"How should I know?"

"In the lowest place you could imagine! The subway! An advertisement in the subway! Why, at the very mention of that hole I wanted to paralyze the fellow!"

"Well," I commented, "I don't know that it's a disgrace to be seen in the subway."

"You think not? Then listen to the rest. The schemster had some nice little testimonial to put my name to. Wanted me to say I always smoked a certain brand of cigarette—I forget which—named after some animal, llama or dromedary or donkey. I was to swear this is the favorite smoke of the twenty-third century accounts for all our progress. Can you imagine such impudence? I told him I considered it an insult!"

"Oh, well, after all, Wormwood," I ventured, soothingly, "it's really meant as a compliment. All great men get such offers. How else do you suppose that manufacturers of soap, radios and toilet articles manage to push ahead? Weren't you to receive liberal compensation?"

"Liberal compensation?" echoed the man from tomorrow, with renewed fury. "As if there could be any compensation for having my face seen in subway pictures! No...no. I'd rather starve. Why, if Maranna and my twenty-third century friends could see me there, what do you suppose they'd say? Would I ever be able to lift up my head among them again? No! No, Professor! I may be forced to live in the twentieth century, but I still have some ideals."

With these words, the man from tomorrow snatched at some gaudily printed circulars left on his table by his recent visitor, and vehemently tore them to bits. "No! No! It's impossible!" he reiterated. "I may be forced to live in the twentieth century, but I will not be corrupted utterly!"

Then, after he had flung the ruins into his overflowing waste paper basket, he turned to me a little more calmly, and remarked, "Well, Professor, I suppose. I really shouldn't be so angry. Doubtless every age has its ruffians and thieves. Now what was it you came to see me about?"

CHAPTER NINETEEN
An Adventure Looms Ahead

I HAVE already mentioned that the man from tomorrow had been living upon gratuities during his first weeks at the Faculty Club. His needs had been slight; he had demanded little more than board and lodging, along with an occasional penny for such incidentals as newspapers, stamps and car fares; and, his requirements having been satisfied at the expense of my colleagues and myself, he apparently gave little thought to the problem of providing for himself. Yet it was obvious that he could not continue to subsist forever upon the charity of his friends; and so one day I asked him, as tactfully as I knew how, whether he did not think it time to ponder the question of making a living.

His eyes were wide with surprise as he turned to me, and, without seeming to understand my meaning, bade me repeat the question.

"Don't you think it time to consider making a living?" I asked again.

"Time to consider making a living?" he softly echoed, uncomprehendingly. "What do you mean? How can a man make a living? If he is alive, he is living—why speak of making that which nature has granted him at birth?"

"Evidently," I said, in exasperation, "the idioms of the English language will have undergone a change by the twenty-third century. To make a living means—well, to support one's self."

"Support one's self?" he thrust back at me, with a blanker expression than ever.

In increasing irritation, I perceived that this idiom also would become obsolete.

But finally, by dint of a great waste of words and a still greater waste of patience, I managed to convey my idea. "Certainly, you do not want to be always a burden on your friends," I suggested. "You are now capable of earning money of your own—in fact, a great many money-making offers have come your way. Wouldn't you feel better satisfied and more independent if you accepted one of these proposals?"

For a moment Wormwood sat stroking his chin and regarding me quizzically, like one who manfully struggles with a new idea.

"It is very good of you to point this out," he remarked, slowly. "Very good of you, indeed. I shall not forget your kindness. I am sorry to say I did not quite understand the situation. In my own times, no man considers it a loss of independence to accept of the generosity of friends, for friendship is thought to involve both giving and taking. It is regarded as an insult to reject a friend's hospitality without just cause; hence I should never have thought of refusing anything from you. But now everything is clear; I shall look at once for some remunerative work. There must be something I can do for the benefit of the twentieth century, even though I am paid for it."

I tried to explain that he should forget "the benefit of the twentieth century" in favor of the benefit of his own income. But, though I argued till the mirror opposite proclaimed me to be red in the face, he did not seem able to grasp my idea. "I'm afraid there's bound to be a sacrifice," he ruminated. "The trouble with remunerative work is that it is so often useless. It benefits only one's self; it is apt to be of small advantage to others. It encourages greed and vice; it is a breeder of the in-growing soul. Ah, well, if I must descend to it I must! Maybe, after all, I can escape the pitfalls and do something worthwhile."

"What sort of work do you think you'd prefer?" I asked, abruptly; for I had little patience with his moral rantings.

"That's what I'm wondering," he admitted, as he rubbed and rubbed his bulging forehead in perplexity. "Something connected with Physical Research, I should say; since that's my specialty. However, I'm so far ahead of this age that I don't know what practical good I could do. It would be as if a twentieth century scientist, shipwrecked without tools or appliances on a South Sea island, were to try to teach the aborigines the marvels of electricity."

"I'll tell you what," I suggested, mentioning an idea that had been in my mind for some time, "why don't you do some writing? Didn't you tell me only the other day that you had received offers from magazines?"

"Yes, but how could I take them seriously? Writing isn't my field," he returned, sadly. "I haven't any skill in it. I haven't any training. I haven't any natural aptitude—"

"My dear man," I broke in, irritated at these pointless excuses, "don't let that stop you! Nowadays no writer let's himself be restrained simply for lack of training or natural aptitude. The modern world has risen above such prejudices. Everyone knows that some of our most popular writers haven't anything to say, and don't know how to say it."

"Well, that would place me among the leaders," reflected the man from tomorrow. "Or no—maybe, after all, it wouldn't. I *have* something to say. I really haven't expressed my opinions of this age. Whole volumes wouldn't exhaust the subject."

"Good!" I approved. "There's your clue, Wormwood. Now I'd advise you to look over your old correspondence again, and see if you haven't some promising offer."

Reluctantly following this suggestion, Wormwood managed with difficulty to resurrect several recent offers from his piles of read and unread letters; and at length, after much deliberation and considerable prodding on my part, he decided to accept the proposal of that well known magazine, *The World's Affairs*, that he write a series of three short articles on "The Twentieth Century Viewed from the Twenty-Third."

Before I left, accordingly, he sat down to write the editor of *The World's Affairs* a letter of acceptance; while, almost immediately afterwards, he began to pen the first of the articles. His efforts were laborious, for he wrote with scrupulous care; and not being able to adapt himself to the present-day typewriter (which, he said, lacked sundry necessary devices, including a "self-renewing ribbon" and an "error eradicator"), he wrote exclusively in longhand. For several days the Campus saw him not, and he refused all invitations indiscriminately, arising at five in the morning and working steadily until evening. But at last, after a vast expenditure of energy and an enormous waste of paper, he had finished and triumphantly mailed the first of the articles; and in due time the second and the third followed and were acknowledged not only with thanks but with a check.

Before the arrival of the letter item, I observed, the man from tomorrow looked conspicuously happy. Whenever I saw him, he would fling out his chest in a jaunty, self-approving manner, would drink deep of the air, and exclaim, "Ah! Now at last I'm free. I'm free! It's a wonderful thing to be free." But, immediately upon the appearance of the check, his contentment seemed to leave him. Once more his face took on a strained and worried expression; one would have said at a glance there here was a man with some secret burden on his mind. "What am I to do now, Professor?" he asked. "What am I to do with all my money? They sent me a thousand dollars, you know. It's more than I have any need of. Do you suppose I should give most of it away?"

"Give most of it away?" I demanded. "What can you be thinking of?"

"Well, it's a great responsibility to have so much money," he explained. "I'd feel so much better to be rid of it. Besides, I don't need the money, and maybe someone else does. In my own age, if I didn't give it away, I'd be scorned by respectable people."

"Well, in this age," I pointed out, "you'd be scorned by respectable people if you *did* give it away. When one has too much money, there are lots of things to do with it. For example, you could buy a motor car—"

Wormwood scowled. "Not if they paid me to take it. Aren't there enough of them already to endanger the public peace and safety...?"

"Or you can invest in some personal finery—some fashionable new clothes," I proceeded. "Go dressed in the latest styles—"

With an angry gesture, Wormwood cut me short. "You don't seem to realize, Professor, that this season's styles are three hundred years out of date for me. What else can I do?"

"Or again," I continued, at a loss for ideas, "you might travel. "Of course, you really haven't money enough—"

"Let's see if I haven't!" he caught up, enthusiastically. "Why not travel? That's precisely the thing! What better way of seeing the twentieth century? Thank you very much, Professor. Yes, I'll travel. I'll travel! That's what I'll do with my money!"

Shaking his own hands as if in self-congratulation, the man from tomorrow did an excited hop, skip and jump about the room. "I'll travel! I'll travel!" he cried, over and over again. "I'll travel! I'll travel! I'll travel!"

"Just one moment there..." I warned, alarmed at his eagerness. "Before you do any planning, you'd better consider your finances. Why, you haven't nearly enough—hardly half enough, for example if you want to go to Europe—"

"Go to Europe?" he challenged. "Europe? What makes you think I'd go there? Not with 1930 methods of transportation! You still haven't instituted transoceanic dirigible travel, have you?"

"Why, no—" I was forced to admit.

"I thought not," he sighed. "I thought not. That is still decades in the future. And do you think I'd trust myself to one of those jerky little steamboats of yours? Why, I don't believe you have a vessel of more than fifty or sixty thousand tons!"

"No, we haven't—yet," I acknowledged.

"And probably they don't make more than twenty or twenty-five knots," he continued. "I remember once reading an essay on the first centuries of steam navigation. It was unbelievable what people had to undergo. Five or six days locked in one of those tossing little tanks! Nothing to do but watch the waters, eat, gossip, and grow seasick! No, thank you, sir. No thank you! When I go traveling, I want to do it for pleasure!"

"Then where, pray do you want to go?"

"Somewhere on land, of course. Almost anywhere on land. Your surface vehicles may be primitive; but at least, one can get out of them when one tires. That's why I'll take a chance. Now all that's left is to decide where to go. Guess I'd better look through the papers. Mind going over them with me, Professor?"

"Not at all," I said, and waited while he fished about in the refuse on the floor to find the "Travel Section" of the previous Sunday's *Leader*. After much vain fumbling amid newspapers and discarded correspondence, he succeeded in locating the desired pages; and together the two of us perused the "Travel Suggestions" and travel advertisements.

Personally, I thought it best for him to take a short and not too costly trip—to Boston, Atlantic City, or perhaps Niagara Falls; but he thought differently. "If I'm to travel," he decided, "I'd better make a thorough-going job of it. Might as well get somewhere."

As he uttered these words, his eyes fell upon an advertisement, which seemed instantly to fascinate him. "There…the very thing!" he exclaimed. "The very thing I've been looking for!"

Snatching the paper from my grasp, he read, in sonorous tones:

"De Luxe Tour of the Continent. Party limited to forty. Accompanied by professional guide. Niagara Falls, the Great Lakes, Yellowstone, Yosemite, Grand Canyon, Zion National Park. Sip the pure air of the Rockies. Marvel at Redwood groves by the blue Pacific. Stroll amid the orange orchards of the balmy Southland. Seven thousand miles of sheer delight through mountain, forest, prairie, and vine-land. Tour to last forty-two days. All expenses included, only $895. Make reservations without delay, Harry Chef & Co., 1100 Fifth Avenue."

"Well," demanded Wormwood, after reaching the eloquent conclusion of this announcement, "what do you think of it? Sounds like the real thing, doesn't it?"

"Oh, I'm not saying it wouldn't be all right," I admitted, hesitatingly. "That is, if one had the money."

"You forget," he protested. "I have more than enough money!"

"Heavens, Wormwood," I protested, "you've only a thousand dollars. Certainly you're not going to spend every penny—"

"Why not?" he demanded. "What's the use of money if you don't spend it? Can't I make more afterwards? Besides, I'll have more than a hundred dollars over."

"But, in a trip like that, one must lay something aside for extras," I pleaded, desperately.

Without appearing to hear me, he had already turned to his writing desk. "You don't mind, do you, if I take just a minute to drop a line to Chef and Company...? I'm so afraid that, if I wait, all their reservations may be taken up."

A moment later while I folded my hands beside me and paced to the window, reflecting on the odd kinks and freaks of twenty-third century psychology, I could hear the pen of the man from tomorrow as it nervously squeaked and raced across the paper.

CHAPTER TWENTY
The Adventure Arrives

WHEN it became generally known that the man from tomorrow was planning a transcontinental tour, several of us who had been supporting him could hardly suppress our grumblings and murmurs of dissatisfaction. "What! He can accept our offerings and then can afford an expensive trip!" was the common complaint. "No doubt he doesn't even intend to pay us back!"

"No doubt he doesn't," I said; for it was useless to explain, and impossible to make the disgruntled ones understand Wormwood's lofty ethical code, which forbade him to pay back what he had received. For that matter, I myself had difficulty in understanding it, and only by the exercise of extreme forbearance was I able to tolerate our visitor's eccentricities.

Unconscious of the reproaches being hurled at him in private, the man from tomorrow went blithely ahead with his plans; he secured his place with the Chef touring party; he made arrangements to leave at an early date; and all the while he would discourse volubly on the prospective joys of the journey to those very persons who had secretly been most vigorous in condemning him. With supreme contempt for any opportunity to accumulate mere lucre, he refused the offers of newspapers which would have paid him a considerable sum for his impressions of the trip; he let it be known in no uncertain terms that he was traveling for purposes of pleasure and education and not for profit; while, from the pose of independence which he struck and the extreme self-assertion of his language, one would have been justified in assuming him to be a millionaire's son.

At last the all-important day arrived. Equipped with a suitcase innocent of anything in the way of suits, but containing an abundance of notebooks and notepaper in addition to a small camera, Wormwood permitted me to hire a taxicab and accompany him to the railroad terminal. After arriving at the station, with its hurrying throngs, its enormous writing rooms, and its high vaulted ceilings, he became so interested in the sights that he loitered at a snail's pace, with eyes cast speculatively upward, and would probably have missed his train had I not continually goaded him on.

"Queer! How very queer," he meditated. "Reminds me a little of some of our smaller airports, except that people seem so very much more in a hurry. Strange, how hushed everything in the twentieth century appears. The world has never before had so many time saving devices, yet one would think no one had time enough to do anything. Now in my own century—"

"Come, come," I urged. "Your train leaves at 5:25, and it is now 5—"

At this point we were interrupted by a porter, who snatched at Wormwood's suitcase and almost succeeded in wresting it out of his grasp. "Great Western Limited, sir?" he inquired.

"Here, what do you mean?" demanded Wormwood, with an angry flush. And then, as sudden realization came to him, "Oh, you want to carry my grip? "Thanks greatly, but you have the wrong party. I'm strong enough to carry it myself."

While the discomfited porter was retreating, my companion turned to me and inquired, "Tell me, do I look sick or infirm, that he thought I couldn't carry my own grip?"

Unfortunately, I had no chance for explanations; although I saw that the man from tomorrow was sadly in need of instruction regarding certain prerequisites of modern travel. By this time we had arrived at the gateway, where a few hurried stragglers were bidding leave of friends and pressing forward to take the 5:25.

And, since the clock informed me that the train would leave in something like two and a half minutes, I was loudly insistent that Wormwood show the gateman his tickets without delay.

Yet, though quivering with excitement, he still seemed in no particular hurry. "Surely, the train won't leave without me!" he said. "I have my reservations, haven't I?"

For another minute he fumbled nervously in his pockets; then, while I foresaw how he would reach the platform just in time to see the train pull out, he put down his grip and wasted another thirty seconds in shaking both my hands vigorously and in assuring me that he would write soon. "Yes, I'll surely write!" he promised. "I'm certain to have worlds of things to tell about."

"Better hurry, if you want to make the train," urged the gateman, for Wormwood was now the last in line.

Whereupon he shot hastily forward, allowed his ticket to be punched, turned back to wave me a final farewell, and was lost in the nether darkness. The last I saw of him, he was taking to his heels—which, I reflected, was probably just as well; for the hand of the clock opposite me was just moving forward to 5:25.

Several days went by while I browsed in the luxuriance of unwonted freedom and ease. Somehow it seemed to me, now that the man from tomorrow had left, that a great weight had been lifted off my mind; for previously I had felt the constant need of counseling and watching over him, the constant fear that he was about to do something reckless or outrageous...

I did, indeed, occasionally wonder how he was faring on his journey; nor had my last few minutes with him encouraged me in the hope that he would make a good traveler. It was therefore not without pleasure that I at length found myself in possession of an envelope addressed in his heavy hand; and it was not without interest that I glanced along the contents, which were peculiarly difficult to read because of the shaky and uncertain writing:

"Honored Professor,

It is very, very hard to write, because of the monstrous jerking of the train, which has jarred my nerves until I feel as if I have been through a war.

"I am now leaving Chicago for the 'great wild west,' which I see described in the advertisements. What a journey I have had! It is only four days, but it seems like four weeks! I had never thought traveling could be such hard work. In my own times, all long trips are made by air; and so it was naturally somewhat of a novelty to me to enter one of your primitive surface coaches. I found the interior as commodious-looking as I could have expected, and for an hour or two I was too interested to mind the swaying and lunging. But after a while I began to feel very sick, and thought I could recognize the symptoms of that ancient disease known as seasickness, which is fortunately almost obsolete in the twenty-third century. I will not describe my sensations for the next hour or two, except to say that I wouldn't have minded if the train had run into the river. But late in the evening, somehow, I began to feel better; though I did miss supper, and also missed seeing the scenery. The worst of my sufferings was in the beginning, when I felt too ill to remain up. Then I asked the conductor where to find the sleeping apartments; but he referred me to an officer known as the porter, a colored man who was very courteous, but surprised me by saying, in a strange dialect whose origin I cannot begin to imagine, 'Yes, sah, dis am de sleepin' car.' He then told me I could not go to bed yet since it was not time to put up the berths. Of course, I thought this ridiculous, but he said I had only an upper berth, and the lady sitting across from me had the lower, which she wanted to use to sit in, so that the berth couldn't be put up without her permission. This seemed queer to me; but I was too sick to try to wonder what it all meant. I simply asked the lady if I might have her permission to go to bed—a question she must have mis-understood, for she looked at me with a horrified glare. 'Sir!' she muttered, in such tones that you would have thought I had run a dagger through her. After that, I didn't try anymore, but simply rolled up on the seat, feeling miserable and wishing I was back in the twenty-third century.

"Later in the evening, when I was a little better, I began to watch that interesting official, the porter. Everybody, I was surprised to find, seemed to know him, for everybody called him 'George.' He was a most obliging and likable chap, and did lots of helpful little things, such as to dust off the men's clothes and shoes and to bring hat-bags and pillows for the ladies. And so, when I saw him coming down the aisle and doing some heavy work that he called 'making up the berths,' I thought it a shame that no one would do anything for him in return. Sick as I was, I suggested to a man across the aisle that we pitch in and help George, who wasn't a very big fellow and was looking fearfully tired. You ought to have seen the look that man across the aisle cast me! You would have thought I was suggesting a murder! I knew I must have said something wrong somehow, but I couldn't imagine what. So I went to George myself and asked if I mightn't help him. I believe I never in all my life saw a man look so surprised! 'Now that's all right, Boss,' he said, still speaking his curious dialect. 'Ah thanks yo' very much, but yo' just remember me in de mornin', and Ah'll thank yo' still mo'.' Now what could he have meant by that?

"Well, at last the berths were all fixed up, and George helped me climb up the ladder into bed. I tell you, that was an experience! How Maranna and my own people would laugh at the idea of taking a ladder to bed! Fortunately, I am a small man as twentieth century people go; but, even so, I had to be something of an athlete as I began to undress on my swaying mattress. How I ever managed it I don't know, but I was feeling seasick again by the time I had finished. 'Is this the pleasure trip I am paying to take?' I asked myself. Yet the worst was only just beginning. What a night I passed! I hardly slept a wink. Once, when I did go to sleep, I awoke in terror, when a passing train went by with such a crashing and screeching that I shook in every limb. And, another time, we stopped short with such violence that I thought there had been a wreck and barely restrained myself from crying out at the top of my voice. 'Alas!' I thought. 'What inconvenience the twentieth century traveler must undergo! Never before had I sighed so longingly for the spacious sleeping apartment of our dirigibles, with their vibration-proof pneumo-etheric screens and their radio-atomic silencers, which make them noiseless as one's own home…!

"However, let me pass on. The following morning we were at Niagara Falls, and there was a great bustling among the members of our party, who, by the way, seem to be a most dull and seedy group, composed largely of sour-looking old women and flat-looking men approaching the Epoch of Decadence. Somehow I felt sorry to have to say goodbye to George, for whom I had taken a real fancy; but I shook his hands heartily, which seemed greatly to surprise him—and, at the same time, I did not lose the opportunity to say a good word for him, and to wish him the best of success in his future undertakings. However—though I may have been mistaken—it seemed to me that George looked disappointed, and even mumbled a bit beneath his breath. 'Say, Boss, ain't yo' forgot something?' he asked—which was very strange, for I looked through my suitcase carefully, and am sure there was nothing missing...

"Now let me tell you about Niagara Falls. That was a sight almost worth coming to the twentieth century to view! Of course, I have frequently been in the vicinity in my own times—but never have I witnessed such a spectacle. Long before the twenty-third century, the waters of the Great Lakes had been so diverted for industrial purposes and their level consequently lowered that there is only the merest trickle running over the falls. Strangely enough, you folks of the twentieth century don't appreciate your advantages in having this great natural marvel still with you!

"Well, I guess this is enough for today. The train is jerking so badly that I'm beginning to feel seasick again. By tomorrow at this time, they tell me, we will be approaching the Rockies.

"Shake Dr. Horn's hand in greeting for me. And give my salutations to Mrs. Howard—and to the fair Miss Whitcomb. With gracious appreciation of past favors,

"Your Friend from the Future."

Following the receipt of this letter, I did not hear from Wormwood for several weeks; and I was growing just a little anxious on his account before finally I received a heavy envelope bearing the postmark of San Diego. "Evidently Wormwood is having a chequered career!" I reflected; and, upon opening the envelope, I found that I was not mistaken in this surmise:

"Most respected friend,

So much has happened since I last wrote that I hardly know where or how to begin. I have had some very enjoyable experiences—and some that were not quite so enjoyable. The thing that has most impressed me is the Western scenery. To be sure, I have often passed through the same territory in my own times—but how different it looks to me now! Although you in the twentieth century have already spoiled much of the natural grandeur of your land, diverting streams and destroying forests, you have not yet ruined it utterly. It is not nearly so bare or barren as in the twenty-third century. The Rockies and the Sierras are not completely bald and treeless; their slopes are not blasted everywhere by the scars of mines; their streams have not dwindled into nothingness, their wild life has not been altogether exterminated. We of the twenty-third century would gladly repair the damage, which was done before our own time—but, alas, it is too late! One might as soon try to give life to a corpse.

"Consequently, it was a real experience—if a rather sad one, for a man who sees into the future—to go traveling across wooded mountains, to drink of the fragrance of pines and redwoods, and to quench one's thirst in cool shady streams undisturbed by the drone of cities. In our own age, unfortunately, the growth of population has blighted many places that were virgin solitudes in yours; I was surprised to pass over some of the sites of coming great cities, and to find nothing at all! Gatesville, with its three million population in my own century, is a mere village of three hundred souls today; while the western metropolis of San Ramona, which is to boast more than ten million, is represented by a sheepherder's home overlooking two wilderness streams! In California, I was particularly impressed at the change wrought by time. How delightful it looks today with its mild brown valleys, its curved brown hills, its orchards, its blue bays, its peaceful distances! It seemed to me to be quaint as some remote dream-place; and I groan to think how it will be despoiled and blasted by the growth of population; how, three hundred years from now, its hillsides will be black with its forty-million population, its forests will be devastated, its valleys will reek with factory smoke, its mountain streams will be polluted by industry; while nowhere on the great shoulders of its snowy ranges or in the depth of its tremendous canyons will one find a spot secure from the smoke and the brawling and the disturbing intrusion of man.

"Yes, my friend, this age has indeed some advantages; but my heart grows heavy when I realize how little you appreciate them, and how little you will protect them from the greed and the numbers and the locust-like ravages of your own citizens...

"Picturesque and imposing as your scenery is, however, I was not able to enjoy it fully. This was because, wherever I went, I had to be attended, like a man with an over-large family, by the forty members of the touring party, who surely must have been recruited from persons mentally in the Epoch of Childhood. They only saw what they were told to see; and what they were told to see they always admired. Usually they had but one word to express their approval; and that word was 'Wonderful!' 'Look at that terrific crashing stream!' our guide would say; and two scores of voices would chime in, 'Wonderful!' 'Look at that enormous cliff!' he would remark; and again one would hear that expressive response, 'Wonderful! Observe that field over there!' he would exclaim, pointing to a flat stretch of ordinary grass. 'It was there that Andrew Jackson routed Benedict Arnold in the War.' And once more you would hear that same impressive chorus, 'Wonderful!'

"At first I found this sort of thing amusing, but after a while its monotony became too much for sensitive nerves to bear. And so I took to wandering off by myself and avoiding the rest of the party whenever I could. This enabled me to see much more of the country, but it also made me very unpopular. I noticed how queerly my fellow travelers would look at me, and how strangely they would nod and point in my direction. Also, once or twice I overheard some curious phrases, such as 'Nobody home there,' and 'That guy is cracked.' I wonder if you would mind informing me what these expressions mean?

"To make matters worse, my tongue would always be getting the better of me and saying things that should have been left unsaid. 'Now where are the invisible glass factories?' I unthinkingly asked in one town, forgetting that they wouldn't be built for two hundred years yet. And in another town I said, 'This place looks so strange without its floating dirigible hangars,' which made everyone stare at me as though I had gone mad, since floating dirigible hangars are an invention of the twenty-third century. Again, when I was shown any object that my fellow travelers thought very modern, I would be apt to forget and declare that it was an interesting antique; while, as if this were not enough, I couldn't help making an occasional reference to the comforts of my own century. And so I have come to have a singular nickname, which I received on the second day of the trip and have kept ever since; 'The guy that thinks he isn't born yet.'

"Well, Professor, let me turn from all this nonsense and come down to serious things. For I really have something very serious to write you about. In one way, the trip has proved a great disappointment. The advertisement of Harry Chef and Company, I am grieved to say, misrepresented sadly in saying that all expenses were included. Alas! I have been to constant expense on my own account; particularly since, not sharing the cannibalistic fare of my fellow sightseers, I have daily had to buy food and sandwiches and other articles to ward off starvation. I must reluctantly report an unhappy bit of news; the two hundred dollars that I had when I set out, and which seemed a little fortune, has been steadily dwindling. At the present moment I have just two one-dollar bills in my pocket, in addition to a few small coins. I wonder, dear Professor, whether you would not forward me a slight amount? I should never forget your kindness, and should be only too glad to repay you in time if you would accept repayment. Looking over my itinerary, I see that you will be able to reach me at the Palace Hotel at the Grand Canyon.

"I salute you warmly, as ever,

"Your friend,
"John."

"P. S. Since writing the above, I saw a charming little souvenir, which I thought just the thing for Miss Whitcomb. Please advise her that she may expect to receive it any day now. One of the other tourists, from whom I borrowed the money, agrees that it is precisely the gift for a lady."

CHAPTER TWENTY-ONE
The Homecoming

AFTER I had wired Wormwood the money he requested, I assumed that he would leave me in peace for the rest of his trip. But no! I was not to be so fortunate; about two weeks later, I was startled to receive a telegram, "Collect." Tearing open the envelope, not without misgivings, I read the following tale of woe:

"Professor Ellery Howard,
46 West 73 St.,
New York City.
"Have missed my train at Chicago. Also missed Chef party, who have tickets. Only forty cents left. Kindly send immediate aid, care Illinois Railroad.
    "John Wormwood."

Here, indeed, was a message to make me stamp about the floor and snort violently. I have always prided myself on being a man who controls his temper; but this was one of the occasions on which I lost it utterly. Now all at once I thought I could appreciate the feelings of a father cursed with an errant and incorrigible son— how avoid the responsibility for Wormwood's irresponsible deeds? Had he not already been as much of a drain on my resources as a new motor car, and as trying to my patience as a very old one? Mrs. Howard, when I showed her the telegram, waxed even more indignant than I, and suggested that I "teach Mr. Wormwood a lesson" by leaving him stranded in Chicago. But I, although not without temptations to follow this advice, was tormented by pictures of the man from tomorrow drooping and dying in a strange city. And so, although I grumbled mightily, I wasted no time about seeking the nearest telegraph office and forwarding the necessary funds.

While waiting for Wormwood to complete his journey, it occurred to me to pay another visit to James Richard Cloud, against whom I felt an unreasonable secret grievance. It was Cloud, and not I, I told myself, who was responsible for Wormwood's presence in this generation; accordingly, it should be he and not I that should shoulder the burden. At the least, I wished him to know how much I was suffering at the indirect result of his Dimension Machine; and it was probably with this idea in the background of my mind that I sought him out in the new quarters where he had been installed ever since receiving the Endersby Award.

As usual, I found him at work on the improved model of his invention. At the moment of my arrival, in fact, he was in a particular state of excitement over the discovery of what he termed an "Adjustable Inter-Dimensional Balance." While, throughout the greater part of my visit, he was busily engaged in testing some instrument that looked like a barometer, but that, instead of "Fair," "Unsettled," and "Stormy," was marked "Super-Spatial Variations," "Dimensional Etheric Pressure," and other things of a similarly incomprehensible nature.

"Well, Professor, I think I'm getting there!" he enthused. "Yes, I really do think I'm getting there! I've got my Dimension Bridge about all ready now. My Dimension Gauge is almost perfected. There are only a few delicate minor balances to complete before I'm ready to venture out into higher space. Do you think you would care to join me, Professor, and have the credit of being one of the first two men—"

"No, thank you," I said, reflecting that I was too old to be seeking honors out of my own dimension.

"Well, at any rate, I want you to know what I've been doing," he continued, as he stepped back a foot or two to regard his Inter-Dimensional Gauge. "I owe that to you—since you were one of the first to appreciate my invention. The machine is already in a condition to test. Thus far, no one except me has seen it in operation, but I'm going to show you now—"

"Not yet, Cloud! Please, not yet!" I protested, raising my hand in alarm. "You'd better stick to this dimension a while longer—"

"Oh, have no fear, Professor!" he laughed. "I'm not going to experiment with myself just now. I won't take any chances till everything has been perfectly adjusted. But I want to demonstrate with some small object."

He paused, while I nodded in silent acquiescence, and his keen eyes appraisingly scanned the room. "Let's see—what will we take?" he meditated. "Almost anything will do. Ah, there—the very thing!"

His gaze had fallen upon a little stiff-backed notebook six or eight inches wide. "The very thing!" he repeated, as he snatched up this object with an avid, zealous expression. "Now for the experiment! I hope to be able to convince you, Professor!"

Wondering what on earth he could be contemplating, I watched how he placed the article in a basket-like wire contrivance at one end of the machine—a contrivance similar to that in which Wormwood had been deposited from the Fourth Dimension.

"Now I want you to see that there's no possible chance for this object to escape by ordinary means," the inventor pointed out, as he closed the container in such a way that the notebook seemed to be held secured as a bird in its cage.

"No, there is no apparent chance—except by opening the wire case," I agreed. And Cloud, looking pleased, mumbled something I could not quite make out, and turned to his experiment.

First he pulled a lever, and there occurred that curious movement and manipulation of the mirrors, which I had observed in the original Dimension Machine. Then he pulled a second lever, and there came an ominous whirring and sparkling at one end of the instrument, and all at once the wire basket began to rotate with tremendous rapidity. So swiftly did it revolve that all that was visible was a gray blur, which itself seemed to grow eerily thinner and thinner as I watched, until I could see the walls through it as plainly as though there were nothing between. "The dimensional contact is about to be formed!" shouted Cloud, his tones barely audible above the vibrant noises of the machine—when all at once I was startled by a heavy crashing sound accompanied by a dazzling flare, and then gradually the rotations of the basket ceased, the sparks and the whirring died away, and silence fell upon us.

"You see? Where is the notebook?" cried Cloud, triumphantly pointing to the wire container.

I looked, and gasped—the notebook was gone!

"It's somewhere in the Fourth Dimension," the inventor continued. "Hundreds and maybe thousands of years away. But now to get it back."

Then once more he pulled the levers; once more the mirrors twisted and paraded back and forth; once more there was a whirring sound, a clattering and a flashing of lights; once more the wire basket rotated so rapidly that it dwindled to invisibility; once more there came the thunderous crash and the brilliant flare—after which the noises and the movements by degrees ceased, and the instrument became silent as before.

But, in one way, it was not as before. "Look!" exclaimed the inventor, pointing enthusiastically to the basket. And I looked, and to my astonishment, beheld the notebook—apparently undamaged by its passage through time or space!

"What can be done with inanimate objects can be done with living men as well," declared Cloud, stroking his chin in self-congratulation, while his eyes were thin fires of enthusiasm. "As you can observe, I've at last perfected the Recall Coils. You see now why I say that, before long, I'll be able to visit the Fourth Dimension myself?"

"Yes, I see," I admitted. But what I did not see was the practical importance the invention was to have. A day or two later the man from tomorrow, looking tired and flustered, arrived by a slow train from Chicago. He returned at once to the Faculty Club, where he was reinstalled in his former quarters; and then, without even taking time to free himself from the dust of the journey, he hastened to my home, where he came unannounced and unexpected.

"I just had to see you, Professor!" he exclaimed. "You're my best friend in this century, and so I just had to see you after being away so long. Heavens but I've had a strenuous time of it! It does feel good to be back home again."

So saying, he stretched his travel-worn form over the full length of a new tapestried sofa, and stared at me out of eyes that brimmed with pleasure, although in the background I seemed to sense unsounded depths of sadness.

"Yes," he said, "that pleasure trip may have been beneficial, but it certainly was hard work! This age doesn't seem to know anything of the real luxury of travel. It thinks that it must take its vacations the way it takes its business deals—in a terrific rush. Heaven forbid that it should have a moment of leisure! The result is that, being unable to assimilate all that it does, it suffers from a sort of sightseers' indigestion—a malady for which no remedy is known to science. To come to think of it, of course, that is just what I should have expected in the Neurotic Age."

"Well, now, Wormwood, suppose you forget all that." I returned, wondering if it were possible for him to pin his mind down to practical questions. "Don't you think you'd better be looking toward the future? You've come back in debt, you know, and the question is what you're to do—"

"Yes, yes, I realize that," he admitted, sadly, as his thin hand disconsolately stroked his uneven chin. "This age, I see, has a prejudice against a man without money. Why, for example, in Chicago, as I was standing on a street corner, not knowing what to do with myself, a policeman accosted me and came near to putting me in handcuffs when he found I had only a few pennies and nothing to do with my time. As if the way to help a man that's down is to kick him! I saved myself a lot of trouble only after assuring that policeman that I was waiting for some money and would leave town in a few hours. Otherwise, I might have had to paralyze him—which, I'm afraid, would have been very embarrassing."

"Thank heaven, you spared him!" I muttered, thinking it would have been still more embarrassing had I received a hurry call to Chicago to rescue my friend from a cell.

"So it's clear enough," Wormwood resumed, "I'll have to earn some more dollars now. Isn't money a queer thing?—seems to curse one like a two-edged sword. It's a torment when you haven't got it, and still more of a torment when you have. No wonder insanity was so prevalent in the Neurotic Age! Well, I must resign myself. I suppose I'll attempt some more writing. Maybe *The World's Affairs* would want me to do some new articles."

"Maybe they would," I agreed. "Why not try them?" Wormwood saw no objection to this idea, and, after a little further urging, promised to write immediately to the editor of *The World's Affairs*.

But there was one problem that still weighed upon his mind. Even after he had risen to leave, he lingered hesitantly, as though reluctant to go without mentioning a secret.

"Have you seen Miss Whitcomb of late?" he finally asked, almost with the diffidence of a schoolboy. And he stammered slightly as he continued, "I—I have been thinking of her often. Of all the ladies I have met in this century, she is the most charming. She would not seem out of place in the twenty-third century. I hope she has received my little souvenir? I have been wondering, for she did not acknowledge it. Do you suppose I might try to see her soon? Think she would be home tonight—"

"Miss Whitcomb is away on her vacation," I stated, sternly. "She has gone to Isolation Lake. Dr. Horn is there also. Probably she will not be back for two or three weeks."

"Really? Well, that is too bad," he sighed, with a woe-begone expression. "Then I shall have to wait. Yes, I shall have to wait. There is no other way, I suppose."

Once more I was about to remonstrate with Wormwood on his undue solicitation about the fiancée of another man; but the thought struck me that my words would be wasted. Besides, there was something so genuinely sorrowful about the spectacle of his drooping lips and eyes that I had not the heart to try to reason with him.

CHAPTER TWENTY-TWO
The Brewing of Disaster

WHEN I look back upon the culminating episode in the twentieth century career of the man from tomorrow, the stream of events seems to have moved so rapidly and strangely that even today, although all that happened is a well-known and often repeated story, I am left a little bewildered and incredulous. Had I not been the personal witness of many of the incidents; did I not have the testimony of unimpeachable observers in regard to those incidents which I did not witness, I should be inclined to dismiss the whole tale as the fabric of a baseless imagination. But there is, unfortunately, no possibility of arguing with facts; and so, while I look back with amazement and dismay upon the scenes immediately preceding Wormwood's exit, I am unable to deny their reality. All that I can attempt is to present them in as simple and as accurate a fashion as possible so that the reader may be able to judge for himself while sharing in the conflicting emotions—the astonishment, the relief, the confusion, the regret—which agitate me even as I write…

The beginning of the end—although who could have suspected that fact—is to be dated from Wormwood's acceptance of a commission to write a new series of articles for *The World's Affairs*.

It was only after prolonged coaxing on my part that the man from tomorrow could be induced to accept the offer. Not that the proposed terms were not liberal enough; not that the suggested work did not suit him, or that he expected to find a more desirable opening elsewhere! It was merely that the editor, in commenting upon Wormwood's previous contributions, had been guilty of a tactless remark.

"Our readers enjoyed your articles exceedingly," he declared in a letter to the man from tomorrow. "Numbers of persons have written in that they have rarely read anything more amusing."

"Now what do you think of that?" demanded Wormwood, as he flung the letter indignantly toward me. "You know me better than to suppose I meant to say anything amusing. Why, I was presenting a serious comparison of my own century and the present one! I pointed out the faults of this age, and tried to show the way to improvement. You don't know how much in earnest I was. How hard I labored over every word. And now people think I'm a humorist!"

"Well, Wormwood," I said, noticing what a disgruntled expression he was wearing, "don't be too downhearted. Isn't it the fate of all great men…to be misunderstood?"

"I'll never write for that editor again. Never. Never!" he swore. "All my efforts would be lost. My good ideas thrown into the waste-heap. Why should I rack my brains to make some adolescent smile? They think me funny, do they? Well, after this they can laugh at some other clown!"

"But, my dear friend," I pleaded, "do you think it will be different if you write for any other magazine? Besides, what harm if people do laugh a bit? I thought you said one of the troubles with the Neurotic Age is that it takes itself too seriously?"

"Well, that is so," he reflected. "Of course, that is so." Yet still he did not seem convinced. It was only by virtue of half an hour's argumentation, during which I again reverted forcibly to the practical necessities of the situation, that he begrudgingly agreed to accept the offer of *The World's Affairs.*

And thus, unwittingly, he paved the way for the bewildering climax of his career.

The articles, which Wormwood was to write, were all to be commentaries on current events. He was to witness various occurrences important and unimportant, and was to give his opinion of them from the point of view of the twenty-third century. Among other things, he was to attend a baseball game; a political meeting; a University Commencement; a reception to some visiting Admirals; a public debate; a literary forum—and in each case he was to try to tell how the event would have seemed in the twenty-third century. Unfortunately, I have not time to linger over his comments, which are available to anyone who will take the trouble to consult the files of *The World's Affairs;* I need only say that, although Wormwood still wrote with serious intent, I could not help agreeing with the editor all to the deliriously funny nature of his articles. Even the dullest reader could hardly have helped chuckling when he attended a conference of leading Senators and Representatives and characterized them all as in their Decadent Epoch; or when he went to a grand opera and mistook it for burlesque owing to the exaggerated gestures of the actors. I believe, indeed, that had it not been for that unexpected circumstances, which overwhelmed all our plans and projects, the man from tomorrow would in a short while have won a reputation as America's leading humorist.

The all-important assignment was one that at first seemed ordinary enough. A notorious murder case had been filling all the newspapers—notorious not because the crime had been exceptionally flagrant, but because there had been considerable question about the criminal intent of the accused, whose case had been appealed and whose sentence had been reprieved time and again, until at last it seemed doubtful whether he actually would go to the electric chair. His crime at worst, his defenders maintained, had been committed not willfully but under the influence of an overmastering passion—which, of course, was not a justification, but did offer arguments for those who believed that his sentence should be commuted. In the end, however, all pleas and investigations had been of no avail, and upon the Governor's refusal for a final petition, Thomas Brogan's remaining days had been reduced to a mere thirty.

It was at this point that the man from tomorrow was commissioned by *The World's Affairs* to visit Sing Sing Penitentiary and interview the doomed party. Permission to enter the Death House had been granted by the prison authorities, and Wormwood duly made ready for the short trip to Ossining. But he did not seem to relish his task; and, before setting out, he expressed himself in no uncertain terms.

"So? In the Neurotic Age, they still considered it right to take human life…? Well, I have often read in our histories of the horrors of those uncivilized days, when punishment was so much more severe and crime so much more plentiful. It was only when the extreme penalty was abolished and human life came into greater respect, that murder ceased to be common. But, of course, one had to expect many murders in an age when men were trained for wholesale killing in warfare."

"Some more conversation in the same vein followed; and then Wormwood, after asking what train to take to Ossining and noting down the directions, shook my hand in his usual enthusiastic manner and jauntily departed…

It was under strikingly altered circumstances that our next meeting occurred. Yet how little intimation I had of the approaching change! On the following day I received a telephone call from Wormwood, who informed me in a cheerful voice that he had been to Ossining, where he had had "some very interesting experiences." He expressed regret at not being able to see me and describe those experiments at present, but declared that he must leave at once for Washington to attend a Congressional Reception, and would probably return at about six or seven the following evening.

All of this, of course, I heard with only a casual interest. It was not before another twenty-four hours that I suddenly understood what importance attached to Wormwood's commonplace words—an importance that he himself came far from realizing.

At about five o'clock on the afternoon of my friend's promised return, I was annoyed by the arrival of two unexpected visitors. They were grim, frigid-looking men, with heavy, thick-boned faces and suspicious eyes; and I did not like the way they scowled at me as I came down to greet them. Nor was I pleased at the stars they showed me beneath their ordinary-looking gray coats. "Well, gentlemen," I said, mechanically, wondering what on earth the officers could want with me, "is there anything I can do for you? Be seated, won't you?"

My visitors thanked me, but remained standing. "Sorry to disturb you, Professor Howard," began the elder of the pair, as he fumbled jerkily at his Derby hat. "Do you know anything of a man named John Wormwood?"

"John Wormwood?" I echoed, astonished. "Why, I—yes, I do know him."

The two policemen exchanged significant glances.

"Now Professor," continued my interviewer, "we get your name at the Faculty Club of your University. They told us you would know where to find Mr. Wormwood. He was not there when we came to call on him, which—er, under the circumstances, we might have expected."

"Under what circumstances?" I demanded, unhappily convinced that the man from tomorrow had gotten into a dangerous scrape.

Disregarding my question, the officer proceeded. "At the Faculty Club, no one seemed to knew where Wormwood was, or when he would return. It's very important to find him, and you, Professor Howard, are the man to help us. If you will give me some clue—"

"Sorry, gentlemen," I interrupted, deciding upon a course of action. "I see that you are upon the wrong track. I can give you no clue. I do not know where Mr. Wormwood is. The last I saw of him was the day before yesterday, and I cannot say when I shall see him again. If, however, I do get track of him eventually, and you wish to be notified—"

"Notified, nothing!" flung back one of the men, with a snarl. "No, we're not asking to be notified! You understand, Professor Howard, the penalties for deliberately withholding information!"

At this impudent outburst, I had an impulse to retort angrily and order my callers out of the house. But, realizing that strategy is the better part of discretion, I managed to control myself, and to assume my sweetest most suave tones:

"You are wasting your time, gentlemen. You may be sure that, if I could, I would do anything to assist you. Here is the best I can arrange—I'll give you the name of someone who is often in touch with Mr. Wormwood and may be able to help you. Better take this down:

The name is Professor Warrington—Charles Warrington—1119 Morningside Drive."

My visitors noted down the name and address; thanked me brusquely; bowed, and departed.

Immediately after they had left, I reached for the telephone, and called a familiar number.

"Tell me, Warrington," one might have heard me saying, "do you know the latest about Wormwood? What sort of mess has he been getting into...? Oh! Read this afternoon's paper, you say! I certainly shall. By the way, I'm afraid you're soon to have two visitors. Receive them warmly, Warrington; express your willingness to help them—but, for heaven's sake, don't give them any information... What's that? You'll pass them on to Professor Carroway? Fine...! Well, I'll be looking now for that paper."

After snapping down the receiver, I reached in excited haste for my hat, and, a moment later, was rushing toward the nearest newspaper stand at such a rate that some of my neighbors, having grown accustomed to my usual leisurely pace, paused to stare at me, as though fearing I had gone mad.

What new bit of insanity had the man from tomorrow perpetrated? I asked myself. Was it that he had gone back to wearing his twenty-third century costume? Or that, in the too-zealous attempt to paralyze someone, he had unintentionally committed murder?

Oppressed by such doubts, I reached the newspaper stand, flung down a few pennies, and picked up a copy of the afternoon Star. At the first glance, I observed nothing to interest me; there was little except the usual news about the riots in India, and about the proposed increase in naval armaments following the successful limitations conference. "Wonder what Warrington could have meant?" I muttered—and then, all at once, I saw! The article had escaped my attention because of its very prominence!

Spread over several columns at the top of the page, the following headlines met my eye:

"RIOT AT SING SING
"DEATH-HOUSE CONVICT FELLS GUARD"
"Checked in Attempt at Escape—Wormwood Sought."

Regardless of the stares of passers-by, I stood openmouthed at the street corner, grasping the paper with trembling fingers, and reading:

"A riot at Sing Sing penitentiary was suppressed this morning with the aid of machine-guns, after Thomas Brogan, under sentence of death for the murder of Frederick Cramm, had broken loose with firearms and overpowered two guards. Brogan, who had secured the weapon surreptitiously and secreted it beneath his clothing, declared, under pressure, that he had received it from John Wormwood, the alleged visitor from the twenty-third century, who had secured admittance recently as interviewer for a well-known magazine. Wormwood is now being sought by the police..."

CHAPTER TWENTY-THREE
Strategy and Flight

WHILE the article in the Star offered me only the vaguest and most unsatisfactory notion of what had happened, I had read enough to know that Wormwood's situation was desperate. I could not imagine how he had managed to secure firearms; much less could I understand what motive he had had in offering the weapons to the prisoner; but one thing at least was clear, agonizingly clear—he was guilty of a gross violation of the law, and was faced with the probability of a long prison term.

From that peril, obviously, he must be saved at any cost. Though no one had suffered more than I from the absurdities of Wormwood's conduct, or had been put to greater expense in time, temper and money, I would have been the last to wish him behind the bars. I must confess, now that I had discovered his danger, that I realized how strangely I was attached to the man from tomorrow; somehow, for all his curious manners and beliefs, he had earned a claim upon my affections, which it was impossible either to reason about or deny.

Yet what could I do to help him? Obviously, he must be warned; for in my telephone conversation with him only yesterday, he had shown no consciousness of danger. Then somehow his whereabouts must be kept from the police; and, above all, he must not return to the Faculty Club—for nothing was more certain than that the detectives would be in waiting for him there.

Yet, if no efforts were made to save him, would he not return from Washington within an hour or two? Would he not hasten back to his room, and thus walk unsuspectingly into the trap the police had set for him?

It was clear that the only course was to reach him and warn him before he had returned to the Faculty Club. But how reach him and warn him? All that I knew was that, according to his own statement, Wormwood expected to be back at about six or seven o'clock—and I could not even say by what train he would travel or by what railroad he would arrive!

Yet half a chance, it seemed to me, was better than none at all; I must go to the railroad terminal by which the man from tomorrow seemed most likely to return, and must scan the passengers arriving from every Washington train. I well knew that I was more than likely to miss Wormwood; that possibly he had arrived already; that possibly he would not arrive at all today, or that in my anxiety I might overlook him even if he did come. But, regardless of such contingencies, I lost no time about going to the Maryland depot and inquiring as to the train schedule from Washington.

"The last train arrived ten minutes ago," the clerk brutally informed me. "The next will be in at 8:04"

Anxiously I glanced at my watch, and saw that it was exactly 6:16. Despondently I told myself that perhaps I had missed Wormwood by a hair's breadth; yet resignedly, in the hope that my friend had been delayed, I faced the prospect of a wait of almost two hours.

During the interval, after trying to snatch a bite at a station lunch counter and finding that I could not eat, I passed most of my minutes in vain speculation as to whether the man from tomorrow would be on the incoming train. Probably after all, I assured myself, Wormwood was already in town, and might even now be falling into the clutches of the police despite my efforts to save him.

This view was confirmed when at length the train—ten minutes late, as if for the sake of tantalizing me—had come rumbling into the station. Certainly, no fond parent or lovelorn swain ever fastened his gaze, more eagerly than did I, upon the throngs trailing through the exit; but alas, though the train seemed to have been well filled and scores of flushed and hastening passengers glided past, there was no familiar face among them all. Finally the streams of travelers began to dwindle; at last only a few slow-footed stragglers were issuing from the gateway. There came a fat lady puffing with a monstrous suitcase; then, for a brief blank interval, no one at all emerged. "You see. He's not coming," I reflected. "How foolish to have waited!" And I was about to leave—when all at once I caught sight of the man from tomorrow.

He was idling along in the most leisurely manner possible, at the side of a perfect giant of a woman with whom he was chatting energetically. In one hand he held a huge traveling hatbox; in the other he swung a covered object that looked like a parrot-cage. "Yes, Madam," he was saying, in tones loud enough to be heard at a distance, "the method of travel by private wing-motor, which hasn't been invented yet—" But it was at this point that I interrupted him.

"Wormwood! Wormwood!" I exclaimed, eagerly, regardless of the fair stranger. "I'm so glad you've come! Quick! I must speak with you…"

I thought I had never before seen such a cold and cutting light in Wormwood's eyes. "Oh, how are you, Professor?" he exclaimed, turning to me in a surprised manner. "What are you doing here today?"

And with that, I believe, he would have passed on, had I not clutched him by the arm, and insisted, "I must speak with you, I say! At once, Wormwood! It's imperative!"

Something in my manner, if not in my words, must have informed him that I was in deadly earnest. None the less, he looked annoyed, and returned, coolly, "Oh, all right. All right. Just one minute, Professor. Can't you see I'm busy now? First I must help this gallant lady with her baggage."

The "gallant lady" burst into a low tittering, and permitted her escort to accompany her as far as the Parcel Room, where he bade her farewell in the demonstrative fashion of the twenty-third century. Since I kept at a respectable distance, I could not hear what they had to say; but I observed that, before making his final bow, Wormwood took out a notebook and pencil and jotted down several words at her dictation.

"A marvelous lady!" he enthused, as he rejoined me. "So kindly and agreeable! Next to Miss Whitcomb, she is the most chivalrous I have met in the twentieth century. I first saw her in the station at Washington. It was on account of her that I missed the train before this. She was most considerate—permitted me to help her with her grips, and even to order her dinner for her. Yes, indeed, her ways are exquisite! Too bad that one of such charm should be wasting herself as saleslady in a millinery shop—"

"Come! Come, Wormwood!" I protested. "I don't doubt that you could tell me her whole family history if we had time, but there are other things to think of just now. I must talk seriously with you."

"How's that?" he demanded, regarding me questioningly. "To come to think of it now, how does it happen that you're here today, Professor?"

I glanced warily to all sides, unhappily conscious that detectives might be observing us. And though apparently we were quite inconspicuous amid the station crowd, I realized that we must spare no precautions. Hence I bent close to Wormwood, and whispered into his ear, "Wait a while. I can't answer now. Come with me, and we'll try to talk things over."

"Why the mystery?" he gasped; and then, evidently resigned to silence, he accompanied me without a word to the taxicab stand at one end of the station. On the way, I almost had heart failure, for we ran face to face with a policeman, who, however, did not seem to recognize either of us as desperate characters. Avoiding this representative of law and order, we managed to gain a cab in safety; while I, at a loss what to say to the driver, flung out this strange request, "Central Park! Any nice secluded spot!"

The startled chauffeur bade me repeat the request; and then, as if uncertain if his ears had not deceived him, he nodded in a puzzled fashion, and set the taxi into motion.

"Now Wormwood," I began, relieved to be temporarily out of danger, "let's get down to business. It seems that you've got yourself into the perfect devil of a predicament. What on earth was it that you did at Sing Sing?"

"At Sing Sing?" he repeated, in tones of undisguised surprise. "Why, I did have some interesting experiences, as I told you. But what makes you think I did anything unusual?"

"Here is what makes me think so," I declared, drawing the newspaper article from all inner pocket. "Judging by the looks of things, they'll be wanting you back at Sing Sing for a lengthy stay."

He took the paper and glanced at it by the uncertain light, while I had temporarily become a little more steady, as the taxicab halted for the traffic signals.

For a second, Wormwood was silent. "What do you think of that? Poor Brogan didn't escape!" he sighed, in tones of vast disappointment. "Poor Brogan! He didn't escape! And I thought he would get away!"

"Forget about Brogan, and read on!" I demanded, indignantly. "How about your own predicament?"

Suddenly Brogan seemed to pass out of Wormwood's mind. "Well, if that isn't the strangest thing!" he blurted out, clutching the paper angrily, while once more we began moving on our way. "What damnable lies! This paper should be made to retract! I'll write them a letter! I'll—I'll—"

With fists clenched and shaking he paused, as if not knowing how to continue.

"Then is it all false?" I inquired, in the calmest tones I could command. "Did you have nothing whatever to do with the prison riot?"

"Riot? I know nothing about the riot!" he exclaimed. Evidently that all happened after I left! All that I know is that the paper prints lies. Lies! Lies! Lies! All lies! I didn't give the convict any firearms!"

"What did you give him?" I asked, perceiving a sudden light.

"Not firearms. Even if I'd had any weapons of the Man-Eating Ages, do you think I'd have given them to anyone? Why, it's bad enough to see them in museums! I'd as soon hug a rattlesnake as handle such utensils! No, my friend! All that I gave that poor unfortunate convict were the paralyzing rays!"

My surprise was strangely confirmed. "Paralyzing rays?" I repeated. "Now I understand! But don't you see, Wormwood, that's against the law!"

"Why?" he demanded, uncomprehendingly. "What have I done against the law? I was merely doing my duty. Any humane person would have done the same. It is true, I sacrificed my rays—but that was in order to save a man's life. In this age, is it punishable to save a life?"

"Under certain circumstances," I declared. "Better tell me all about it, Wormwood. Then we may know better what to do for you."

"Well," he returned, leaning back in his seat with a grave, reminiscent expression, "it's all very simple. I saw this poor wretch, Thomas Brogan, who, I was surprised to find, was a human being like you and me—not half so vicious-looking as many men you pass on the street. I rather took a liking to the unlucky devil; he was the sort I might have made a friend of, if he hadn't been caged like a wolf. It made me almost shed tears to think how, in less than a month, he was to be coldly and mechanically taken out and shriveled to death. Think of the horror of the long waiting! He would have to die not one death but a hundred! It seemed to me that no man, no matter how guilty, should be submitted to such torture. And so I resolved to help him. Now you know that I had only one vial of the paralyzing rays, which I couldn't replace—but, just the same, I didn't have to think twice before giving them to this poor Brogan. I waited till the jail-keeper seemed momentarily off his guard; then I slyly passed them to the prisoner, and whispered, 'Watch for your chance, then point this at the jailer's breast, and press the little button near the top.' And Brogan took the rays; but though he couldn't say anything in reply, the expression in his eyes was reward enough for me."

"Now I see what has happened!" I said, slowly. "Now I see! Brogan waited a day or two before finding his chance, then paralyzed two of the jailers and tried to escape. The other guards, coming up and seeing the ray-instrument, thought it was a pistol. That's how the report about the firearms got circulated. Well, the whole affair is most unfortunate, Wormwood. Most unfortunate!"

"Yes, most unfortunate!" he agreed mournfully. "Poor old Brogan didn't even get away!"

By this time we were gliding among the winding drives of Central Park. Suddenly, in a fairly well wooded section, the car stopped short and the driver asked whether we wished to go any further. "No," I decided, emphatically. "This place is ideal." And after descending with my companion and paying the fare, I led Wormwood aside into a clump of shrubbery where, it seemed to me, we would be free to continue our discussion without fear of a dangerous intrusion.

Never had I felt so much like a criminal, as when we began our whispered conversation in that shadowy retreat. It seemed to me almost as if it were I, and not Wormwood, that was being sought by the police; I could have half-believed myself a fugitive from justice, for the darkness and secrecy of the night combined to create a sense of mystery, and I was strangely transported back to the imaginings of my early youth, when I had pictured myself involved in daring and piratical adventures...

"Now Wormwood," I began, as I huddled close to him with my back in uncomfortable proximity to a projecting rock, "we've got to get you out of your predicament—which means we must save you from the police. But how is that possible? There is nowhere in this country you can go; your twenty-third century ways would be certain to make you conspicuous. Hence, although I'm sorry to say so, there's only one course left. You've got to get out of this century."

"Got to get out of this century?" echoed the startled Wormwood, as he nervously began to rustle some dead leaves in the dark.

"Not so much noise there! Please!" I muttered. "You'll be giving yourself away," And, after he had grown silent again, I continued with, "Yes, Wormwood, you've got to get out of this century. The only safe thing will be to return the way you came—to go back to your own age, your own people."

"Ah, if only I could!" he sighed. "How often I've thought of it—how often I've been homesick for it! My hyperspace observatory—a natural life once more, with natural food, natural clothing, and a natural place to sleep. And natural people to live with—and Maranna among them! Yes, I've often been homesick for it, though it's only a dream that can never come true!"

"It's much more than a dream," I dissented. "It can come true." And briefly I told of Cloud's invention for projecting a man into the Fourth Dimension.

Wormwood, however, did not seem impressed. "In my own times," he declared, "it was mere child's play to get into the Fourth Dimension. But how is that possible for you twentieth century folk? As I've told you before, you have no molecular compressors, no radio-propeller gauges, no—"

"But all that doesn't matter!" I broke in, abruptly. And I described the experiment I had witnessed, in which a small notebook had been whirled out of our dimension, and then recovered.

"Well, yes—in a crude way, maybe it is possible for you to get into the Fourth Dimension," Wormwood conceded, begrudgingly. "What makes me most doubtful is though I've made a study of the subject, that I can't remember reading that any successful Dimension Traversers were invented so early as the twentieth century. However, being really anxious to get back to my own times, I'd be ready to do anything reckless. Yes, I'd even take a chance with one of your primitive models."

"Good," I said, as I shifted my position slightly and painfully scratched my hands on some invisible creeper. "Then shall we pay a visit to Mr. Cloud?"

"Well, yes, perhaps. But aren't you being just a little hasty?" he argued. "It's all right to leave this century, but I don't like to be exactly rushed out of it. I think it's only fair to take a few minutes before deciding on a change of three hundred years. There are several things still weighing on my mind."

"What things?" I inquired, wondering what there could be to weigh upon his mind by comparison with the fact that he was wanted by the police.

For several seconds he was silent. In the darkness, unfortunately, I could not see the expression of his face; eventually something that sounded like a sigh issued from between his lips. He shifted uneasily; he cleared his throat, then coughed before continuing:

"Well, you see, Professor, it's this way. There is a lovely lady who—er—whom I don't like to be deserting. Can't you guess whom I mean?"

"Alice Whitcomb!" I caught up, impatiently. "Well, forget about her, Wormwood! She's not for you! Why, she wouldn't care what century you're sent to!"

"Now it would be a terrible thing," he continued, mournfully, "to get back to my own century, and then to remember that the charming Alice Whitcomb is dead—dead for nearly three hundred years. No, I could never bear that thought. What if it does cause me some suffering? I'll be loyal! I'll stay in this century! I'll take my chances of going to prison! For her sake, I'll take my chances!"

In his excitement, the man from tomorrow lifted his voice to such a pitch, that I began to fear we would be discovered. At the same time, he swung out his arms in eloquent gesticulations, barely missing my nose in the dark, and not missing the shrubbery, with which his hands collided with a sharp, threshing sound.

"For heaven's sake, Wormwood, be quiet!" I cautioned. "If you keep on that way, you'll never get back to your own times…"

Then all at once, as I recalled a letter that I had received yesterday or the day before and deposited in my portfolio, I began to fumble about anxiously in my pocket.

"Look at this, Wormwood," I pointed out, striking a match and dimly making out the envelope by the momentary glow. "I want to show you how much cause you have to be thinking of Miss Whitcomb."

Wormwood leaned close to me; while, striking a second match, I showed him a tiny notation. "This letter, you see, is from Dr. Horn."

"Yes, I see," he acknowledged, as the light fluttered into darkness. "But what has that to do with me?"

"Now notice what Dr. Horn says," I continued, while, with shaking hands, I lit a third match, and, in my nervousness, nearly set fire to the paper.

The match flared, flickered, and went out; but, by its dying illumination, the man from tomorrow was able to decipher the first words of the letter. "Dear Professor," he read, in a shaky voice, "Alice and I were married last night—"

As we plunged once more into darkness, a low, distinct moan came from Wormwood's throat. I felt his hand grasping my wrist with a shuddering intensity; I felt the quivers that ran through his whole body; I heard his mournful words, "So! So she has betrayed me. She was not loyal. She would not give me a chance. She would not wait for me. She took another instead! Oh, that is unworthy of her. How much, much less chivalrous than I had thought!"

I said nothing, but waited for the outburst to subside.

"Why did she have to be in ever such a hurry? Why? Oh Why?" he continued, most passionately. "Why did she have to take him...to take him...when she could have had someone like me? Oh, how greatly disappointed I am in her. How disappointed! Not even to let me know. Never, never have I been so betrayed before..."

The man from tomorrow bent low, his face buried in his sleeves; despite his silence, I could have half-imagined that he was giving way to sobs.

But after a few moments, he suddenly flung his head upward, and, with a resigned gesture and in a changed voice, resumed. "Come. Take me back to my own age, Professor. Take me back! I have seen enough of this century! It has robbed and cheated me too much. It has robbed and cheated me, and has given nothing in return! I want my own age, and Maranna—I want Maranna once more…"

He stared off into the distance a few moments longer, then abruptly rose to leave. By the vague light of the ascending moon, I saw that his eyes were mistily shining; while he walked with face downcast, and his shoulders drooped as though beneath some intolerable weight.

CHAPTER TWENTY-FOUR
The Disappearance

By the time that we had reached Cloud's apartment, it was after ten o'clock. I did not know whether the inventor would be at home, or whether, on the other hand, we should have to disturb his slumbers; but, in any event, I considered our mission urgent enough to justify the unexpectedness of our call.

As we alighted from the taxicab, I was able to glance up toward Cloud's windows, which were on the second floor left. Much to my relief, I could see bright chinks of light issuing from behind the drawn shades; as a result of which I became so excited that I did not even wait for my change from the taxicab driver, but flutteringly hastened with Wormwood into the building and up the stairs.

A moment later, upon pressing the inventor's doorbell, I was disconcerted to hear something that sounded like a growl from within. A minute passed, and the door was not opened; I was forced to ring a second time, and even a third, before I could evoke any response. "Who the devil is there?" finally came an irritated voice. "What do you want?"

I am afraid that my own voice sounded more than a little irritated as I called back, "It's we, Cloud! Can't you let us in?"

Abruptly the door opened, to reveal an annoyed-looking Cloud, clad in a dressing gown discolored with chemicals.

"Oh, you, Professor!" he exclaimed, in evident surprise, as he took my hand. "And you, Mr. Wormwood. I thought it was the landlord. He always picks the most ungodly hours to call for the rent. Well, come in and make yourselves at home."

Without another word he led us into his laboratory, where the Dimension Machine gleamed and glittered with rods and mirrors unbared. Since I had last seen it, I noticed, several changes had been made, of which the most conspicuous was in the shape of a wire container, more than five feet in height and several feet across, which replaced the smaller receptacle used in the experiment with the notebook. At the opposite end of the machine a series of blue and purplish sparks was flickering and buzzing; while, close at hand, a mad confusion of tongs, pliers and other tools lay strewn about the floor.

"Just now, when you got here," stated Cloud, as we entered the room. "I was at work on a Dimensional Inter-calculator. Another little kink or two smoothed out, and it will be perfect. An idea had occurred to me just as you rang the bell. You don't mind waiting a few minutes, do you?"

"Not at all!" I was bound to assure him. Yet I was quivering with such impatience that every moment of delay was certain to be a moment in Purgatory.

With glittering-eyed eagerness, Cloud went back to his pliers; and, seemingly forgetful of our presence, began to work once more at his machine. The sparks lashed and scintillated; the levers moved and rattled; the inventor's face glowed with an excited interest; but the clock on the wall continued to tick and tick and tick and tick never-endingly, while Wormwood and I fidgeted and waited.

Nearly an hour had gone by before at last the inventor gave a triumphant whoop. "It's done!" he ejaculated. "Done! The Inter-calculator is finished! Look at that, will you? Works like a charm! Come, want to see?"

"Not now! Please, not just now, Mr. Cloud," I protested. "We have something much more urgent to consult you about."

"More urgent?" he repeated, in surprise, seeming for the first time to realize that there may have been a reason for our visit. And then, all at once penitent, he apologized. "I'm sorry, I had forgotten about your coming here. I was so interested in the Inter-calculator that I couldn't pin my thoughts down to anything else. You really must pardon me. Now let's hear what's on your mind, Professor."

Solemnly I took a seat opposite the inventor; while Wormwood stood looking on speechlessly, I launched into a full description of the events of the day, from the visit of the detectives to Wormwood's acceptance of my plan to send him back to the twenty-third century.

"Now, Mr. Cloud," I concluded, "it seems to me the question to decide is whether the machine is ready for Wormwood's return. Judging from what you told me when I was here last, and from what I myself saw—"

"Yes, yes, I understand," Cloud interrupted, with a thoughtful wave of the hand. "The Dimension Bridge, of course, is complete, so that it will be possible to leave this dimension at any time now. I myself was planning to make the experiment within a few days. But there's just one little question in my mind. That is to there is just one little trouble."

"What trouble?" I demanded, anxiously. "Nothing serious, I hope?"

Cloud hesitated perceptibly. "No, nothing really serious. It's only a technical detail—the Reverse Brakes need a little adjustment. You realize what would happen if they should fail. After sending a man out of this century, we couldn't be sure of ever being able get him back again."

"Oh, is that all?" I laughed. "Well, that's all right. Once Wormwood has left this century, I'm sure he won't want to return."

"I can imagine no more terrible misfortune than to have to come back," affirmed Wormwood. "So, you see, I'm not at all sorry the Reverse Brakes are out of Order."

"Oh, well, if that's the way you feel about it," agreed Cloud, "no doubt I can help you. Since you're all ready to leave, we can commence at once. There will be only a few preliminaries to arrange."

"All right. Go ahead, arrange the preliminaries," sighed Wormwood. And then, as he caught sight of his reflection in one of the mirrors, he sighed again, and murmured, "Too bad! I'm really not in any condition at all to go on such a long journey. Couldn't we possibly—couldn't we possibly wait till tomorrow?"

"Wait till tomorrow?" I cried, as Cloud began a final critical inspection of the mirrors and levers. "Are you crazy? Tomorrow you may not be permitted to leave."

"Well," he explained, as he dolefully regarded himself in the mirror, "I was just thinking that if we waited till tomorrow, I might be able to get my own clothes back. I mean, the suit I came here in. Can you imagine what the people of my own century will say if they see me in these things? Can you imagine how Maranna will laugh? Why, wouldn't you laugh yourself if you saw a man all locked up in a fifteenth century coat of mail? When you come to think of it, wouldn't it be much better to wear nothing at all?"

With that, Wormwood started to slough off his coat. I fear that, had I not made a motion to restrain him, he would not have checked himself until every other garment had followed.

"Better give me a few minutes more," Cloud requested, as he bent down to tighten a screw on one of the mirrors. "I want to make sure that everything is in place. There's no telling what would happen if even one rod or lever got loose."

"You know, Cloud," I encouraged, "I'm coming to admire your work more and more each day. After you've done a good job for Wormwood, you may be sure my colleagues and I will spare no efforts to bring your achievements world-wide recognition."

Cloud smiled, thanked me, and proceeded with his work with increased gusto.

Meanwhile the man from tomorrow, his thin face drawn into a funereal expression, had come to me and firmly taken both my hands.

"Professor," he declared—and, as he spoke, there were tears in his eyes. "I want you to know how hard this parting will be for me. I have greatly appreciated your friendship, and for your sake I would almost be willing to remain in this century. I shall not forget you in my own age; it will be a deep sorrow to know how long you have been dead. But I shall revere your memory, Professor. Yes, you may be sure I shall revere your memory."

I thanked him rather coldly, I fear; for I was not exactly anxious to be reduced to a mere memory.

"After I get back to the twenty-third century," Wormwood continued, meditatively, "I wonder how long I will seem to have been away. Perhaps not an hour; perhaps not even a minute. I may not seem to have been gone at all. They may tell me my adventures in the twentieth century were only a dream. Ah, well! Maybe that's what they really are. Already they seem pretty much like a dream to me. After I've been back a while, I may even be ready to laugh at them myself. But, at any rate, I may tell of them to Maranna occasionally on summer evenings when we sit together in the moon-parlor of the Observatory, or go flying around Mount Holrood on our private tri-plane. And Maranna at least will be real enough. After all, Professor, the ladies of the twenty-third century are the most honorable, the most steadfast. I'm coming to the conclusion that it's really a mistake to love out of one's own century."

"It's a mistake to do anything at all out of one's own century," I was on the point of remarking—when Cloud announced that he had finished his inspection of the machine and had found it in perfect readiness for the experiment.

"Now we'll set the Dimension Gauge for three hundred years ahead," continued the inventor, turning to a device like an enlarged radio dial. "You see, it's an improvement on the old apparatus, which was likely to be century or two off in its bearings. With this new contrivance, we can gauge our time down to the fraction of a year."

"I should hope so," mumbled Wormwood, anxiously. It would be a trifle annoying to be deposited by mistake in the twenty-fourth century—or in the twenty-second."

"Oh, never fear!" Cloud consoled him, as he cautiously adjusted the dial. "Now there...it's all fixed. Nothing left but to get into the Dimension Carrier and set things going!"

With these words, the inventor stepped toward the large wire case at one end of the machine. "Guess I'd better show you in what position to lie, so as to avoid dangerous after-effects," he proceeded. And, stepping onto a chair, he let himself down into a wire apparatus, in the bottom of which he curled up like a snail.

Then it was that, while I stood staring questioningly at Cloud, there occurred that unexpected event, the recollection of which bewilders and torments me even today.

As the inventor climbed into the wire container, Wormwood's excitement was rising by leaps and bounds. A flush had come into his face; his limbs were quivering; his fingers restlessly tapped and tapped at his clothing; his eyes were a-glitter with a wild, impatient fire. I believe that, in his agitation, he momentarily lost control of himself; at all events, he certainly did not take time to reason, but gave way to the unbridled impulses of the moment. When he saw Cloud at the bottom of the wire cage and heard the shouted words, "All right…all right now," he evidently misunderstood, and did not pause to consider that what Cloud meant was that his demonstration of the proper position was all right. Hearing, apparently, only what he desired to hear, he assumed that he had been directed to enter the machine. With disconcerting haste, he leaped on the chair, his hands grasping the steel supports of the container, and began to let himself down beside the inventor.

Now things began to happen with lightning rapidity. At first Cloud, seeing the man from tomorrow entering the wire cage was merely startled and annoyed. "Wait a minute, there!" he cried. "Let me out first! You're making things hard—"

But, almost immediately, his annoyance gave place to alarm. "For God's sake!" he yelled, as he sprang to his feet—and all at once his face went white. "For God's sake, get your foot off there! Don't, don't touch that!"

His warning had come too late. "Don't touch what?" cried the man from tomorrow, already more than half in the container. But, even as he spoke, he had raised his foot against a little half-concealed knob. And, with that, the damage had been done.

Suddenly there came a violent hissing sound; suddenly the atmosphere began to flare with the scintillation of blue sparks. The levers of the machine commenced to twist and unlock, the wires to buzz and clatter, the mirrors to turn and rotate; a confusion of indescribable reflections met my eyes, and I was aware that the wire cage, with Cloud and Wormwood in it, was beginning to revolve at a dizzying rate.

"Oh, my God, now you've done it!" came the frantic voice of Cloud. "Professor! Professor! Pull the reverse! Quick Pull the reverse! Quick…before it's too late!"

With frenzied speed, and at the risk of losing a hand beneath the swiftly propelled rods, I pulled what I imagined to be the proper lever. But, in my haste, I must have touched off the accelerator by mistake; for instantly the sparks and sputtering grew much more violent; the levers began to vibrate more rapidly than ever, the mirrors to rotate at a delirious rate. And the wire container, with its two human occupants, whirled round and round faster and faster, faster and faster, and ever faster. Vaguely, above the clattering of the bars and glasses, I could hear the terrified cries of the imprisoned men but I had lost sight of them utterly; so swiftly were they being swung round and round that they made but a mottled blur through which, after a moment, the yellow blankness of the opposite wall became visible.

I shall never be able to say how that mad scene came to an end. I do not believe that more than sixty seconds went by before it was all over; but I was scarcely aware of what I saw, heard, or did; I acted with the mechanical fury of a wild man. Ignorant as I was of Cloud's machine, I fumbled recklessly with the knobs and levers, in the crazed hope that chance might show me the Reverse; I turned dials; I pressed buttons; I shifted rods; I switched on electric bulbs. Yet everything that I did seemed only to increase the speed and fury of the rotating mirrors and the insane haste of the whirling wire container. Had I been in possession of my senses, the straining, cracking noises of the overstressed machine would have warned me of danger; but, in my panic, I had no ear for warnings, and continued crazily to press buttons and pull levers—until all at once, with such suddenness that I cannot account for it even now, there came a deafening report. A flash of fire seemed to leap across the room and through my very brain; I was conscious of a dull, reeling sensation, as though I had been struck by a club; then instantly all things went blank before me, and I was swept into oblivion.

When I came to myself again, my head was still oppressed by a dull sensation, and I was vaguely aware that there were bandages above my eyes. My first feeling was one of utter confusion, as though I were dreaming, or had died and awakened in another world; and it was only by degrees that I recognized that I was in bed, and made out the details of a neat, white-walled room that seemed strangely unfamiliar. Not until the entrance of a woman in scrupulous white, with the precise and orderly manners of a trained nurse, did it dawn upon my clouded consciousness that I was in the hospital; and then for some time I could not make out the reason for being in such a place.

"Be quiet and try to sleep," the woman whispered to me. "You are still very weak. You have been through a severe strain..."

Several days later, when my wounds were healing and I was well enough to sit up in bed, I was told what had happened. The explosion that had felled me had been so loud as to send several of the neighbors rushing in alarm to Cloud's apartment. Summoning a policeman, they had broken down the door; and, entering, they had found me cut and bruised and apparently lifeless on the floor, in the midst of a wilderness of shattered mirrors, twisted steel rods, and broken wires and coils. At first they had given me up for dead, and it had been hours before I had shown signs of returning consciousness; indeed, I had survived only by a miracle, for the explosion had occurred with such violence as to bury steel bolts and screws deep in the walls and to wreck the Dimension Machine beyond possibility of repair.

Almost the first question I asked, when again capable of speaking, was whether any other human beings had been found in the room. But my informant looked surprised, and assured me, "No, you were quite alone. There was no sign that anyone else had been present."

So, after all, I reflected, the man from tomorrow had left this dimension. But the worst of it was that Cloud had left with him! He would never reap the fruits of his genius; his miraculous invention was lost irredeemably!

Yet had he and Wormwood actually gone to the twenty-third century? What if, owing to my interference, the machine had been thrown out of gear, depositing them in the twenty-first century—or in the twenty-eighth? Alas, either possibility might have come to pass, and the truth would never be known to me!

The police, however, report that they are following several important clues.

If I was mystified, however, I was not alone in my doubts. In testimony to the fact, I quote from a newspaper article, which is only typical of many that appeared a short while after the disaster:

"MYSTERIOUS DISAPPEARANCE OF WORMWOOD

"Man Wanted on Felony Charge Eludes Police."

The local police profess themselves still baffled at the disappearance of John Wormwood, known as 'The Man from Tomorrow,' who is wanted on a charge of inciting a riot at Sing Sing Penitentiary. Descriptions and photographs of the alleged felon have been flashed to every city on the continent, and departing trains and steamers are being carefully watched. Several arrests have been made, but in every case the suspect has had to be released. Professor Ellery Howard, who is reputed to have been intimate with Wormwood, and who is now at Vanderbrook Hospital recovering from a recent accident, refuses to make any statement except that he has no knowledge of the missing man's whereabouts and expect within a few days to have the supposed culprit safely behind the bars."

THE END

If you've enjoyed this book, you will not want to miss these terrific titles...

ARMCHAIR SCI-FI, FANTASY, & HORROR DOUBLE NOVELS, $12.95 each

D-1   **THE GALAXY RAIDERS** by William P. McGivern
          SPACE STATION #1 by Frank Belknap Long

D-2   **THE PROGRAMMED PEOPLE** by Jack Sharkey
          SLAVES OF THE CRYSTAL BRAIN by William Carter Sawtelle

D-3   **YOU'RE ALL ALONE** by Fritz Leiber
          THE LIQUID MAN by Bernard C. Gilford

D-4   **CITADEL OF THE STAR LORDS** by Edmund Hamilton
          VOYAGE TO ETERNITY by Milton Lesser

D-5   **IRON MEN OF VENUS** by Don Wilcox
          THE MAN WITH ABSOLUTE MOTION by Noel Loomis

D-6   **WHO SOWS THE WIND...** by Rog Phillips
          THE PUZZLE PLANET by Robert A. W. Lowndes

D-7   **PLANET OF DREAD** by Murray Leinster
          TWICE UPON A TIME by Charles L. Fontenay

D-8   **THE TERROR OUT OF SPACE** by Dwight V. Swain
          QUEST OF THE GOLDEN APE by Ivar Jorgensen and Adam Chase

D-9   **SECRET OF MARRACOTT DEEP** by Henry Slesar
          PAWN OF THE BLACK FLEET by Mark Clifton.

D-10 **BEYOND THE RINGS OF SATURN** by Robert Moore Williams
          A MAN OBSESSED by Alan E. Nourse

ARMCHAIR SCIENCE FICTION CLASSICS, $12.95 each

C-1   **THE GREEN MAN**
          by Harold M. Sherman

C-2   **A TRACE OF MEMORY**
          By Keith Laumer

C-3   **INTO PLUTONIAN DEPTHS**
          by Stanton A. Coblentz

ARMCHAIR MASTERS OF SCIENCE FICTION SERIES, $16.95 each

M-1   **MASTERS OF SCIENCE FICTION, Vol. One**
          Bryce Walton—"Dark of the Moon" and other tales

M-2   **MASTERS OF SCIENCE FICTION, Vol. Two**
          Jerome Bixby—"One Way Street" and other tales

If you've enjoyed this book, you will not want to miss these terrific titles…

ARMCHAIR SCI-FI & HORROR DOUBLE NOVELS, $12.95 each

D-11   **PERIL OF THE STARMEN** by Kris Neville
THE STRANGE INVASION by Murray Leinster

D-12   **THE STAR LORD** by Boyd Ellanby
CAPTIVES OF THE FLAME by Samuel R. Delany

D-13   **MEN OF THE MORNING STAR** by Edmund Hamilton
PLANET FOR PLUNDER by Hal Clement and Sam Merwin, Jr.

D-14   **ICE CITY OF THE GORGON** by Chester S. Geier and Richard Shaver
WHEN THE WORLD TOTTERED by Lester del Rey

D-15   **WORLDS WITHOUT END** by Clifford D. Simak
THE LAVENDER VINE OF DEATH by Don Wilcox

D-16   **SHADOW ON THE MOON** by Joe Gibson
ARMAGEDDON EARTH by Geoff St. Reynard

D-17   **THE GIRL WHO LOVED DEATH** by Paul W. Fairman
SLAVE PLANET by Laurence M. Janifer

D-18   **SECOND CHANCE** by J. F. Bone
MISSION TO A DISTANT STAR by Frank Belknap Long

D-19   **THE SYNDIC** by C. M. Kornbluth
FLIGHT TO FOREVER by Poul Anderson

D-20   **SOMEWHERE I'LL FIND YOU** by Milton Lesser
THE TIME ARMADA by Fox B. Holden

ARMCHAIR SCIENCE FICTION CLASSICS, $12.95 each

C-4   **CORPUS EARTHLING**
by Louis Charbonneau

C-5   **THE TIME DISSOLVER**
by Jerry Sohl

C-6   **WEST OF THE SUN**
by Edgar Pangborn

ARMCHAIR SCIENCE FICTION & HORROR GEMS SERIES, $12.95 each

G-1   **SCIENCE FICTION GEMS, Vol. One**
Isaac Asimov and others

G-2   **HORROR GEMS, Vol. One**
Carl Jacobi and others

If you've enjoyed this book, you will not want to miss these terrific titles...

ARMCHAIR SCI-FI, FANTASY, & HORROR DOUBLE NOVELS, $12.95 each

D-41   **FULL CYCLE** by Clifford D. Simak
         IT WAS THE DAY OF THE ROBOT by Frank Belknap Long

D-42   **THIS CROWDED EARTH** by Robert Bloch
         REIGN OF THE TELEPUPPETS by Daniel Galouye

D-43   **THE CRISPIN AFFAIR** by Jack Sharkey
         THE RED HELL OF JUPITER by Paul Ernst

D-44   **PLANET OF DREAD** by Dwight V. Swain
         WE THE MACHINE by Gerald Vance

D-45   **THE STAR HUNTER** by Edmond Hamilton
         THE ALIEN by Raymond F. Jones

D-46   **WORLD OF IF** by Rog Phillips
         SLAVE RAIDERS FROM MERCURY by Don Wilcox

D-47   **THE ULTIMATE PERIL** by Robert Abernathy
         PLANET OF SHAME by Bruce Elliot

D-48   **THE FLYING EYES** by J. Hunter Holly
         SOME FABULOUS YONDER by Phillip Jose Farmer

D-49   **THE COSMIC BUNGLARS** by Geoff St. Reynard
         THE BUTTONED SKY by Geoff St. Reynard

D-50   **TYRANTS OF TIME** by Milton Lesser
         PARIAH PLANET by Murray Leinster

ARMCHAIR SCIENCE FICTION CLASSICS, $12.95 each

C-13   **SUNKEN WORLD**
         by Stanton A. Coblentz

C-14   **THE LAST VIAL**
         by Sam McClatchie, M. D.

C-15   **WE WHO SURVIVED (THE FIFTH ICE AGE)**
         by Sterling Noel

ARMCHAIR MASTERS OF SCIENCE FICTION SERIES, $16.95 each

MS-5   **MASTERS OF SCIENCE FICTION, Vol. Five**
         Winston K. Marks—Test Colony and other tales

MS-6   **MASTERS OF SCIENCE FICTION, Vol. Six**
         Fritz Leiber—Deadly Moon and other tales

If you've enjoyed this book, you will not want to miss these terrific titles...

ARMCHAIR SCI-FI & HORROR DOUBLE NOVELS, $12.95 each

D-51   **A GOD NAMED SMITH** by Henry Slesar
         WORLDS OF THE IMPERIUM by Keith Laumer

D-52   **CRAIG'S BOOK** by Don Wilcox
         EDGE OF THE KNIFE by H. Beam Piper

D-53   **THE SHINING CITY** by Rena M. Vale
         THE RED PLANET by Russ Winterbotham

D-54   **THE MAN WHO LIVED TWICE** by Rog Phillips
         VALLEY OF THE CROEN by Lee Tarbell

D-55   **OPERATION DISASTER** by Milton Lesser
         LAND OF THE DAMNED by Berkeley Livingston

D-56   **CAPTIVE OF THE CENTAURIANESS** by Poul Anderson
         A PRINCESS OF MARS by Edgar Rice Burroughs

D-57   **THE NON-STATISTICAL MAN** by Raymond F. Jones
         MISSION FROM MARS by Rick Conroy

D-58   **INTRUDERS FROM THE STARS** by Ross Rocklynne
         FLIGHT OF THE STARLING by Chester S. Geier

D-59   **COSMIC SABOTEUR** by Frank M. Robinson
         LOOK TO THE STARS by Willard Hawkins

D-60   **THE MOON IS HELL!** by John W. Campbell, Jr.
         THE GREEN WORLD by Hal Clement

ARMCHAIR SCIENCE FICTION CLASSICS, $12.95 each

C-16   **THE SHAVER MYSTERY, Book Three**
         by Richard S. Shaver

C-17   **THE PLANET STRAPPERS**
         by Raymond Z. Gallun

C-18   **THE FOURTH "R"**
         by George O. Smith

ARMCHAIR SCIENCE FICTION & HORROR GEMS SERIES, $12.95 each

G-5   **SCIENCE FICTION GEMS, Vol. Three**
        C. M. Kornbluth and others

G-6   **HORROR GEMS, Vol. Three**
        August Derleth and others

If you've enjoyed this book, you will not want to miss these terrific titles...

ARMCHAIR SCI-FI & HORROR DOUBLE NOVELS, $12.95 each

ARMCHAIR SCIENCE FICTION & FANTASY CLASSICS, $12.95 each

If you've enjoyed this book, you will not want to miss these terrific titles...

ARMCHAIR SCI-FI & HORROR DOUBLE NOVELS, $12.95 each

D-71   **THE DEEP END** by Gregory Luce
TO WATCH BY NIGHT by Robert Moore Williams

D-72   **SWORDSMAN OF LOST TERRA** by Poul Anderson
PLANET OF GHOSTS by David V. Reed

D-73   **MOON OF BATTLE** by J. J. Allerton
THE MUTANT WEAPON by Murray Leinster

D-74   **OLD SPACEMEN NEVER DIE!** John Jakes
RETURN TO EARTH by Bryan Berry

D-75   **THE THING FROM UNDERNEATH** by Milton Lesser
OPERATION INTERSTELLAR by George O. Smith

D-76   **THE BURNING WORLD** by Algis Budrys
FOREVER IS TOO LONG by Chester S. Geier

D-77   **THE COSMIC JUNKMAN** by Rog Phillips
THE ULTIMATE WEAPON by John W. Campbell

D-78   **THE TIES OF EARTH** by James H. Schmitz
CUE FOR QUIET by Thomas L. Sherred

D-79   **SECRET OF THE MARTIANS** by Paul W. Fairman
THE VARIABLE MAN by Philip K. Dick

D-80   **THE GREEN GIRL** by Jack Williamson
THE ROBOT PERIL by Don Wilcox

ARMCHAIR SCIENCE FICTION CLASSICS, $12.95 each

C-25   **THE STAR KINGS**
by Edmond Hamilton

C-26   **NOT IN SOLITUDE**
by Kenneth Gantz

C-32   **PROMETHEUS II**
by S. J. Byrne

ARMCHAIR SCIENCE FICTION & HORROR GEMS SERIES, $12.95 each

G-7   **SCIENCE FICTION GEMS, Vol. Seven**
Jack Sharkey and others

G-8   **HORROR GEMS, Vol. Eight**
Seabury Quinn and others

If you've enjoyed this book, you will not want to miss these terrific titles…

ARMCHAIR SCI-FI, FANTASY, & HORROR DOUBLE NOVELS, $12.95 each

D-81   **THE LAST PLEA** by Robert Bloch
OMEGA by Robert Sheckley

D-82   **WOMAN FROM ANOTHER PLANET** by Frank Belknap Long
HOMECALLING by Judith Merril

D-83   **WHEN TWO WORLDS MEET** by Robert Moore Williams
THE MAN WHO HAD NO BRAINS by Jeff Sutton

D-84   **THE SPECTRE OF SUICIDE SWAMP** by E. K. Jarvis
IT'S MAGIC, YOU DOPE! by Jack Sharkey

D-85   **THE STARSHIP FROM SIRIUS** by Rog Phillips
THE FINAL WEAPON by Everett Cole

D-86   **TREASURE ON THUNDER MOON** by Edmond Hamilton
TRAIL OF THE ASTROGAR by Henry Hasse

D-87   **THE VENUS ENIGMA** by Joe Gibson
THE WOMAN IN SKIN 13 by Paul W. Fairman

D-88   **THE MAD ROBOT** by William P. McGivern
THE RUNNING MAN by J. Holly Hunter

D-89   **VENGEANCE OF KYVOR** by Randall Garrett
AT THE EARTH'S CORE by Edgar Rice Burroughs

D-90   **DWELLERS OF THE DEEP** by Don Wilcox
NIGHT OF THE LONG KNIVES by Fritz Leiber

ARMCHAIR SCIENCE FICTION CLASSICS, $12.95 each

C-28   **THE MAN FROM TOMORROW**
by Stanton A. Coblentz

C-29   **THE GREEN MAN OF GRAYPEC**
by Festus Pragnell

C-30   **THE SHAVER MYSTERY, Book Four**
by Richard S. Shaver

ARMCHAIR MASTERS OF SCIENCE FICTION SERIES, $16.95 each

MS-7   **MASTERS OF SCIENCE FICTION AND FANTASY, Vol. Seven**
Lester del Rey, "The Band Played On" and other tales

MS-8   **MASTERS OF SCIENCE FICTION, Vol. Eight**
Milton Lesser, "'A' is for Android" and other tales

www.ingramcontent.com/pod-product-compliance
Lightning Source LLC
Chambersburg PA
CBHW030333180626
46810CB00003B/1339